MW01611872

Trial by Sabotage

Hartman & Malone Mystery Series, Volume 1

Paige H. Perry

Published by Paige H. Perry, 2020.

TRIAL BY SABOTAGE

First edition. January 13, 2020.

Written by Paige H. Perry.

Chapter 1

Saturday 8:00 AM

"MARIE, ARE YOU READY yet?" Anna asked.

When the doorbell rang before her sister replied, Anna frowned and jerked the door open. Her frown disappeared the moment she saw her best friend standing on her doorstep. She held a single flower in her hand and a small slip of paper that she was staring at with a smile.

"Claire!" Anna said. "What's with the flower?"

"According to this note, your boyfriend left it here," Claire said. "That's so sweet!"

A smile spread across Anna's face as she took the flower and scanned her eyes across the sweet note.

"Ahh, he said he will miss me this weekend!"

"I read it," Claire said. "If I ever decide I want a boyfriend, I will find me one like Alex."

"Ha! Claire, you and boyfriend don't compute in my vocabulary. You'll run them off within a day."

"Yeah, well. They'll just need to learn how to treat me, then."

Anna shook her head and laughed. When she realized Claire wasn't holding a bag, she frowned.

"Where's your suitcase?"

"Oh, honey," Claire said and swept past her into the apartment. "We are stopping at my apartment before we head out. There's no way I'm lugging my suitcases over here."

"Suitcases?" Anna asked.

"Sorry, ladies," Marie interrupted. "I had to wrap up some work things. I'm almost ready."

Claire perched herself on the edge of their couch. "Well, you need to get a move on. The spa awaits, ladies."

Anna laughed, shook her head, and turned to her sister.

"We need to run by Claire's apartment and pick up her bags before we pick up Frankie."

Marie stopped packing documents into her briefcase and turned to frown back at Anna. "Bags? Claire, we're only leaving for two days. Plus, we will be at the spa, so we don't need that many clothes. Why are you bringing more than one bag?"

"I like to be prepared." Claire glared at the bag Marie was taking. "Speaking of bags. Why are you packing your briefcase? I didn't invite work on our girls' weekend trip."

Marie shook her head.

"I go to trial on Tuesday," she said. "I need to have my paperwork with me in case something comes up."

"The life of a lawyer," Claire said and rolled her eyes.

Marie ignored her, grabbed her bag, and said, "All right. Let's get out of here. This case has me wound up. I need some time to relax."

"I'm driving," Anna said.

She scooped up her own small bag and headed to the parking lot, her sister and best friend following close behind her. After throwing their bags in her trunk, she drove just around the corner and walked with Claire back to her apartment to retrieve her bags. Claire opened the door, and Anna glared down at the four bags sitting by the door.

"Claire," she said. "Why do you have four bags?"

"I said I like to be prepared, silly!"

Anna rolled her eyes and helped Claire lug her bags back to the car. When both were back inside, Anna looked over at her sister.

"Let's hope that Frankie packed light or we won't have enough room in here for us," she said.

Marie shook her head and grinned at Claire in the backseat.

"You just can't ever pack light, can you?"

"What are you talking about?" Claire asked and pulled a compact out of her purse and examined her appearance. "That is packing light."

Anna rolled her eyes again and sped across town to Frankie's apartment. When she saw Frankie waiting on her doorstep with a single duffle bag, she looked at her sister relieved.

"See," Marie said. "MY best friend knows how to pack for a weekend trip."

Marie got out of the car to greet her friend and help her put the bag in the trunk. Once all four were back inside, Anna pulled out of the parking lot and headed through town, the Virginian sun sparkling down on them as they drove.

Anna swept through their sleepy town, enjoying the quiet drive and the company of her sister and friends. A smile spread across her face as she gazed in her rearview mirror at the others and glanced over at her sister. Before turning her attention back to the road, she looked in the rearview mirror a second time, her gaze darkening as she noticed an odd vehicle behind her.

"That's strange," she thought. *"I saw that car at our apartment and at Frankie's."*

With a frown, Anna made a few turns to dislodge the idea that they were being followed from her mind. When the car stayed on her tail, she glanced over at her sister. Marie seemed distracted and had yet to notice her sister's perplexed state or the strange turns she'd been making.

"Marie, why are we being followed?"

Anna's inquisitive eyes passed across her sister's face before turning to study the dark blue Impala in her rearview mirror. Marie's face dropped three shades in color and her mouth dropped, but she didn't answer her sister. Anna frowned when Marie didn't seem surprised by the tail and gave her an expectant glance while maneuvering her red Mustang around the curves in the road.

"This is not how girls' weekend should start out," Claire said from the backseat.

"Shut up, Claire," Marie mumbled under her breath.

Her hands opened the passenger visor, and she gazed at the Impala. Anna's scowl deepened when Marie still refused to meet her gaze and instead fished around in her purse, her hands emerging with a hair tie.

"Marie?" Anna asked. "They've been following us for at least 15 minutes. What's going on?"

Her blue eyes implored her sister for more information. When she didn't receive an immediate answer, Anna gripped the steering wheel and gritted her teeth, glowering at her sister and making her gulp.

"I might be under investigation," Marie said.

Anna mulled the situation over in her mind. Marie continued peering at the car behind them in her visor while pulling her brown hair into a ponytail. Anna continued to drive, cursing when the sedan matched her moves.

"Well, they aren't being too secretive," Anna grumbled after making a complete circle around the block with the Impala staying a car's length behind her.

"It's the FBI," Marie added when Anna couldn't shake the Impala.

Anna ran a hand through her blonde hair and groaned.

"Marie Hartman!" Frankie said. "What in the world is going on?"

Anna kept her eyes on the road while her sister turned to speak with Claire and Frankie. Claire sighed, emphasizing the fact she didn't appreciate something messing with her weekend plans while Frankie crossed her arms and glared at Marie.

"I'm sorry, Frankie," Marie said. "I didn't intend on dragging you and Claire into this mess."

"Oh, thanks," Anna said. "You just wanted to drag me into it, I guess. Now, whatever you've done, I'm an accomplice, since I'm the getaway driver."

Marie turned and put her head in her hands. Anna grew even more annoyed with her sister's insistence on still not meeting her eyes. She again gripped the wheel before jabbing her foot on the accelerator, causing everyone to fly back in their seats with a thud.

"You've got to tell me what's going on," Anna demanded as she made a quick left and glanced in the rearview mirror again, cursing under her breath when the Impala did the same.

"There's a case I'm working on," Marie said. "But I can't tell you anything."

Anna slammed on the brakes, bringing her car to a complete stop. The Impala faltered, the driver surprised at this new tactic, and stopped short a few feet back.

"So, there's a case, you can't tell me anything, and you're under investigation. Does that sum things up?" Anna pointed her thumb at the Impala. "Should I just go ask them what's going on?"

Marie held up her hands. "No. Don't do that. I'll tell you what I can, but just drive."

"Am I losing these jokers?" Anna asked, not taking her foot off the brake.

Claire and Frankie gasped from the backseat and threw on their seatbelts.

Marie hesitated.

"MARIE! Am I losing them?"

Anna focused on her sister, ignoring the car behind her and the passenger who had gotten out of it. She waited while her sister thought through their options. Marie's eyes focused on the passenger mirror as a man approached Anna's car. He was at the left bumper before she decided.

"Yeah. Lose them."

Anna slammed on the gas, her tires squealing in protest. She glanced behind her one last time and saw the man outside the vehicle throw himself back inside the Impala. Tires screeched, and soon they were hot on Anna's tail. Her passengers squealed as she took off and threw the car around the nearest corner.

Already in a precarious residential area of town, Anna watched for signs of danger. Even though she understood the limits of her car, she remained tense as her car drifted around corners and sped through stop signs, the buildings and vehicles outside her window flying by.

None of her passengers dared interrupt Anna's laser focus as she led the Impala on a quick tour of their city. The pair of cars flew through the residential streets as Anna headed towards the center of town, looking for her chance to lose her pursuer.

The two in the backseat squealed again as Anna slid left around one corner and right around the next, the Impala's tires screeched as the driver followed suit. Anna took a quick glance in the rearview mirror and glared at the car behind her. She pushed her foot harder on her accelerator and realized her car didn't have much more to give her.

"Come on," she whispered. "Just a tad more, girl."

Her encouragement appeared to spur more life into the small car. She smiled as it lurched further ahead of the Impala. The vehicle was still close enough for her to make out the frustrated and furious expression on the driver's face when she peered back at him in the rearview mirror.

The stakes were high and dangerous, and Anna did her best to stay calm and reduce stress for herself and her passengers. But she couldn't help but notice Marie glaring at her. A nervous pit began forming in Anna's stomach as she tried to think of a way to explain her driving skills to Marie.

Anna turned her full attention back to the road, ignoring the sound of Frankie muttering to herself. Early morning traffic was picking up, and there was now more to consider than just herself and her passengers.

Anna's eyes flitted from one side of the road to the other looking to escape the determined FBI agents while she zipped through traffic. After a few hasty turns with the Impala following close behind, Anna saw her opening.

A group of cars slowed in front of her when the light changed, but Anna swerved around them and jerked the wheel and her emergency brake. The car slid around the corner of the intersection at breakneck speeds. She flinched at the sound of her tires squealing while leaving a streak of rubber burned into the asphalt.

While the Impala tried to repeat her quick moves, horns blared and traffic started moving again, leaving them trapped on the wrong side of the street. Anna glanced back in her rearview mirror and smiled as she realized they wouldn't be seeing them for a while.

"Everyone all right?" Anna glanced at the terrified pair in her backseat.

They only nodded back at her. Marie's eyes bored a hole through Anna, but she ignored her anger and began plotting their next move.

"Where am I going, Marie? We need to figure this out."

"Where did you learn to drive like that?"

"You don't want to know," Anna said. "Besides, I believe we have more pressing matters to tend to. Where am I going?"

"There's a place we can go." Marie jerked her phone from her purse and began tapping on the screen. "But don't think I'm dropping this conversation. I have a co-worker who has been helping me with this case. His name is Bryant Malone. He can help with this too."

"Plug his address into the GPS, Marie." Anna glanced in her rearview mirror to check for company. "It needs to be quick, Marie. Those guys will catch up with us soon."

"You don't think I should call him first?" Marie asked. "Warn him we are coming?"

Anna shook her head. "We don't have time to ask for permission. Oh, and we need to turn off our phones. We don't want to give those agents a direct way to track us. That should buy us a few minutes of privacy, at least."

Claire's instinct to protest the loss of her phone ended when Anna looked back at her with a stern expression on her face. Without another word, she turned off her phone and chunked it back into her purse. Frankie sighed and followed suit.

Oblivious to the drama, Marie plugged the residence into the GPS before turning to gaze out the window. Once the car calculated her destination, Anna's foot shoved the accelerator closer to the floor again. Her car lurched forward and tires protested the abuse.

After zipping through a few more streets and somehow avoiding being pulled over, Anna reached the driveway of Marie's co-worker and threw her car into it, gravel and dirt flying around them in her wake.

Chapter 2

ANNA PUT THE CAR IN park and killed the engine. Before the dust cleared around her car, Anna tossed the door open and began pulling open her fuse box. While crawling onto the floorboard under her steering wheel to disconnect her GPS, she began barking orders to the petrified women in her car.

"Grab my laptop bag out of the trunk, Marie," Anna said, her voice muffled. "Claire, Frankie, there's a car cover under the passenger seat. Can you get it for me? We need to hide my car."

"Um, can I help you?"

Anna jumped and bumped her head on the steering wheel. She frowned up at the sound and rubbed her head for a second before jerking her GPS cord free from the fuse box and standing to her feet. She had to peer up at him to meet his eyes. She pulled her hand up to shade her face from the sun and to inspect the man better. His amused smile caused her to throw her hands on her hips and frown.

"You sure can! Help me cover my car."

The man in front of her was tall with rugged good looks. His piercing blue eyes looked back at her, confusion floating through them. He ran a hand through his dark brown hair, and he stared back at Anna. Claire jumped between them.

"Well, hello!" A twinkle lit up her eyes as she smiled at the man. "I'm Claire! Who...Are...YOU?"

Anna rolled her eyes and snapped her fingers in front of Claire's face.

"Claire, we don't have time for that," she said.

Claire pouted and glared at Anna before turning to help Frankie wrestle the car cover over Anna's car.

"I'm so sorry!" Marie said and pushed Anna out of her way. "Bryant and I work together. You must be his brother. Joe, isn't it? I'm Marie."

Joe nodded, still looking confused by the intrusion, his eyes shifting from Anna to the car and back again.

"I need Bryant's help," Marie said. "Is he home?"

Joe met her eyes and frowned. "Uh, yeah. He's inside the house. Why don't we find him? This sounds...urgent?"

They followed Joe toward the house. Anna and Marie walked side by side, Claire and Frankie followed close behind.

"So much for girls' weekend," Frankie said.

Marie ducked her head but ignored her.

"Well, we might still get some entertainment." Claire eyed Joe again, and Anna shook her head at her.

Frankie groaned and gave Claire a look of disapproval. "Anna, don't you think you should call Alex?"

Anna looked back over her shoulder and laughed before shaking her head.

"What should I tell him? That his girlfriend just broke 7, no 8, traffic laws while running from the FBI? I don't think he would approve."

Joe snickered and glanced back at Anna.

"He might could find out what's going on?" Frankie suggested.

"No, we are leaving him out of whatever pickle Marie has gotten us into," Anna scowled. "Alex likes his job. No need to make him change careers by bringing him into the middle of this mess."

"What does Alex do?" Joe asked.

"He's a cop," Marie answered.

"S.W.A.T.," Anna added.

Anna noticed Joe's steps falter at her comment. Instead of replying, he turned his attention back to the front door and swept it open for them, regaining the slight slip of his composure with a smile.

"This is the most interesting Saturday I've had in a LONG time," Joe grinned and led them inside to locate his brother.

They found Bryant reading the paper in the family room.

Joe plopped down on the couch next to him. "Brought you a present, Bryant."

He threw his feet up on the coffee table and laced his fingers together behind his head.

"Well, four of them, I guess."

Bryant was just as handsome as his brother, and Claire looked ready to pounce on either of them if given a chance. Anna grabbed her arm and gave her a warning glare to stop her from flirting with him. Claire glared back at her and folded her arms across her chest but stayed quiet.

"Marie?" Bryant asked. "What are you doing here?"

"There's a problem with the Haskell trial."

Bryant raised his eyebrows. "A problem? One requiring a weekend house call?"

"A problem large enough that garnered FBI attention," Anna grumbled.

Marie and Bryant both turned toward Anna.

"This is my sister Anna. Anna, Bryant Malone."

Anna nodded at Bryant, and he returned to his conversation with Marie.

"The FBI?" Bryant asked. "What is going on, Marie?"

Marie sighed. "I think someone's messing with the case and the witnesses."

"Someone's been talking to our client other than us?" Bryant asked.

"No," Marie said. "With the other witnesses. I suspect someone is trying to get Haskell off and blame everything on our client, but I'm uncertain about that."

"It makes little sense for someone to try that, Marie," Bryant said. "The evidence is unambiguous. We've known that from the start."

"Whoever is behind the tampering is falling hard on the whole case," Marie said. "I've spent the last two days recovering evidence they tried to erase."

"Why didn't you come to me sooner with this?" Bryant asked. "Everything was fine when I left the office on Wednesday. What could have happened in the two days I wasn't there?"

"Everything happened so fast," Marie said. "One minute I was putting a nice bow on the whole thing and the next I was running around trying to rescue our evidence and getting followed by the FBI."

"I'm confused, Marie," Bryant said. "Can you start at the beginning?"

"Just like we'd planned, I started working on verifying the evidence and getting the statements ready for court while you were out. But, when I came in Thursday morning, my copy of the witness statements was missing from my file cabinet. I had to get the copy out of your office. I thought nothing of it at first, but it confused me how they could have gone missing because they were the last thing I worked on the night before."

"Strange. Then what happened."

"The next day our entire flash drive worth of evidence was missing. Not in your office and not in mine either."

"But you got it back?"

"I had to go to the D.A.'s office to get a copy yesterday morning," Marie said. "It set me behind getting the statements ready, but I finished them before I left. For safety, I took all our documents with me."

Bryant glanced at the briefcase she brought in. "What about the FBI and the witness tampering? How did you find out about that?"

"Right before I went home last night, an agent called asking if I would set up a meeting to have a chat about something they were investigating."

"That could have been about anything, though."

"That's what I thought too, but this morning the prosecutor sent me an email asking why I had been in touch with one of his witnesses. When I said that I hadn't, he said that the evidence the FBI is gathering says otherwise."

"Do you have the specifics of the evidence the FBI gathered?" Bryant asked.

Marie shook her head and said, "When I asked for specifics from the prosecutor, he reiterated that the FBI would be in touch Monday, but it appears they aren't waiting around to investigate."

Bryant rubbed his temples with his fingertips and looked distressed.

"They won't let you anywhere near the evidence, I'm sure," he said, "and whoever is doing the tampering will do everything they can to keep you in the dark."

"Right," Marie said. "And, to make matters worse, if they throw even a glimmer of doubt onto this case, our client, or the evidence, Haskell will walk."

"Then everyone is in danger," Bryant said before turning toward Anna and saying, "Hey, what are you doing?"

Marie turned to see Anna had taken control of a desk in the corner and was typing on her laptop. Anna ignored Bryant's question.

Joe walked up behind her to watch her work. "It appears she's hacking into the FBI's evidence warehouse and our Wi-Fi network. Remind me to change our password later, Bryant."

"You can't do that!" Marie and Bryant said in unison.

"Why not?" Anna asked and continued typing. "You need information on their evidence. I'm getting it."

"Anna!" Marie said. "That's illegal! If you get caught..."

"I won't," Anna said.

Joe reached into his pocket, pulled out a small rubber band, and began twirling it around his fingers while watching her screen.

"Oh, don't do that."

Anna paused.

"Oh, you're right, what if I...," she said.

"No, that won't work either." He stepped closer to her and examined her screen. "What about this?"

Anna sat back as Joe leaned across her and hit a few keys on her keyboard.

"Nope, I already thought of that," Anna said before he finished.

"Hey, what about...!" Joe started.

"Why didn't I think of that?" Anna said. "You are a genius!"

"He didn't even say anything!" Frankie said from her place on the couch.

Anna and Joe both glanced at her and then at each other before turning their attention back to the computer screen.

"What just happened?" Bryant asked and looked to Marie for answers, but she shrugged in response.

Anna punched a few more keys and gave Joe a triumphant high-five.

"Got it!"

Marie put her head in her hands. "I can't believe you just did that."

"How does she even know how to hack into the FBI's evidence warehouse?" Bryant whispered to Marie.

"I don't know, and I don't want to know."

"Do you want the info or not?" Anna asked.

Bryant looked at Marie and shrugged before heading over to Anna's computer and taking her seat.

"Let's see," he said. "Looks as though the visitor's log shows you visiting Sussex State Prison Monday at 2."

Marie stood behind him and peered over his shoulder. "Not possible. I was in court then."

"We shouldn't have a problem proving that," Bryant said. "We'll just need to get the court records."

"What else do they have?" Marie asked.

"Uh, oh," he said. "This one will be tougher. Payments are coming out of the office's petty cash that you signed off on. They might think it went to pay bribes."

"I didn't approve any petty cash payments," Marie grumbled.

"We can get copies of the authorizations and prove they were forgeries," Bryant said and continued his search.

"What are those?" Marie asked.

She pointed to image thumbnails to the side of the screen. Bryant opened them one at a time and scrutinized them.

"Those are pictures of you delivering paperwork to someone in a parking lot," he said. "That's a good picture of you, but he's fuzzy."

"That's our paralegal, Callen." Marie leaned closer to study the images. "I was giving him documents to file the next morning. You can read the label on the envelope I'm holding."

"We'll need copies of this paperwork and proof the case label doesn't coincide with the Haskell trial," Bryant said. "So far, I don't see any solid evidence for them to cause much serious trouble."

"Except they still have enough to investigate me," Marie said. "And if they manufacture more evidence, we might spend weeks chasing around paperwork."

"Meanwhile, we won't be able to work on the case and everything will go out the window."

"Plus," Marie said, "it won't be long before they drag you into this too since we are working the case together."

"Sounds as though you two could use help finding out who is behind this before they wreck your case," Joe said.

"No," Bryant said. "We are NOT bringing anyone else into this."

Anna shot a concerned glance her sister's direction. "If you ask me, we already are right in the middle of it."

Marie shook her head.

"You are in enough trouble as it is."

"What else is new?" Anna asked.

She folded her arms across her chest and threw a cocky grin at her sister. Marie frowned back at her, a worried and uncertain expression crossing her face.

"Oh, come on," she continued when Marie didn't reply. "When am I ever going to say I helped you out of a legal mess? Just think of it as a deposit for the next time I need help with one."

"Are you expecting to be in a legal mess soon?" Joe whispered.

Anna glanced at him and shrugged. "You never know."

Joe laughed and shook his head at her before turning his attention back to his brother. Before long, Anna was certain Marie and Bryant were coming to the same conclusion.

"Fine," Bryant said. "But I want you both far from the action."

"That means, no risk-taking," Marie said, looking at Anna.

"What's the fun in that?" Joe said under his breath.

Anna shot him a coy smile of her own.

"What's the plan?" Frankie asked.

"Yeah, how can we help?" Claire added.

"You can help by taking my car and heading to the hotel." Anna dug her keys out of her pocket. "If you hurry, you can still make it in time to have a nice weekend. Just the two of you."

"You're sending us away?" Frankie asked. "You don't think we can help?"

"The fewer involved, the better," Marie said. "I prefer to keep at least some of my friends and family safe from this."

"Besides," Anna said, tossing her keys to Frankie. "The spa is far more enjoyable for you than here, Claire."

Claire glanced at the guys before stomping toward the front door, complaining. "But it doesn't have the same company!"

Anna rolled her eyes at Frankie who shook her head and stood to follow Claire. But, before they disappeared in Anna's car, a knock sounded on the front door.

Chapter 3

"YOU LADIES ARE HARD to find," a smug FBI agent in a suit said after Joe cracked open the door.

Joe crossed his arms over his chest and said with a no-nonsense tone, "Do you have ID?"

The men looked at each other, sighed, and pulled their badges out of their pockets for him to examine. Anna leaned against the wall behind Joe and watched the men. They looked different in person than they did in her rearview mirror.

"What can we help you with, Agents Hoage and Kamera?" Joe asked, after peering a second time at the names listed on their badges.

"Please, call me Carver," the shorter of the two said before sticking out his hand in Joe's direction. "This is Renato."

Not taking the bait, Joe ignored Carver's outstretched hand and continued to glare at him instead.

"We're considering taking Ms. Hartman in for the 15 traffic violations she committed earlier today," Carver said, dropping his hand and glaring over at Anna.

Anna took a step forward, her anger boiling. Marie lunged forward to grab Anna's arm and tried to rein in her sister's temper, but Anna shook her off, stepped up beside Joe, and put her hands on her hips.

"15?" she asked. "That's excessive, don't you think?"

"It's the truth," Carver said. "We can take you in right now unless everyone wants to cooperate with our investigation."

"No, you can't," Anna said.

"Can't, what?" he asked, his voice sounding both annoyed and surprised.

"Take me in," Anna said. "You don't have a warrant, and you don't have jurisdiction over traffic violations. Besides, you never identified yourself. For all I knew, you were human traffickers."

"Human traffickers? How about we go have a chat with the local PD about your antics? I'm sure they'll write up a warrant?" Carver crossed his arms and glowered at her.

Sarcasm dripped out of Anna's voice. "Maybe you should. I'll wait right here for you."

A dumbfounded look crossed Carver's face as he turned to his partner for support. Before he said more on the matter, Joe ended the argument.

"We aren't inviting you in." Joe said and slammed the door in his face.

Through the window, Anna watched as Carver and his partner marched to their car and drove away. She cringed at the thought of them heading off to find a warrant for her.

"Well, it looks as though we will have to move," Bryant said. "Can't stay here if those guys are coming back."

Marie glared at her sister. Anna looked to Claire for support, but with one sharp glance from Marie, she slunk away from her friend's defense, choosing to bury her head in her hands to avoid involving herself. Frankie hadn't stopped shaking her head since Joe had opened the door.

"What were you thinking, Anna?" Marie demanded. "Were you trying to give them a fresh target?"

Anna shrugged. "That will keep them busy for a while, at least."

"I think you need to go with Frankie and Claire," Marie said.

"Oh, yes, please!" Claire said. "Please come with us, Anna! I don't belong in jail. I can't be visiting you there. I'll get my good shoes dirty!"

"Why, so I can wait around to get arrested at the spa? No thanks, Marie."

Anna glared back at her sister, not willing to yield to her demands. With her mind made up, she waited for Marie to concede the argument to her. Still fuming, Marie threw her hands in the air.

"I hope Alex will get you out of jail because it might come to that," she said through gritted teeth.

"Let's hope it doesn't."

Marie rolled her eyes before turning to Claire and Frankie.

"Come on," she said. "I guess Anna and I need to get our stuff out of her car so you can get out of here."

Frankie stood to follow Marie but looked back when Claire didn't follow her. Claire jerked her purse on her arm with a sigh, spun around, blew a quick kiss to Bryant and Joe, and sashayed after the others. Embarrassed, Anna shook her head and popped her sunglasses on her nose before stepping out on the porch.

The sun warming her skin, she strode to her car and pulled off the car cover before opening the trunk and pulling Claire's suitcases out of the way. Frankie popped herself into the driver's seat and started the engine.

"Are you sure this will work out?" Frankie asked Marie while she waited for Anna to finish up. "I mean, what if something happens and you can't get this straightened out? What are we supposed to do then?"

"Don't worry," Marie said. "This is my mess, and I'll clean it up."

Anna pulled their bags from her trunk and hugged both Claire and Frankie goodbye. Anna watched her friends leave and sighed. Marie gave her an apologetic look and led her back inside. When Marie and Anna returned with their bags, both Joe and Bryant were gathering pieces of technology and other items they might need.

"I think you and I should start gathering documents to disprove the evidence they have on you first," Bryant told Marie as he jotted a note for his parents. "Joe and Anna can trace the evidence back to see who might have generated it. If you don't mind separating."

Anna shrugged, and Marie nodded.

"Sounds good to us," Marie said.

"I don't like you being involved in this, Anna," Marie whispered while they waited for Bryant and Joe to finish.

"You'd help me if I got into trouble," Anna said. "In fact, you've helped me out of a few jams over the years, if I recall."

"But this is my job. And now you're in trouble with me, and I couldn't forgive myself if something happened to you because of this."

"Marie, you're my sister. What did you expect me to do? Go have a weekend at the spa while you tried to stay out of FBI custody?"

Marie sighed. "But now I'm sending you off to work with a stranger."

"You want me hanging out with you?" Anna asked. "It makes no sense for me to tag along to the places you are going. It will just raise questions, and you won't get the answers you need."

"I guess."

"My question is, how do you know you can trust Bryant?" Anna whispered.

"We've worked together on this since the beginning. There's no way he'd sabotage our case. I know him better than that."

Before they could discuss the predicament further, Bryant and Joe reappeared with two bags each.

"So, where are we headed?" Anna asked, ending her analysis of Bryant's loyalty.

"You and Joe will go rent a hotel room for the night while Marie and I head to the office to pick up the case file we are working on," Bryant said. "Having somewhere to think and regroup will be helpful. When we get there, we will fill you in on the case."

Marie gasped and shook her head before attempting to interject.

"Marie," he chided. "We HAVE to tell them some things about the case if we expect them to help."

Marie's nervous face didn't convince anyone she was on board, but she dropped her argument for the time being and followed the others back outdoors. Bryant squinted at the sun and glanced over at the detached garage by the side of the house and sighed.

"Anna," he said. "I need to apologize for my brother's choice and upkeep of vehicle in advance."

"There's nothing wrong with my jeep!" Joe said.

The expression on his brother's face caused Joe to hang his head.

"I guess it might be a little dirty," he said.

Bryant marched over to the garage and raised the door, revealing a mud-covered jeep. His eyebrows raised at his brother, Bryant motioned to the jeep with both hands and shook his head.

"I'd hate to see REALLY dirty," Marie whispered to Anna.

Anna covered her mouth with her hand to suppress a laugh and looked the jeep over, trying to find a spot not covered in dried mud.

"Looks like you had fun, at least," she said.

No longer able to hold back her laughter, Anna uncovered her mouth and smiled at him.

"I was going to wash it today," Joe said, "but my plans changed because of this distraction you two brought with you."

"Mmm-hmm," Anna grinned. "Well, let's go then."

Anna opened the passenger door and watched a clump of mud fall from the door onto her shoe. Joe jumped in the driver's side and began throwing things from the passenger seat into the back floorboard, so Anna had a place to sit. She spent the time dusting the mud off her shoes.

Bryant shook his head before leading Marie to his much-cleaner sedan.

"New mission," he shouted. "Go clean that thing first."

Anna climbed in the jeep and looked at Joe, amused.

"I really was going to clean it today."

"It's fine, really." Anna laughed, closed the passenger door, and put on her seatbelt.

Bryant was still shaking his head as the two vehicles pulled out of the driveway in separate directions. A few miles later, Joe whipped into an automatic car wash, causing Anna to chuckle. As the water washed the dirt away, she peered at the hood of the jeep.

"Ah, it's blue," she grinned. "I couldn't tell."

"Shut up." Joe said side-eyeing her, but Anna's playful smile made it difficult for him not to laugh.

"So," he said, trying to shift the focus back on her. "How does one break eight traffic laws at once?"

"Well," Anna said, "there was speeding involved. And, I ran a stop sign, and a red light or two. Passing in a no-passing zone, which involved driving into oncoming traffic..."

Anna stopped when she realized Joe was laughing.

"That's a lot of action," he said between bouts of laughter.

"Marie told me to lose them," Anna shrugged.

"How do you know how to drive like that?"

"Don't tell Marie, but I've dabbled in a little street racing from time to time."

"You're pulling my leg."

"Nope."

"I think we could get into trouble together," he said.

When the car wash finished up, he sped away and pulled into the parking lot of a cheap motel after driving a few miles. After paying for and finding their room, Anna and Joe tossed their bags on the floor, turned on a few lights, and texted their siblings the hotel's location and room number.

"Now what?" Anna asked.

"Now," Joe said, lying on one bed. "We wait."

Anna sighed and laid on the other bed, staring at the ceiling. After a few minutes, she propped her head on her elbow and looked over at Joe.

"So," she said. "What do you do? When you aren't playing in the mud with your jeep, of course."

Joe laughed before turning his head to peer at her.

"Cyber freelancing. I finished my digital forensics degree almost three years ago, but I'm lying low for now. I'm not in any hurry to get a permanent gig going."

"It sounds like you and Bryant live at home with your parents."

Joe mimicked Anna's pose and said, "Uh, no. Don't say it like that. That's NOT how it is."

Anna laughed.

"Well, how is it, then?"

"Bryant and I were planning to get an apartment together after he passed the bar last year. But they diagnosed dad with cancer, and mom needed our help at home, so we waited."

"Oh," Anna said. "I'm sorry to hear that. Having a sick parent is not fun."

"Yeah," Joe said. "It's been rough on mom. But I'm glad we've been able to help around the house and take shifts with him at the hospital. He only has a few treatments left, and it's going well."

"Well, that's good," Anna said.

"How about you?" Joe asked. "What do you do? When you aren't street racing and running from the FBI, of course."

Anna laughed again.

"I'm in college. I finish up my criminology degree next semester."

"Ahh, with a focus on technology I presume."

"You presume correctly."

"Do you live with your parents, too?"

Anna felt the smile fade from her face, and she glanced away from him to hide the painful manifestation passing through her eyes.

"Nope, Marie and I share an apartment. Dad's a salesman, and he's never home," she said.

She tried to keep her casual tone of voice when she said, "Mom's gone."

Before Joe responded, she continued with a forced smile, "It was interesting when Eddie wanted to propose to Marie. He insisted on asking Dad first, but he's never in the country, so that was difficult. He wound up having to meet him in Chicago for lunch when Dad was on a layover."

"Sounds like he went out of his way to get your dad's approval," Joe said.

"He did," Anna said. "But it was sweet, honestly. And Marie loved it. And dad."

"I guess you and Marie get along well living together? I often wonder if Bryant and I will kill each other."

"We have our challenges," she said. "But it works out."

A knock sounded on the door, interrupting their conversation. Joe rose from the bed and peered out the peephole before opening it to Marie and Bryant. Bryant barged in with a briefcase and got to work sorting out paperwork and copies of documents.

"I see you washed the jeep," he said to his brother with a grin.

Joe rolled his eyes.

"Such a charming place you two picked," Marie said and gazed at the dingy bed covers.

"Well, when you have to use every piece of cash you have to rent a room, you don't have a choice on the quality of the accommodations," Anna said, annoyed.

"Besides," Joe added. "The penthouse was taken."

"All right, guys," Bryant said, ignoring the room and the conversation altogether. "Here's what we have."

He handed papers to Anna and Joe to familiarize themselves with the case. Anna frowned as she read through the pages. It had the makings of an open and shut case.

Three witnesses had seen or heard the defendant, Jim Haskell, order to have the victim killed. Security footage corroborated the suggested timeline. Plus, there was DNA at the crime-scene tying the murderer back to the scene, and he confessed and pointed the finger at Haskell as being the one who ordered the hit.

Anna glanced over at Joe, who had pulled another rubber band from his pocket and was stretching it between his thumb and forefinger. Noticing Anna watching him, he stuffed it in his pocket.

"This sounds airtight to me," Joe said.

"That's what we thought," Bryant said.

"Now it looks like someone is trying to make it appear otherwise by paying off witnesses," Marie said.

"I'm sure the other side is arranging all of that," Bryant told Marie. "Maybe they are paying someone in our office to change things up."

"Speaking of the other side," Joe said. "What can you tell us about that?"

"I think we should stick to the basics for now," Marie said. "I don't like you two having too much information about that side of things."

"That's not much to go on."

"I know," Bryant said. "But like I said. I want the two of you as far from this thing as possible. Just stick with narrowing down who is creating this fake evidence."

Joe frowned and looked at Anna.

"Looks as though our job will be to narrow our list of suspects to who might need extra money," he said.

"Sounds like it," Anna agreed.

"We will need a list of your coworkers and their basic information. Where can we get that?" Joe asked.

"The only place with that is our HR department," Bryant said, "which we outsource."

Marie dug through her purse and pulled out a business card for the firm's HR partner. Joe looked it over and put it in his back pocket.

"Up for a road trip?" Joe asked Anna.

"Yep," she said. "Let's just hope we can figure out how to pull this off before we get there."

"I guess you guys get to work on clearing out what evidence they've already generated on Marie," Joe told his brother. "We'll touch base with you as soon as we get more information."

Marie shook her head and hugged Anna before she and Joe could disappear out the door.

"Two hours ago, we were heading to the spa," she grumbled. "Now, I'm stuck in a crappy motel room doing work that might end my career."

"Hey, at least we are still getting to spend quality time together."

"Great!" Marie said. "The next time we see each other, it will be through a plated glass window."

"Nah," Anna said with a playful smile. "You'll get a nice low-security prison cell. I'll be able to give you a hug when I come to visit every other weekend."

Chapter 4

Saturday 10:00 AM - Joe and Anna

ANNA AND JOE ROLLED down the highway in search of the HR firm with the information they needed. Neither had a clue how they planned to get inside to get it, but action is always better than inaction, so they kept driving.

From time to time, Anna glanced at her phone, surprised Alex hadn't called yet. Alex would see if a warrant was issued for her. Why he hadn't called her yet was baffling. To Anna, it showed the agents weren't as successful with their plan as they had hoped.

As they drove, a comfortable silence formed between Anna and Joe, but she sensed him glancing at her from time to time. Grateful for his silence, she let her thoughts stray to her sister's predicament and the weekend's turn of events. But the more she pondered things, the more helpless she became.

Not wanting to let the growing ball of worry gnaw at her stomach any longer, she forced herself to gaze out the window and read the passing road signs instead. When the highway leading to the spa passed by her window, she groaned to herself.

Her stress growing out of her control, Anna leaned against the passenger window and propped her head against her hand before glancing at her phone yet again. Frustrated at her inability to make her mind focus, she dropped the device into Joe's cupholder and pulled one of her feet up under her leg, accentuating the rip in her jeans where her knee was.

"Do we have a plan?" she asked.

She turned her back to rest against the door and faced Joe.

"I was hoping you had one."

"I guess let's wait and find out what kind of place we are dealing with when we get there," Anna said. "Maybe we can hack into their computer system or something."

"We could always just break-in," Joe said.

"Yeah, why not? Add breaking and entering to the list of crimes I've already committed today. Sounds great!"

Joe laughed and made a left onto a residential street, followed by an immediate right. They found themselves in an upscale commercial section of town. The Saturday traffic was minimal, and Joe took advantage of the lack of traffic to get them to their destination a little faster.

When they arrived at the address on Marie's business card, it surprised them to see several cars in the parking lot. They hadn't planned for company.

"Hmm, this is interesting," Joe said as he pulled into a secluded parking spot.

"No, kidding," Anna said. "I wonder what businesses are inside this building to warrant this many cars on a Saturday."

"Let's find out, shall we?" Joe said and pulled out his laptop from a bag he had sat on the back seat. "I have a portable hotspot in the glove box. Hand it to me, please?"

After Anna handed him the device, he connected and got to work.

"They need to update their security," he said after a few keystrokes. "HR firms should be more careful."

Anna laughed and watched his screen as he worked.

"We might be in luck," Joe said. "It looks like they are having a customer appreciation day at our HR firm here. That might be our ticket in."

"You want to just waltz in there and ask for the information?"

"Well, I don't know about asking, but if you have a better idea, I'm all ears," he said, still typing on the keyboard. "Man, they even have the guest list on their intranet. This job couldn't be any easier."

"We need a good cover story," Anna said.

"Ahh, check this out, one company didn't send anyone," Joe said with a smile.

"That's so sad. We have to make sure we represent them."

"All right," he said growing serious. "The missing company is a tech firm, so we should be able to pull this off. River Networks is the business name. It looks like they manage a bunch of servers and stuff for their customers."

"Virtual cloud servers, or the real thing?"

"Looks like a little of both," Joe said after clicking through more of the website. "Computer networking, security, IT repairs, help desk. Oh, and it looks like they just signed a contract with them last month, so we should be able to skirt through unnoticed."

"Cool," Anna said. "What names are we going with?"

"You can be Mary, and I'll be John. That's simple to remember, right?"

"John works for you!" Anna said as she pulled down the visor and peered at herself in the mirror. "I don't think I'm giving off a 'Mary' vibe, though."

Joe laughed. "Definitely not a Mary, but let's go with it."

The pair stepped out of the jeep, and Anna started walking toward the building.

"Oh, wait!" Joe dove back inside the jeep, coming back out with a handful of rubber bands he stuffed in his pocket.

"OK." Anna raised an eyebrow at him. "You've got to tell me about the rubber band thing."

"One thing you will learn about me is I ALWAYS have rubber bands on me. You wouldn't believe how handy they are."

"That's the strangest thing I've ever heard in my life."

Joe laughed a little and said, "Trust me. You'll see. Rubber bands are a lifesaver."

"If you say so," Anna said. "I bet your mother loves you. There's no way you remember to get them all out of your pockets."

Joe scoffed at her. "Please. I'm old enough to do my own laundry, thank you very much. But, yes, Mom is not a fan of the rubber band habit."

Anna was still shaking her head as they walked to the front door of the building and smiled at the receptionist who greeted them.

"Hello!" she said. "Welcome to Robinhouse HR Group. What company are you with?"

"Hi," Joe said. "I'm John, and this is Mary. We are with River Networks."

"Ah, yes," she said, scrolling through the list on her computer screen. "I don't have the most updated list, so we don't have name tags for you! I can make you up some real quick. Sit tight."

The woman reached into a drawer and pulled out a sheet of labels and a marker, writing each of their fake names on one and handing it back to them to wear.

"If you'll follow me," she said and rose from her desk. "The gathering is in the conference room. I'll show you the way."

Joe and Anna followed the receptionist while glancing around at the other areas of the office, trying to get an idea where and how to find the data they needed.

"Here we are," the receptionist said. "Let me introduce you to our owner, Jake Robin, if you haven't met him already. Oh, and I'm Janice."

Janice led them to a powerful-looking man in the center of the conference room. He sipped the drink in his hand while looking Anna up and down. Anna pretended not to notice, as did Janice. However, she felt Joe stiffen as Jake's eyes swept over her. She tried to catch his eye, but he ignored her and held Jake's gaze.

"Mr. Robin," Janice said. "This is Mary and John from River Networks."

"Ah, such a pleasure to meet you. Please call me Jake," he said, taking Anna's hand in his.

Joe stuck out his hand, forcing Jake to release Anna's hand to shake his.

"Nice to meet you," Joe said.

Jake somewhat puffed out his chest and glowered back into Joe's eyes.

"I can't say I remember meeting either of you when we set up the River Networks account," he said, staring down Joe as he spoke.

Joe looked him in the eye, not backing down.

"Hmm," Joe said. "I can't say we had the pleasure of meeting with you either."

"Well, I believe it is a new account." Jake's eyes narrowed. "I'm just not familiar enough with everyone at your company yet. I will make sure I get over there to meet your team in the next few weeks."

"Um, yes," Anna said, breaking the men's staring contest. "We've only been with Robinhouse about a month. We transferred after a break-in at our old HR firm. It was quite a fiasco!"

Jake laughed.

"Well, I can assure you, my dear, you don't have to worry about any security issue here."

Anna bit her lip and pretended to appear worried.

"I have to say," she said. "Since we've had our data compromised before, it sure makes me worry about having it off-site. I think we should go back to having an in-house team, John."

"That's a lot of work, Mary," Joe said. "We would have to hire too many people."

"I know," Anna said, letting her voice sound pained. "I just can't help but worry since I'm not positive our data isn't secure!"

Jake sat his drink down at a nearby table and put his arm around Anna's shoulders.

"Let me help," he said. "Let me show you how secure our facility is."

"Oh, you would do that?" Anna gushed in mock surprise. "That would make me feel better."

"Of course! That's what we have these meet and greets for — to help our customers be secure in their business relationships with us."

Anna allowed Jake to guide her through the office. She sensed Joe's tenseness as Jake took them to a back room and unlocked the door with the badge connected to his belt. Jake turned the handle, and he ushered the two of them inside a room filled with labeled filing cabinets.

"There," he said, standing a little too close to Anna. "Everything is secure inside this room. We encrypt the data stored on our computers, and only our employees can access it. Everything is secure."

Anna cleared her throat to cover up the snicker she heard escape from Joe's lips. Mentally rolling her eyes at Jake's pretentiousness, she kept Jake's attention on herself. Anna continued to flirt with him and held his attention as she moved throughout the room, only stopping when his back was to Joe and the door.

Joe pulled one of the rubber bands from his pocket, sent a grin Anna's direction, and placed it around the door handle, preventing it from locking them out. Still staying in tune with Jake, Anna watched out of the corner of her eye as Joe checked his handiwork and gave her a thumb's up sign behind Jake's back.

"Thank you so much for helping put my fears to bed," she told Jake before leading him back toward the door. "That was so nice of you!"

"Anytime, Mary," Jake said with a giant grin on his face. "I guess we should get back to the party now. I would hate to neglect all the other guests!"

Joe opened the door and held it open for Anna and Jake to pass through before following behind them and allowing the door to close behind him.

"I need to make a trip to the restroom," he said. "Can you point me in the right direction, Jake?"

Jake appeared eager to be alone with Anna for a few moments.

"It's down the hall to the right. I'll take Mary back to the party and keep her company while she waits for you."

Jake took Anna's arm and guided her back toward the conference room, making the trip a long one. She wasn't too keen on him being this close to her but stuck with him until she saw Joe swoop back into the room with a triumphant look in his eyes.

"I'm sorry, Jake," Joe said when he approached. "Mary and I will have to leave early! I seem to have eaten something that didn't sit well, and I'm not feeling that great."

"Oh, no!" Jake said. "I hate to see you two leave. Here, let me give you my personal number in case you need any more reassurances regarding your data, Mary."

"Thank you so much," Anna said in a sugary voice, taking his card and reading it over. "I will call if I need anything from you!"

"I'm looking forward to it," Jake said with a seductive smile.

Joe took Anna's arm and pretended to appear ill. Janice looked surprised to see them leaving so soon, but after hearing about Joe's illness, she stepped away from him and shooed them out the door of the office. Anna and Joe tried to stay calm even though both their hearts were racing, and they wanted to run to the jeep to escape.

After what seemed like an eternity, they were inside the jeep and pulling away. Once they were out of view of the office building, Joe pulled a few sheets of paper from under his shirt and handed them to Anna.

"They were just sitting there in a file cabinet," he said. "They didn't even lock it, and didn't have any security cameras in there, either."

"That was brilliant!"

Anna grinned from ear to ear as she looked through the pages filled with names, social security numbers, bank accounts, and other essential information about Marie's coworkers. "I can't believe we pulled that off."

"Piece of cake," Joe laughed. "Told you those rubber bands would come in handy."

Anna shook her head at him but laughed too.

"You're unbelievable," she said.

"Jake was the unbelievable one," Joe growled. "Someone should take guys like that out back and teach them a lesson."

Anna shrugged off his anger and said, "I'm used to it. Nothing I couldn't handle."

"Well, you shouldn't have to handle it!"

Anna diverted the conversation and said, "Let's get somewhere with a good Wi-Fi connection and start figuring out what we are dealing with."

"How about the library?" Joe said. "That's a quiet place."

Anna nodded, already poring through the papers Joe had handed her. The sound of Anna's phone ringing, which startled both Anna and Joe, brought Anna from her musings. Anna glanced down to see Alex's name and sighed. It was the call she had been expecting all day.

With what she hoped was a cheerful tone, she answered with, "Hey, you!"

On the other end of the line, Alex whispered, "Anna. Do you want to tell me why an arrest warrant for you just came across my desk?"

Anna hesitated.

"Anna?" Alex asked a little louder and sterner.

She sighed, "Marie's in a bit of a jam. I'm trying to help her out of it."

"What type of jam? I thought you were going to the spa!"

"I can't tell you," Anna said. "Marie's already told me more than she should have, and you see where that's gotten me."

"Yeah, with an arrest warrant! "Where are you?"

"Um, I'm not telling you that either."

"Anna..."

Anna cringed at the anger she heard in his voice.

"Alex, look," Anna said, stopping him in mid-sentence. "I'm not telling you because you'll either have to come get me and take me in or make the moral decision to break your police code. I'm not doing that."

Alex sighed, "Fine. I can't keep them away from you, though. They will search for you. If you get stopped or caught..."

"I know," Anna said. "It'll be ok. I promise. Don't worry."

"You know I will worry," Alex said.

"Well," Anna said. "Let's just hope we get everything straightened out in a few hours, and we won't have to worry about it anymore."

"I love you, Anna," Alex said. "Please be careful."

"I love you, too," Anna said with a smile. "And I will."

Chapter 5

Saturday 10:00 AM - Bryant and Marie

MARIE FLIPPED THROUGH the papers in her lap, trying to make sense of what was going on. It had all seemed so simple when she and Bryant had taken this case. All they did was get a deal for their client and make sure he was ready to testify. How everything had become so complicated was beyond her.

After Joe and Anna left, Bryant spent the next several minutes pacing around the hotel room. From time to time he stopped, rifled through the papers he and Marie had retrieved from the office, jotted something down on a legal pad and continue pacing again. It was quite a while before he got his thoughts in order enough to share them with Marie.

"All right," he said. "Our first approach should be to get a copy of the visitor's log. Do you remember the last time you visited Mr. Shaw?"

"The last time I saw him was when you and I both had a chat with him this past Wednesday. We both had to sign in, so my signature should be on the list."

"Good," Bryant said. "That means we have something to compare your signature to. Let's go to the jail first for the visitor log. Then, we can find the file you gave Callen."

Marie tilted her head in confusion. "We'll need a warrant for that."

"Already on it," Bryant said. "I had Jason fax over a request for a warrant about an hour ago. We need to swing by Judge Reigner's house to pick it up."

"How did you convince the intern to come in on a Saturday?" Marie asked.

"He owed me a favor," Bryant said. "I got him tickets to a playoff game last month. He wanted to propose to his girlfriend on the kiss cam."

"Did she say yes, at least?"

Bryant looked embarrassed.

"I don't know. I never asked him."

Marie shook her head and laughed.

Bryant changed the subject and said, "With the copy of the petty cash authorization and the visitor's log record, we should be well on our way to getting you, and me, out of this mess."

Marie nodded and gathered up the documents they had retrieved so far before following Bryant back to his vehicle. Inside, Marie sighed and shuffled through the paperwork. Bryant sensed her discomfort and tried to draw her away from the case.

"So, what's Eddie up to these days?" he asked.

"Oh, no!" Marie said, remembering her fiancé for the first time.

She glanced at her watch alarmed and continued without waiting for Bryant to reply. "Eddie is finishing up USMLE today! He's supposed to call me when he's done!"

"I'm sure he's not finished yet. Doctor certification tests take a while," Bryant said. "How much longer does he have before he finishes up and earns his certification?"

"Ugh, so much has happened already today I feel like it's the end of the day," she said. "He has one year left on his residency. We are putting off the wedding until he's finished. At the rate I'm going, he might have to fish me out of jail first, though."

"It might surprise you how easy it will be to clear our names in all of this. Whoever is behind it wants to keep us busy, not blame you for anything. Otherwise, they would have tried harder to get better evidence against you."

"I guess that's true," Marie said, as they pulled into Judge Reigner's driveway.

Bryant rang the doorbell, and Marie watched through the window for the judge to appear. During the wait, she thought back over the case and the strategic deal they had worked hard to get. She'd taken a liking to their client, pitying him and the difficult choices his boss had forced him to make over the years.

Even though he hadn't always done right, he was attempting to ensure no one else got hurt because of him. Marie sighed, wondering if they could follow through with their promise to help him get out and put an end to being trapped in a life of crime.

When a furious Judge Reigner appeared at the door in his bathrobe, Marie forced her thoughts back to the situation at hand. She and Bryant looked at each other with dread before turning their full attention to the judge as he greeted them at the door.

"I hope you realize I had to pass up a game of golf with the president of the country club for this," he said.

"Believe me, Judge," Bryant said. "If we had any other option, we would have taken it. Time is of the essence."

"So, I understand," the Judge said. "This little witch hunt of yours better not get me into any trouble, Malone. Do you hear me?"

"We're trying to clear a few things up, Judge," Marie said. "We'll get out of your hair so you can get back to whatever you were doing."

Judge Reigner didn't even wait for them to say goodbye before shutting the door in their face and shuffling back down the hall. Marie looked at Bryant flustered, knowing he wasn't too confident in the situation himself. Both Marie and Bryant tried to push their negative feelings aside as they drove across town to the jail. When they arrived, the guard was as excited to see them as Judge Reigner.

"Who are you here to see?" she asked, motioning for them to sign the log.

"We need a copy of the visitor's log from Monday and also the one from four days ago."

"You need a warrant," she said, preparing to close the window in their faces.

"We have one," Marie presented the document in question.

"Can't this wait until Monday?" she asked.

"Nope."

The woman sighed and looked over the papers Marie had handed her. Satisfied they were in order, she sighed and rose from her chair.

"Stay right here."

When she returned, Marie was sure she had taken much longer to retrieve the documents than was necessary. Before they thanked her for her help, she had already closed the plastic protection divider and turned her attention back to the paperwork she was working on when they had first arrived. The moment they were back in Bryant's car, Marie began comparing signatures.

"This is a forgery," she said. "A court of law wouldn't fall for any of this nonsense."

Bryant looked over her shoulder at the signatures and nodded in agreement.

"At least it's making our job easier," he said. "Now, we need to get the file from Callen, and we can plan our next steps."

"I guess the best option is to swing by his apartment," Marie said, looking at the screen of her phone. "I had to take something to him before, so I should have his address in here."

Bryant waited until she put the address in the GPS before pulling out of the parking lot. On the drive to Callen's apartment, Marie spent the time comparing the forged signatures on both the petty cash receipt and the visitor's log with her own.

"Well, they are consistent," she mumbled, impressed with how similar the forgeries were to one another.

"That shows the same person is doing the dirty work," Bryant said, navigating the parking lot of the apartment complex. "Let's hope Joe and Anna can narrow down who's behind this."

"And why," Marie said as they got out of the car.

"It looks like our FBI friends have caught up with us," Bryant said, nodding at the dark sedan pulling into the parking lot behind them.

"Ugh," Marie said, glancing at the car while picking up her pace. "Let's hurry and get this over with, and maybe we can get them off our back."

Callen answered his door and looked surprised to see them.

"I need the file I gave you the other day," Marie said, getting straight to the point. "The one on the Anderson case. It wasn't at the office."

"I have it here," he said. "Come in, and I'll get it for you."

He led them inside his apartment and headed toward the coffee table in the small living room. Marie closed the door behind them, hoping to confuse the FBI agents she was sure had followed them inside.

"You know," Callen said, reaching into his briefcase. "It's ironic you would show up looking for this case file."

"How's that?"

"I had no intention of bringing it home!" he said. "When you gave it to me, I put it in the file cabinet as I always do. But somehow, it ended up in my briefcase when I went home."

"That is strange," Bryant said as the three of them peered at the file in Callen's hand.

"It's almost as though someone didn't want this file at the office," Marie said.

"I don't know why," Callen said. "It's not as though anything significant is going on in this case."

Marie took the file and began flipping through the pages. It was as she had remembered it. And, as Callen pointed out, nothing significant. A client with a simple robbery charge, nothing more.

While Marie flipped through the papers, Bryant paced the apartment thinking through the situation, Marie followed him distracted by the movement.

The pair wound up stopped in front of Callen's couch, their back to his large picture window Marie was sure he had paid a premium to get. This time, however, when Marie looked back at Callen to ask him another question, she saw a horrifying sight.

A small red dot had formed on the breast pocket of Callen's shirt. Noticing the dot at the same time as Marie, Bryant threw his arms around her waist, pulling her down behind the couch while yelling, "Get down!" at Callen.

As they hit the floor with a thud, bullets and glass started shredding through the small apartment destroying furniture, pictures, and couch cushions in their wake.

Bryant and Marie put their arms over their heads, waiting for the stream of bullets to subside. After a few moments, silence reached their ears, and they raised their heads to look at each other in shock.

It wasn't but a few moments later when the FBI agents burst through the door with their guns drawn.

"Stay down," they barked at Bryant and Marie before clearing the apartment and gazing at the building across the way. Carver pulled out his cellphone and called in for back-up, instructing a team to clear both buildings.

Marie peered out from behind the couch at Callen's life-less body on the floor. Blood flowed across the wood floor toward her, and she pushed away, closing her eyes to shut out the image.

"Time to go," Carver ordered. "This is a crime scene now."

"Come to our office and answer some questions," Renato said.

Renato grabbed Marie's arm and pulled her to her feet while shielding her from the potential threat of more flying bullets. Not giving them a chance to argue, he gave Bryant a stern look before pushing Marie toward the door.

"Let me get our evidence out of my car, first," Bryant raised his hands.

"We can trust you to follow us," said Carver. "No funny business, though, or there will be hell to pay."

Marie held tight to the case file they had retrieved from Callen and allowed Renato to remove her from the apart-ment, Bryant and Carver following close behind. Both at-tempted to avoid glancing at their colleague, but it was diffi-cult. The moment they were in the hallway, one agent began securing the scene and calling for an investigation team while the other took possession of Bryant and Marie's cell phones.

"Wouldn't want you two communicating with anyone before we chat, now would we?" he said.

He glanced at the file in Marie's hand but made no move to take it from her. Bryant and Marie waited for what seemed like an eternity, but for what was no longer than 30 minutes. After a team arrived, the two agents filled them in on the situation before motioning for Bryant and Marie to follow them outside.

Once they arrived at Bryant's car, which the agents had blocked in its space, they gave them an address and led them out of the parking lot. Marie and Bryant spoke little on the ride, both pondering what they had witnessed in Callen's apartment. Before long, Carver and Renato placed them in separate interview rooms at the FBI's office and Marie faced off with Carver alone.

"Witness tampering is a federal crime, Ms. Hartman," the agent said, taking advantage of her frazzled state to push for information.

Marie pushed the image of Callen's body from her mind and narrowed her eyes at the agent.

"Carver," Marie said, bristling at the accusation. "Why would you think I tampered with witnesses?"

"Well, for starters, you signed out some petty cash we think you used to pay one of those witnesses."

"Forgery." Marie sat back and crossed her arms over her chest. "A simple glance at my true signature will prove forgery."

"All right," Carver said. "What about the visit to one witness in prison on Monday?"

"I was in court all day, Monday," Marie said, her gaze not wavering from his. "You can check the court records. Also, I suspect the visitor's log will prove to be a forgery."

"Hmmm," Carver said, unsure of his evidence. "Well, what about that dead fella over in that apartment?"

Anger shot through Marie's body and reflected in both her brown eyes and her voice.

"If you are referring to Callen," she said. "He's not some 'dead fella.' He was a co-worker and a big part of my team. Speaking of which, what are you doing about Callen? Are you notifying his family? What about the shooter? Have you found him yet?"

"Hold your horses." Carver raised his hands. "I can't give you any information about an ongoing investigation, but I can assure you we will inform his family."

Marie looked away for a moment. Carver became more sympathetic towards her.

"I am sorry for your loss," he mumbled. "But that doesn't change the fact I need to understand what you were doing at his apartment."

"Picking up a file," Marie said through gritted teeth.

"It wouldn't be the file they saw you give someone in a parking lot the other day, would it?"

Marie said nothing.

"It appears you already know what evidence we have on you," the agent said, examining her. "How would that be?"

"This conversation is over," Marie said. "It will take about five minutes to prove the evidence you have is a sham."

"What was in the file you picked up from Callen?" the agent asked, eyeing the file still in her arms.

"I'm not at liberty to say," Marie said. "Attorney/client privilege. But I can assure you it doesn't relate to the witness tampering case, and my office will sign an affidavit on the fact."

"This is far from over, Ms. Hartman, but I suppose you are free to go," he relented. "Sit tight, and I'll go see if I can find your partner."

He left Marie alone with her own thoughts for several minutes and only appeared at her door again when he'd retrieved Bryant. After shooting a glare Carver's direction, Marie exited the room and joined Bryant in the hallway.

"You all right?" he whispered.

"Yeah," she said. "What did they tell you?"

"Nothing," he shook his head and rolled his eyes. "Tried to say you were talking and insinuated we had a romantic relationship, but other than that, nothing."

Marie groaned.

"That's ridiculous," she whispered. "Besides, there's nothing to talk about."

"I know. Let's get out of here."

Marie and Bryant followed Carver and Renato through the FBI office and toward the parking lot, neither willing to discuss the situation further in front of the agents. Marie clutched Callen's file and followed Bryant from the building. She could feel the agents' eyes following them as they walked through the parking lot.

Bryant shifted the briefcase with the rest of their evidence from one hand to the other and reached inside his pocket to search for his car keys. Once they were in his hand, he pressed the button to unlock the car. To everyone's surprise, the vehicle erupted in a fireball, the explosion knocking both Marie and Bryant to the ground.

Chapter 6

Saturday Noon - Joe and Anna

"YOU FIND ANYTHING YET?" Anna's voice was just above a whisper.

The librarian didn't appreciate her elevated tone and lifted her head to glare at Anna, but she ignored her. Joe flipped through the list of names in front of them and sighed, causing the librarian to roll her eyes and shift her glare to him instead.

"Not yet," he said.

He peered over the top of his laptop at her. They had gone through the first eight names on the list and felt they were getting nowhere. They had spent the past couple of hours going through social media accounts, public records, court records, and every other outlet to find a connection. Just when they thought they were getting somewhere, something would disprove all their theories, and they would have to start again.

"What we should have done," Anna said and picked up the list of random names, "is have Bryant and Marie sort these for us. How do we even know who might be close enough to all this?"

"Good point," Joe said. "I can't believe I didn't think about that myself."

"We might spend all day going through these names!"

Joe rubbed his eyes with his fingers. "How about we take a break? I could use some food."

Anna rested her chin on her hand and closed her eyes. "Me too. And, a drink."

Joe laughed. "We'd better hold off on the drinking for now."

"If you insist," Anna said, gathering her things.

"There's a good hotdog stand nearby," Joe said when they were back in the Jeep. "How about we grab a few and rest for a bit and regroup?"

"Rest? In the jeep?" Anna hesitated.

"Unless you want to drive all the way back to the hotel..." Joe said.

Anna shook her head and frowned, "No, that's silly. Yeah, your plan sounds good. Let's go."

Joe parked the jeep in a parking lot near the hot dog stand but left it running.

"Why don't you wait here? I'll bring us back some hotdogs. No sense in both of us making the trek over there."

"Sure," Anna said, not being able to keep the tired tone from affecting her voice.

Joe tossed his keys on the driver's seat and jogged across the street toward the hotdog stand. Anna watched him for a moment before settling deeper into her seat, preparing to take a quick nap to refresh her mind. Just as her eyes fluttered shut, she caught sight of movement nearby.

Startled, she lowered her head below the window. Only her eyes and the top of her head visible, Anna watched a man walk across the street on the same path Joe had taken moments ago. She watched as the man adjusted his shirt, which brough the back of it up far enough for her to spot a gun tucked into the back of the waistband of his pants.

"THAT isn't good."

She killed the engine of the jeep, secured the doors and followed Joe and the man down the sidewalk. The man ambled down the sidewalk, which gave Anna plenty of time to catch up with him. Joe seemed oblivious of his shadow, and the man walked up behind him as he waited in line at the hotdog stand.

The man reached behind him to grasp the grip of the revolver only to utter a hiss of shock when he found the gun missing. Surprised, he turned to examine the path he'd just taken for his gun but soon learned it had found its way into Anna's hand.

As he stared down the barrel of his own gun, the man lifted his hands and said, "Easy, love."

The noise caught Joe's attention, and he turned, his eyes widened in confusion when he saw the gun in Anna's hand.

"Um, Anna?" he said. "Any reason you are pointing a gun at a stranger?"

"Oh, it's not mine," Anna said, her eyes never leaving the man. "It's his."

Anna moved the gun a little closer to the man to make him a tad more uncomfortable and asked, "You want to tell me why you pulled out this beauty while following my friend here?"

Joe's eyes narrowed and jaw clenched when he realized what had happened. When the man didn't answer, Joe folded his arms across his chest and glared at him.

"Look," Anna said. "I'm tired, hungry, and starting to get cranky. If you could give me an answer before I must use too much energy to get them, I would appreciate it."

"Besides," Joe said and looked toward the hot dog stand. "I'm sure the police will show up soon and want to know what's going on."

The patrons of the hot dog stand began fleeing the moment they noticed the gun in Anna's hand, and the proprietor had ducked behind the counter in fear. There was no doubt in Anna's, Joe's, or the man's mind the police would soon be on their way if they weren't already.

"You wouldn't shoot me," the man said.

"Try me." Anna said and put her finger on the trigger.

The man took a step back, almost running into Joe, who grabbed his shoulders and spun him around to face him.

"How about I help you out here?" Joe took a step forward and clocked the man on the chin with his fist, causing him to drop to the ground.

Anna lowered the gun and shook her head.

"Now, how are we going to figure out what he wanted?"

"I'm sure this is a better option than you shooting him."

Anna shrugged and put the gun in the waistband of her pants.

"Uh, how about I hang onto that for you?" Joe said.

Anna raised an eyebrow at him.

"As grateful as I am that you saved my life, I'm a little concerned you might find more strangers to point it at."

Anna rolled her eyes but handed the gun over before looking down at the man.

"What do we do with him?" she asked.

"I guess we could take him with us," Joe said.

"Make him answer some questions when he wakes up?" Joe shrugged.

"So much for hot dogs," Anna sighed and bent down to pick up the man's ankles.

Joe and Anna lugged the man back to the jeep, surprised they hadn't heard police sirens yet. After securing the man with Joe's assortment of towing cables and ropes, they hopped in the jeep and pulled out of the parking lot as soon as possible.

"I guess we need to call Marie and Bryant now," Joe said. "I'm sure they will not like this at all."

Before the words came out of his mouth, Anna's phone started ringing.

"I'm sorry," she said, looking at Joe with a horrified expression on her face after she'd answered her phone, "say that again."

Joe looked over at her, his eyes imploring her for information while navigating the road.

"Uh, Bryant's car exploded?" Anna said.

"WHAT?!?!" Joe gripped the steering wheel and had a difficult time keeping the jeep on the road.

Anna listened for a second and said, "Everyone's all right."

Joe breathed a sigh of relief and relaxed a bit but continued to glance over at Anna with an anxious expression on his face as she listened to the voice on the other end of the line.

"Where are you at?" she asked.

Anna started shaking her head, and Joe watched as she brought her hand to her mouth, shock passing across her face.

"Wow, Marie," she whispered. "This has gone to the next level."

Joe nodded to the backseat, reminding Anna of the predicament they were in. Anna grimaced and peered in the back floorboard at the man, who was still unconscious.

"At least, your crazy afternoon trumps ours," she said. "And, maybe it will make what we need to tell you not that bad."

"Not that bad?" Joe mouthed at her.

Anna shrugged and put a hand over the mouthpiece of her phone.

"Just wait until you hear what they've been doing," she said. "It makes this look like we were out shopping for living room curtains."

Joe raised an eyebrow and whispered, "Where am I going?"

"Where are we going, Marie?" Anna asked, turning her attention back to her phone.

After listening for a few moments, Anna popped the address into Joe's GPS, and he sped away toward their destination.

"All right, we are on our way," Anna said before hanging up with her sister.

"What is at this address, Anna?" Joe asked.

Anna grimaced before saying, "The FBI office."

"Anna!" Joe slowed the jeep a bit. "We can't go to the FBI office. We have a kidnapped man on the floorboard."

"Either he comes with us, or he comes after us," Anna shrugged. "Which is it going to be?"

Joe gritted his teeth and sped the jeep back up again.

"Also," Anna said. "That guy Marie gave the file to, the paralegal they had to go visit — he's dead. Someone shot up his apartment with Bryant and Marie inside and caught him in the crossfire."

"What the hell is going on?" Joe asked.

All Anna could do was stare back at him with a confused expression on her face.

JOE'S JEEP FLEW INTO the parking lot of the FBI office and bounced over a curb, causing the man in his back floorboard to bounce and utter a grunt. Joe glanced at Anna when he located Marie and Bryant sitting in the back of an ambulance, and she returned his relieved gaze. The parking lot was swarming with investigators who were combing through remnants of Bryant's car.

Anna and Joe glanced back at the man in the backseat, who still appeared unconscious, grimaced at one another and shrugged. The damage already done, Joe threw on his child locks to keep the man confined in the backseat, and he and Anna made a beeline for their siblings.

Bryant held a bag of ice to his head, and Marie clutched a blanket around her shoulders and looked dazed. The FBI agents who had been following them began protesting their presence.

"Calm down," Bryant said. "You knew they would show up."

"This is an active crime scene," Carver growled.

A frustrated paramedic followed him, trying to get his arm into a sling. Anna and Joe both glared at him, daring him to ask them to leave. He relented but stood nearby as he gave in to the paramedic's demands.

"What is going on?" Joe asked his brother.

Bryant shrugged.

"Your guess is as good as mine."

"You haven't figured out anything?"

Bryant put the ice pack back on his head.

"Nothing other than someone really, REALLY wants to kill us."

"Yeah, no kidding," Joe said, glancing back at his jeep, remembering the cargo he had stored there.

Anna turned to Marie and frowned at her dazed expression.

"Marie," she whispered. "Are you ok?"

Marie just looked back at her sister with a blank expression on her face.

"What happened?" Anna demanded, turning her attention back to Bryant.

"After they almost killed us in Callen's apartment, the agents took us back here for questioning," Bryant said. "We had enough evidence by then to get them to let us go. When we were leaving, the car just blew up."

"Thank God, you weren't in it!" Anna said, looking back at her sister.

A sudden commotion caught everyone's attention, including that of Carver and Renato. Joe and Anna looked at each other and back at Joe's now shaking jeep. Bryant gave them a look.

"We might have had a situation pop up," Joe said.

Carver and Renato pounced on them.

"You two want to tell us what's going on over there?" Carver demanded.

"Well," Joe said. "Just before Marie called Anna, a man attacked us."

"So, you put him in your jeep?"

Bryant stared at his brother.

"Please elaborate, Joe," he said.

Joe turned his attention back to his brother.

"We were leaving to get something to eat and to take a break because our original plan wasn't working out well, but we'll talk about that later."

He glanced at the agents who narrowed their eyes at him.

"Anyway," Anna continued for him. "We had stopped, and Joe went to get us some hotdogs. I see this guy follow him, and he pulled out a gun."

"What?!" the agents and Bryant said in unison.

Joe rolled his eyes. "Everything turned out all right. We were trying to figure out what he wanted when Marie called Anna, and we had to leave."

"You didn't think he was just trying to mug you or something?" Renato asked.

Anna shook her head and said, "His clothing was too nice for that. And his gun looked expensive and had a suppressor on it. He looked comfortable with it."

"Uh, what did you do with the gun?" Carver asked.

Joe hesitated, causing Carver to hold out an evidence bag. Joe sighed and pulled the gun from the back of his pants and put it in the agent's bag. Bryant glared at him in shock.

"Please tell me you didn't bring a gun into the FBI's parking lot," he hissed.

"Not to mention a kidnapping victim." Carver examined the weapon before handing it to Renato.

"Let's go check out your friend over there," he said, pointing at the jeep. "I will assume you were bringing him here to turn him over for proper questioning?"

"Uh, why else would we keep him?" Anna hesitated.

Carver turned to glare at her and said, "Exactly."

The moment Joe unlocked the Jeep, and the agents opened the doors, the man started trying to kick his way free from the ropes and chains Anna and Joe had used to secure him.

"What in the world do you do with all of this?" Carver asked.

"They are for off-roading," Joe said.

Confused, Carver and Renato stared at him.

"Oh, uh, you use them to get pulled out if you get stuck in the mud," Joe said.

"Hmmm," Carver said, turning his attention back to the man on the floorboard.

"These people kidnapped me!" he yelled. "I was just trying to get a hotdog, and she pulled a gun on me. He stuffed me back here!"

"You mean to tell me, a girl got the best of you," Carver laughed.

"But it was all a setup!" the man said. "They trapped me, and I couldn't get away!"

"Well, you can file a formal complaint inside," Renato said.

"Inside?"

"Inside our office," Carver said. "The FBI office."

The man's face dropped three shades in color when he realized where Joe and Anna had taken him.

"I want a lawyer," he said, dropping his victim act.

"We'll get you one," Carver said, "but we are a little busy right now. It will take a bit."

Renato hauled the man to his feet and marched him through the crime scene toward the office. Carver watched him go for a minute before turning to Joe and Anna.

"I will let this one slide, for now," he said. "But I want to have a little chat with the two of you later regarding all these antics you've been pulling."

Anna and Joe looked at the ground, knowing they were in trouble.

"For now, take your siblings and get out of here while we clear out this crime scene," he said. "Don't go too far, though. We'll be in touch."

Joe and Anna looked at each other surprised but didn't stick around long enough for Carver to change his mind. They grabbed Bryant and Marie, and the four of them headed back to the hotel to regroup. The moment they were back in one room, Anna and Joe crashed on the beds, and Marie sat on the office chair in the room. Marie's silence concerned Anna, but she was too tired to put much emphasis on trying to help her. Bryant took to pacing again.

"All right," he said. "What are we working with? Joe, did you two figure anything out?"

Joe shook his head without lifting it off the bed.

"We got a copy of the list of workers at your firm," Anna said.

"But it will take too much time to go through them all," Joe added.

"How did you guys get that?" Marie asked, speaking for the first time since the explosion.

"You don't want to know," Anna said with a non-humorous laugh.

"If you have any say over it, I would get a new HR company ASAP," Joe interjected. "Especially if that guy will deal with women at your office. He's a bit handsy."

"We'll keep that in mind," Bryant said, raising an eyebrow at Marie.

"What about you?" Anna asked, picking her head up to glance at her sister. "What in the world happened today?"

Marie shuddered and let Bryant fill them in on their day. He looked tired when he had finished recounting all the drama and sat down on the edge of the desk.

"We can't go to trial. There is no way we will be ready on Tuesday. After losing..." Marie's voice trailed off, and tears flooded her eyes. Anna got up to put an arm around her sister, but Marie brushed her off and rushed to the bathroom, closing herself up inside.

"She's right," Bryant said. "We will have to file a delay."

"How are you going to do that?" Joe asked.

"We'll have to go to the office," Bryant said. "We don't have a choice."

"Uh, since it appears someone is trying to kill you, shouldn't you lie low for a bit?" Anna asked.

"Well, if we want to stop them, we need to get this case figured out."

"I guess," Anna said.

"What are we going to do in the meantime?" Joe asked.

"Well, you said there were too many people on your list, so how about you work backward," Bryant said. "Start with the people we work closest with on the case and work from there."

"Here." Joe handed his brother the list of names. "How about you mark which order you want us to work from?"

Bryant got to work filtering through the list and making notes next to names on the list so Anna and Joe could tell who they were dealing with. About the time he was finishing up, Marie emerged from the bathroom.

"I would pay special attention to Callen and those who had access to him," she said. "Whoever did this knew about his involvement in the case and had access to his belongings since they got the file back into his briefcase."

"Good point," Bryant said. "I think that will just about do it."

"How are we going to get around with your car destroyed, Bryant?" Marie asked.

"How about we take you to get your car, Marie?" Anna asked.

"Great, you and Joe can get to work on the list without having to worry about driving us around," Bryant said before gathering up their belongings and leading them outside.

Back in the jeep, Joe started the ignition before stopping to chuckle to himself.

"What?" Bryant asked.

Joe looked at his brother.

"I was just thinking. You know, when I fantasized about driving sisters back and forth from a hotel, this is not what I had in mind. And, you were NOT involved."

"JOE!" Bryant slapped his still laughing brother on the back of the head.

Chapter 7

Saturday 2:00 PM - Joe and Anna

ANNA GLANCED AT THE clock in Joe's jeep and groaned. It felt much later than 2 o'clock. She rubbed her forehead and closed her eyes for a moment. Tiredness was never something Anna tolerated well, but it appeared she would have to put up with it for at least a little while longer.

"You ok?" she heard Joe say, causing her eyes to lurch open.

"Yeah," she said. "Just tired."

"You know, we still haven't eaten. I'm sure a little food will do us both a world of good."

Anna laughed. "How about we stick with a drive-thru this time?"

Joe grinned and whipped through a burger joint. Both he and Anna took a deep breath as the smell of burgers filled the jeep.

"You think it's safe to sit in the parking lot this time?" Joe joked as he pulled into a shopping center's parking lot.

Anna stiffened a bit and hesitated, her mind plummeting into a world of panic.

"What?" Joe asked, giving her a funny look.

"This will sound crazy," she said, not looking at him. "But can we park somewhere else?"

"Sure," Joe said, pulling back out of the parking lot again, a confused expression on his face.

Thankful he did not question her yet again, Anna relaxed a little as they pulled out of the parking lot and drove a few miles down the road. She rolled down the passenger window and took a few deep breaths of air as it rushed through the window.

"How about the park?" he asked, still watching her out of the corner of his eye.

"That's fine."

He drove for a few minutes before pulling into a shaded parking spot. Anna opened her door and threw off her seatbelt before reaching for her burger. They ate in silence, Anna trying to ignore the inquisitive and concerned looks Joe threw her direction.

When they had finished, Joe asked, "Are you ready to get this research finished before the library closes?"

"Let's do it," Anna said. She cringed when she heard the tiredness echo through her own voice and hoped he didn't know her well enough to notice it.

"It will take about 20 minutes to get there if you want to close your eyes for a bit."

"That's a good idea."

Anna rubbed a hand across her face. Before Joe even pulled out of the parking space, she leaned her head back and closed her eyes. Within two miles, she had drifted off to sleep.

As promised, 20 minutes later, he pulled into a spot at the library and threw the jeep in park. She didn't notice the change in momentum, however, and kept her eyes closed.

"Anna?" Joe whispered.

He touched her elbow when she didn't wake up. Anna jerked awake, and Joe jumped back surprised as he tried to avoid her swinging fists.

"I guess, if we were trying to determine if you had a fight-or-flight response, we now know yours is fight," he said, trying to lighten the mood.

Anna wrapped her arms around her head and growled in frustration.

"Are you sure you're okay?" Joe asked, voicing his concern for her aloud.

After a moment of silence, Anna sat up, grabbed the papers and her bag, and hopped out of the jeep.

"I'm fine," she said. "Let's go."

Joe raised an eyebrow at her, but she seemed back to normal again, so he didn't press the issue. They had work to do and could sort out problems later. Inside, the librarian glared at them when her eyes caught them walking through the doors again. She cleared her throat and straightened the sign on her desk that read, "Quiet, please!" Both Joe and Anna ignored her, sat down, and started whispering.

"All right," Anna said. "Let's start with Callen."

"I'll go through his social media pages, and you look for connections between him and the others on Bryant and Marie's team," Joe said.

"I just ran his court records," Anna said, already typing away on her laptop. "Nothing here."

The sound of her phone ringing interrupted their conversation. The librarian shot up out of her chair and glared at Anna, who silenced the offending device and walked outside. She hesitated to answer it when she saw Alex's name pop up on the screen.

"Anna," Alex said when she answered. "What is going on?"

Anna sighed, "I know, Alex. It doesn't look good, but I promise, everything is all right."

"How is everything all right? Your sister almost died twice in two hours."

Anna sat down on the library's steps before she answered him.

"I can't argue with that," she mumbled. "But I can't just let Marie go through this alone."

"I realize that," he sighed. "But that doesn't mean I have to like it."

Anna smiled, comforted by the sound of his voice.

"Where are you right now?" he asked. "Are you at least safe?"

"I'm at the library," she said. "Doing research."

"Which library?"

"I can't tell you that," she said. "I can't have you coming down here trying to keep me out of this."

"Anna, work with me here," he said, frustration dripping through his voice.

"Can you trust me when I say I'm not in danger?"

"No."

"Come on, Alex, please?"

Silence met Anna on the other end of the line.

"How about this?" he said. "If I get wind of one more thing going wrong or if you are even remotely in harm's way, you'll have to deal with me."

"But what about Marie?"

"At the end of the day, Anna, I don't care about Marie," he said. "I couldn't live with myself if you got hurt, and there was something I could have done to prevent it."

"And I couldn't live with myself if something happened to Marie and I didn't help her."

"I know," Alex said. "I just — I love you, Anna."

Anna smiled. "I love you, too."

"Please be careful."

"I will."

Anna hung up and looked at Alex's image on her phone for a minute. She hated making him go through the stress of the mess she had gotten herself into but knew there wasn't anything she could do about it at this point. She sighed, shoved her phone back in her pocket, and headed back inside.

"You find anything?" she whispered to Joe when she sat back at the table.

"I hacked into his phone, and he has a lot of hidden pictures in it with a woman, but I can't seem to figure out who she is."

"Hmm, let's text a picture of her to Marie and Bryant and see what they think."

Marie responded by saying the woman was Lindsay Sprout, and she also worked in their office. However, Marie was unaware Callen and Lindsay were seeing each other. Callen was a private person, and Marie wasn't close to Lindsay in the least. In fact, she had never said three or four sentences to the woman.

"Well, it looks like we need to look into Lindsay," Joe murmured, already getting to work.

"It would be nice if we could see what type of financial situation she was in," Anna said.

"But we need a warrant first, right?"

Anna side-eyed him and began typing without another word. Joe smiled and surfed through the woman's social media pages. The librarian eyed them but settled down a bit when they stopped talking.

After several minutes, Joe peeked up at the librarian, noticed she was busy with someone else and glanced over at Anna's screen.

"You find anything?" he asked.

Anna frowned. "Well, for what her pay scale is, she doesn't have much money."

"Where's it all going?"

"She has all the normal stuff — car, house, student loans, small credit card balance, a few medical bills, but nothing too major."

"Where is all her money going?"

"That's just it," Anna said. "I can't find where her money's going at all. Either there is an account I'm missing, or she's diverting her paycheck elsewhere."

"Let me visit our friend Jake's super-secure system and find out if she has a second account not listed on the sheet," Joe said.

"Remind me if I'm ever in charge of choosing a human resource system, I don't go with whatever gem those guys are using," Anna said as Joe manipulated their system.

"No, kidding."

After a few clicks of a mouse, Joe had all the information they needed on Lindsay Sprout. The account the HR firm had printed on the employee information sheet and the bank account where her paycheck landed were not the same. In fact, Lindsay wasn't the only name on her direct deposit account.

"Well, it looks like Lindsay was playing the field a bit," Joe said after writing down the name of the man who shared the account with the woman. "Let's see who this guy is."

Anna scrolled through Lindsay's account, looking for anything out of the ordinary while Joe fished for information on the mystery man. Anna filled the time by jotting down a few of the more significant transactions.

"Looks like this guy, Audrick Walker, is the CEO of a holding company," Joe said.

"How are we going to figure out if he's connected to anything?" Anna asked. "They have a few fishy looking transactions coming into and going out of their account, but it will take some legwork to figure out what they go to."

"We need more information from Bryant and Marie," Joe said. "Not much we can do without all the information we need to make connections."

Anna rubbed her temples.

"This is like a never-ending circle of nonsense," she grumbled.

"How about this?" Joe asked. "Let's go back to the hotel, get some rest, and wait for Bryant and Marie to finish up. Then we can see what else they can give us."

"Ugh, sounds good," Anna said, nodding and already gathering her belongings.

The librarian looked relieved when they disappeared through the doors and out of her hair.

Saturday 2:00 PM - Bryant and Marie

"HOW ARE WE GOING TO convince the court to continue this case, Bryant?" Marie asked. "It's not like we can explain WHY we need to continue it."

"Well, the courts are closed, so we can't file it until Monday. Maybe the judge will delay it because we can't schedule a hearing before the original court date and time."

"True," Marie said. "Or we might show up for the hearing, and he denies it and expects us to continue with our case as scheduled."

"We must make our continuance convincing enough to warrant a delay."

"At the very least, I guess we could request a delay because of Callen's death."

"Let's start there," Bryant said.

While Bryant typed on the computer, Marie walked around their office, trying to think of something that would help. She stopped in front of Callen's desk. Saddened by the sudden loss of her co-worker, she sat down and looked at the items on his desk.

Everything seemed impersonal. Marie didn't see any pictures of himself and friends or family anywhere. She saw nothing showing a love life. If he was seeing Lindsay, she didn't see proof of the relationship. Marie put her curiosity to the test by going through the things in Callen's desk.

The first two drawers held mundane items you'd expect to find in a paralegal's desk. At first, Marie believed the third contained more of the same until she closed it in frustration. As the drawer slid shut, Marie noticed something impeded its path.

"Well, that's interesting."

Marie ducked her head below the desk and began feeling around the drawer. Her fingers caught on a manila envelope taped to the underside. The tape securing it had failed to do its job when Marie had shoved the drawer back in place.

"Got something," she said and held the envelope up for Bryant to see.

Bryant raised an eyebrow at her and said, "Callen seems to have some interesting secrets we didn't know about."

Marie spilled out the contents on the top of the desk where Bryant was working.

"Oh, my!" Marie flipped through the pictures that tumbled out. Each image was of Lindsay, with a variety of men, including some prominent politicians around town who both Marie and Bryant recognized.

"What is going on around here?" Bryant asked as he picked up a few of the photos and scrutinized them.

Marie didn't have any answers for him, so she continued to flip through the photos in confusion. Most showed Lindsay in risqué situations with the men. Embarrassed, Marie turned the worst of them upside down on the desk to save her co-worker's modesty.

"Was Callen blackmailing Lindsay?" Bryant asked.

"That seems preposterous," Marie said. "But everything about this case seems crazy at this point!"

Bryant thought for a moment before saying, "I think we need to think of a way to speak with Lindsay."

"How in the world would we get away with that?" Marie asked. "We have no reason to know about her relationship with Callen."

"We could say Callen mentioned something about her, and we wanted to make sure she was all right after what happened?"

"If she's involved in this, that's too dangerous," Marie said.

"What choice do we have, Marie?"

Marie sighed.

"How about we do some research, and we talk to her first thing Monday morning," she conceded. "I don't want to go into this conversation blind."

"Good idea," Bryant said. "Let me finish up here, and we can head back to the hotel to see what Joe and Anna have figured out."

Marie passed the time by snooping through Lindsay's desk, hoping to find something to give them more guidance. But whatever secrets Lindsay had, she kept them elsewhere. Marie found nothing suspicious in her desk. She noticed that, like Callen, Lindsay kept few personal details about her life on display.

Before she could think the situation over any longer, Bryant had completed as much as possible on the continuance request and was ready to go. Marie sighed and looked around the office hoping the next time she wound up inside it, her outlook on the future would appear much brighter.

Chapter 8

Saturday 4:00 PM

ANNA TRIED TO LET THE melody of Joe typing sing her off to sleep, but no matter how hard she tried, she couldn't quiet her racing mind. Worrying about and trying to help her sister's situation had taken a lot from her, and she knew her job was far from over. She sighed, shifted in the bed, and threw her forearm over her eyes, longing for a comfort she knew wouldn't come.

She couldn't measure the amount of relief she felt when she heard Marie and Bryant enter the room. Marie frowned when she saw her sister lying on the bed and sat down next to her.

"Are you all right?" she whispered.

Anna pulled her arm away from her face and gave her sister what she hoped to be a convincing smile. From the look on Marie's face, Anna knew it wasn't convincing enough.

"I'm fine," she lied. "Just a little tired."

"Maybe you should get some sleep?"

"That was the plan."

Anna put her arm back over her eyes but remained restless and could feel Marie observing her. Anna was thankful when Bryant and Joe's conversation soon became a welcome distraction and took Marie's attention off her for the time being.

"We just need more information, Bryant," Joe complained. "I don't know what I'm looking for, so I can't figure out how to find what you need."

Bryant looked over at Marie and said, "I think he's right, Marie. We need to let them have everything if we want them to help us figure out what is going on."

"Fine," Marie said after looking back and forth between Bryant and Joe. "I guess we don't have a choice."

Bryant sighed and pulled a file out of his briefcase. Anna sat up, folded her legs underneath her, and did her best to pay attention. She couldn't help but feel her sister watching her and noticed Joe throwing her a few concerned looks of his own.

"*I must look awful,*" she thought to herself.

"All right," Bryant said, oblivious to any of the issues going on with his team. "Dominique Shaw is our client. He works for a local 'businessman,' Santino Haskell, who allegedly had another local 'businessman' killed earlier this year."

"What's with the air quotes?" Joe asked, mimicking his brother's gestures.

"They are in organized crime," Marie said. "They own a bunch of businesses that aren't exactly improving the communities they are part of."

Bryant continued, "They are so well protected by dirty cops and politicians that no one can touch them."

"But we don't care about any of that," Marie said. "We don't work for Haskell. We work for his associate, who is testifying against him in court."

Bryant nodded. "Our client is a high-level member of Haskell's crime establishment. His job is to take care of issues."

"He ran into some trouble early in his life, and Haskell stepped in to save him," Marie said. "He's been paying Haskell back ever since. But now he's trying to get out of the situation and bring an end to the whole thing."

"He flipped on the whole organization," Bryant said. "That's why it's a federal case. Haskell is being charged with racketeering, money laundering, murder, and many other things based on our guy's testimony and the evidence he's provided."

"We don't know everything, and the authorities haven't been able to fill in all the missing pieces," Marie said. "But the D.A. has built a strong case against Haskell and several of his other top-level guys."

"And the government agreed to a deal because of his testimony?" Joe asked.

"Yes, but he isn't getting off free and clear," Bryant said. "He'll spend the rest of his life in witness protection, so he is giving up everything."

"There are also a few witnesses who can corroborate his testimony and a bunch of evidence, so it's a rather simple process," Marie added. "We were to go in on Tuesday to make things official."

Bryant mused, "I suspect the deal won't be on the table any longer when we go in on Tuesday, however."

Bryant and Marie exchanged a frustrated look. After all the work they'd put into getting the deal, the thought of losing it on the whim of one of their coworkers was exhausting. Anna and Joe looked at each other before sighing and going back to looking through the case's paperwork.

Anna held up one photo from the pile Marie had found earlier. "What are these pictures?"

"Those are pictures of one of our coworkers," Bryant said. "Callen had them in his desk."

Anna whistled as she flipped through them, causing Joe to look over her shoulder at them, a surprised look crossing over his face.

"Who are these guys?" he asked.

"The ones we recognize are politicians, judges, and lawyers throughout the town," Marie said.

"How does this play into this whole ordeal?" Anna asked.

"We don't know," Bryant said, shaking his head. "We assume Callen was blackmailing her or something, but we don't have proof. Marie and I plan to talk to her on Monday. If we can figure out a way to bring up the subject."

The group was silent for a moment, thinking about the next proper step. Finding a connection between all the key players looked impossible, but they at least felt they had the right tools to make it happen.

Joe blew some air out of his mouth in frustration and said, "I suppose this Haskell guy has a long list of businesses, doesn't he?"

Bryant nodded.

"Well, do you have a list?"

Bryant flipped through the pages in his file and pulled out a stack of paper, glancing at it before handing it to his brother. Joe pursed his lips and started turning the pages as a scowl crossed his face.

"There has to be 75 to 100 businesses listed here!"

Bryant nodded, "88."

"I bet some of them connect to that guy on your co-worker Lindsay's account," Anna said. "How can we sort through them to find out?"

"That will take forever," Joe groaned. "I will have to build an algorithm to sort through all this mess. That's the only way I can think of that will help us find a link."

"What do you need?" Bryant asked.

"About 10 hours of sleep and 10 hours of free time to let the algorithm run," Joe said, rubbing his eyes.

"Well, tomorrow is Sunday," Marie said, glancing at her sister, who had once again closed her eyes. "How about we get some sleep and let this algorithm of yours run while Bryant and I chase other leads?"

"Yeah, and I need to file a claim for my car," Bryant said, remembering the melted piece of metal that had once been his mode of transportation.

Before any of the team could discuss their plans further, Marie's phone began ringing. Not recognizing the number, she hesitated but ultimately sighed and answered the phone. When she realized who was on the other end of the line, a surprised look passed across her face.

The group watched her, eager to hear the other half of her conversation.

After a few confused questions, Marie said, "I will need to discuss it with the others first. Should I call you back?"

Shaking her head at the reply, she ended the call and turned to face the rest of the group.

"That was Agent Hoage," she said. "He wants us to meet him. He said they have something they want to talk to us about."

"Yeah," Joe scoffed. "I'm sure he has an arrest warrant for both me and Anna at this point."

"They want us to meet them at your house." Marie looked at Bryant. "They have some information they need to share with us."

"Hmm," Joe said, glancing at Anna. "That still seems dangerous considering some of us might not have been doing EVERYTHING by the book."

"You know," Bryant said, giving him a look. "We never gave you permission to break the law."

Joe shrugged, and Anna looked down and smiled a bit.

"Well, you almost got blown up," Joe said.

Bryant shook his head and turned his attention from his brother back to Marie.

"How about we have them stay back a bit and make sure it's safe first?" he said.

"So," Anna said with a smile, "you are giving us permission to run from the FBI now?"

Her comment caused Joe to snicker but drew glares from both Bryant and Marie.

Bryant ignored Anna. "We can talk to the FBI before letting them in on it."

Joe and Anna looked at each other and shrugged, both too tired to keep arguing with their siblings. They gathered up their evidence and other belongings, checked out of the hotel, and followed Marie and Bryant back home. Joe kept the jeep running and watched as Marie and Bryant talked with the two FBI agents. Several times either Bryant or Marie would glance over at them and give them a funny look.

"I sure would love to know what they are talking about," Joe said.

"Looks like we are fixing to find out," Anna said as Marie started waving them over.

"Should I leave the jeep running, so we can make a run for it if something goes down?"

"I'm too tired to run," Anna laughed. "I'll just sleep in jail for a while."

"Nice of you to join us," Carver said as Anna and Joe approached.

"Didn't want to interrupt your conversation too soon," Joe said, still not convinced they weren't trying to trap him and Anna.

Anna gave Carver a sweet smile and nodded at his sling-free arm. "I see your arm is all healed up!"

"Yeah, I didn't need that thing. They just put my arm in it for precaution," Carver said and frowned at her. "Hey, are you trying to butter me up?"

"She's just seeing how limber you are in case we need to make a run for it," Joe said.

"Relax," said Renato. "You two are fine. Water under the bridge at this point."

"Your buddy had a lot to say about things," said Carver. "It appears the information we have isn't all it's cut out to be."

"You don't say," Joe said.

Bryant gave him a look.

"It appears Ms. Hartman here is being set up," Carver continued. "We don't know by who, but we've thrown your friend in holding and might have spread a rumor about him to help speed up how fast he's willing to talk. I'm sure it will only be a matter of time before he spills everything he knows."

"I think we need to put all of you in protective custody until we figure out what is going on around here," Renato said.

"That's not happening." Anna folded her arms across her chest.

"Yeah," Joe added. "I've seen how you protect people. No, thanks."

Carver and Renato looked at each other.

"We said the same thing," Bryant said. "I think we would prefer to take our chances."

"We've been able to take care of ourselves just fine so far," Marie pleaded.

The agents hesitated, unconvinced it was the right decision.

"We'll be careful," Bryant said, trying to convince them.

"Well, it's your funeral," Carver said. "But, if ANYTHING goes down, I want to be the first to know about it."

"Can't make any promises, Chief," Joe said.

Bryant talked over him and said, "We understand, Agent Hoage. We'll keep you in the loop."

The agents shook their heads at the team but said no more before walking back to their vehicle and pulling out of the driveway. Anna sat down in Joe and Bryant's front yard and leaned back against the dogwood tree near the front of their house.

"You know we can go inside, right?" Joe teased.

"You and I were inside all day today," Anna said. "A little outside time sounds nice."

Marie was already busy dialing a number on her phone.

"I've got to call Eddie," Marie said.

"And, I need to file an insurance claim," Bryant said, walking away while reaching for his phone.

Joe laid down in the grass by Anna and closed his eyes.

"Don't you have an algorithm to build?" Anna joked.

"Ahh," he said with his eyes still closed. "Building the thing will only take an hour or two depending on how long it takes to get all the businesses into the parameters. It'll be running the thing that will take the longest. I won't start on any of that mess until in the morning."

"Good," Anna said. "That means I can sleep in."

Joe laughed and covered his face with his arm to block out the sun. Anna sighed, leaned back against the tree, and closed her eyes, allowing the breeze to cool her skin as the sun tried to warm it. It felt nice to enjoy the beautiful summer day after being cooped up in the library all day.

Her eyes were still closed when she heard a car driving down the road. She looked up just in time to see Alex's familiar car stop in the driveway. Before he could get out of the vehicle, Anna was already flying across the yard to meet him.

He swept her up in a hug, picking her up so her feet dangled a few inches from the ground, her eyes even with his.

"What are you doing here?" she asked, gazing into his dark eyes. "How did you even know where we were?"

"Marie called me," he said, studying her eyes, "since you didn't."

"Of course, she did," Anna said. "I was trying to keep you out of this!"

"I hear you've had quite an interesting day," he said and turned to look at Bryant and Joe and the house behind them. "And met some new friends, I see."

"I'll introduce you in a minute," Anna smiled. "First, I need you to kiss me."

He kissed her on the nose and grinned at her before capturing her lips with his for a longer embrace. She pulled away breathless, and he put her down. Frowning, he gripped her chin with his thumb and index finger and made her look up at him.

"You look tired," he said.

"Why does everyone keep saying that?" Anna said with a small smile. "I'm fine."

"You are not fine," he said. "I'm taking you home to bed."

"How am I going to get any sleep that way?" Anna asked with a sly smile.

Neither Alex nor Anna noticed Joe scrutinizing them. It wasn't until Anna pulled Alex behind her to meet her new friends that she saw something was amiss.

"Do I know you from somewhere?" Alex asked, trying to jog his own memory. "You look familiar."

"Apparently not," Joe said before trudging into his house and slamming the door behind him.

"What was that?" Anna asked Alex, confusion playing out on her face as she watched Joe storm inside the house.

When he didn't reply, Anna turned her attention back to her boyfriend.

"Oh my gosh," Alex gasped.

"What?"

"There was this case I worked on right after I joined S.W.A.T.," Alex said. "It was a bank robbery. Almost two years ago now, I think."

"What does that have to do with Joe?"

"If I remember correctly, his girlfriend was in the bank when it happened. The robbers took her hostage. He was there at the scene when it went down."

"You're kidding me," Anna said.

"I thought he looked familiar, but it's been so long, it took me a minute."

"What happened to his girlfriend?"

"The robbers took off with her in a getaway car but crashed a few miles up the road. They had a big shootout with the police before S.W.A.T. could get there, and she got caught in the crossfire."

Anna stared back at Alex not finding words to say to him.

"He pulled her out of the car," he whispered and looked at the ground.

"And you didn't remember him?" she asked.

He hung his head. "I know, Anna. I'm sorry."

Without another word, Anna turned on her heels and followed Joe inside the house, ignoring the strange looks Marie and Bryant were sending her way. Not knowing Joe well, she didn't know where he would go, so she had to guess. Kitchen? No. Living room? No. She even took the risk and checked the bathroom. She found him sitting against a wall in a darkened back bedroom.

"It's fine," Joe said. "I'll be fine. Just give me a minute."

Anna ignored him and sat down on the floor next to him.

"When I was five," Anna said, "about a week before school started, my mom took me shopping for my first back-pack."

"Anna, if this is one of those sob stories that doesn't relate to what I've gone through, save it," Joe said.

Anna didn't miss the annoyance she heard in his voice.

"Just shut up and listen to me," Anna said before continuing. "Mom loved the start of school and made a huge deal about it with Marie. So, she wanted to make the start of my school career fun and special too."

Anna glanced at Joe to make sure he was still listening to her before continuing.

"She meant it to be a bonding trip for me and her. I still remember how excited I was about the backpack I picked out. It was a Rainbow Brite one. She wasn't as excited about it because it was white and thought it might hold stains. I remember her saying that in the store."

Anna felt her emotions welling up inside her and stopped talking. Out of the corner of her eye, she saw Joe looking at her, a look of concern on his face, so she cleared her throat and tried to continue.

"Sorry," she said, her voice cracking a bit. "I don't talk about this much anymore."

"It's ok."

They sat in silence for a few more moments before Anna found herself capable of continuing.

"Anyway," she said after taking a deep breath. "I was happy as a clam holding onto that thing. Mom wanted to put it in the trunk, but I didn't want it out of my sight."

She smiled a little at the memory.

"So, she let me hang onto it in the car." Anna closed her eyes again. "She had just got me buckled in when two men came up and wanted the car. I was too young to understand I needed to get out."

Anna looked down at her hands in her lap as Joe inspected her face.

"She wasn't about to let them have the car and me, so she reached inside and jerked me out through the window before they stabbed her seven times and took the keys out of her hand."

"That's why you didn't like that shopping center, isn't it?" Joe asked.

Anna nodded and spent some time collecting her thoughts again for a minute.

"Yeah, it only bothers me when I'm tired and stressed, or on her birthday, or the anniversary," she said. "Hell, I guess I don't have a good handle on it most of the time."

Joe was silent for a few moments while he waited for her to continue.

"I know if one of those police officers who showed up that day didn't remember me, I don't know how I would feel because I remember each one of their faces."

Neither Joe nor Anna had any words left, so Joe put his arm around her, and she leaned into him, both thankful for the comfort.

Chapter 9

ANNA FOLLOWED JOE BACK outside and met Alex's eyes. When he saw her, he hung his head and approached them.

"I'm so sorry," Alex said. "I should have remembered."

"It's all right," Joe said.

Anna raised an eyebrow at Alex.

"No, really," he pleaded. "I am sorry."

Joe relented. "It is all right. I'm sure you deal with lots of victims and family members and many things none of us would want to remember."

Trying to bring the controversy to an end, Bryant changed the subject.

"So, what's the plan tomorrow?" he asked.

"Well, I have to finish up that algorithm," Joe said. "And it needs the whole day to run. Maybe it will finish up in the afternoon?"

"Bryant, you and I can continue building our case for a continuance," Marie said.

"I get to sleep in," Anna said, smiling at Alex.

Alex sighed in relief as it seemed Anna had already forgiven his earlier misstep.

"How about we get some dinner and some sleep?" he asked, taking her hand.

The pair bid adieu to the rest of the group, and Anna hopped in Alex's car. He put his arm around her and drove to her apartment, picking up some takeout on the way. Once the food was in the car, Anna began popping French fries in her mouth, most of which were gone by the time the sacks made it to the kitchen table and the rest of the food was separated.

"You were hungry," Alex said, watching her devour her meal.

"I know!" she said. "We had quite the day, and we didn't have much time to stop and eat."

"You should have let me come help you," he said. "I could have at least made sure you didn't starve yourself today."

Anna smiled and poked another fry into her mouth.

"You don't have to worry that much."

Alex reached across the table and brushed a strand of hair out of her eyes.

"What kind of boyfriend would I be if I didn't worry about you?" he whispered.

Anna smiled at him again and went back to eating. She tried to keep the tiredness she felt out of her eyes but felt them growing heavier by the second. When she'd had her fill of the food, Alex took her hand and stroked it with his thumb.

"Well, at least I can take care of something for you," he said. "Not much of a date, but at least I fed you."

"We have had better dates," Anna said.

"Well, the night's not over yet," Alex said. "I still have to put you to bed."

"Are you planning to join me, Mr. Vega?"

Anna's heart quickened as she stared back into his dark eyes, the need for him growing out of her control.

"I don't know," he teased. "You spent your entire day avoiding me."

"Oh, I'm not avoiding you now," Anna said. "In fact, I want all of you I can get."

"Is that so?" Alex asked rising to his feet and stepping around the table.

Anna gazed up at him, her heart racing and breath growing ragged. Alex took her hand and pulled her to her feet.

"I'm sure you're too tired," he said.

"I'm not THAT tired," she whispered.

He smiled and brushed his lips against hers. Anna pouted when he pulled away from her.

"I'm not tired either," he grinned and swooped her up into his arms and toted her towards the bedroom. By the time they reached the door, the leftovers on the kitchen table were long forgotten.

Chapter 10

Sunday 7:00 AM - Anna

ANNA JERKED AWAKE IN her bed, her heart and mind racing. The memory of the nightmare was fresh and terrifying. She felt for Alex beside her in bed only to panic when she found his side of the bed empty. With determination, she began the process to slow her rapid breathing and regain her sense of focus.

She squinted as she noticed for the first time the sun streaming in through her bedroom window. As her other senses began to return to her, she began moving her eyes around her bedroom looking for a source of comfort and stability. The fan above her was on, and she could hear it whirring. It put off a breeze that chilled her exposed skin and she pulled the surrounding covers a little tighter.

Anna laid on her back and watched the fan spin in circles, desperate to get her mind to cooperate with her efforts to calm it. Instead, it was as though she were spinning out of control, and everything bombarded her at once. The worry about Marie, the memory of her mother, every emotion from the entire weekend pounded on her tired mind, threatening to throw her over the edge.

After what seemed like an eternity, Alex emerged from her bathroom with a towel wrapped around his waist and gave her a strange look.

"Are you all right?" he asked.

Trying to compose herself so he wouldn't worry, she gave him a thumbs-up sign but couldn't manage much more than that. Not convinced, he approached her side of the bed and bent down to give her a kiss.

"Are you sure?"

"I would be better if you stayed," she said.

She cursed the needy sound her voice had taken. The last thing she wanted was for him to have just one more reason to worry about her. Holding her breath, she peered up into his eyes and hoped he would reconsider going into work that day.

"I'm sorry, honey," he said. "You know I have a shift today. I don't have a good reason to use sick time."

Anna stared in his eyes, willing him to change his mind, even though she already knew he wouldn't. She caught sight of the worry creeping up in his eyes and blinked a few times to push whatever he was seeing in hers away. Trying to put his mind at ease, she smiled and wrapped her arms around him, pulling him back into bed with her.

Alex laughed. "Anna, I have to get ready for work."

"Ahh," Anna pouted, "but I'm lonely in here."

Alex kissed her again but pulled away. He lingered above her, peering in her eyes with a look of concern.

"I'll be back later tonight," he said. "Why don't you stay there and sleep some today before you go gallivanting around trying to help your sister?"

Anna continued pouting but dropped the subject and instead watched him get ready for work. The closer he got to leaving her, the faster her heart raced. By the time he was ready to walk out the door, Anna was sure her pulse would run away with her once and for all.

"I've got to go," Alex hesitated.

Trying to put on a brave face, Anna said, "It's all right."

"I love you," he said.

Anna sat up in bed and smiled back at him as he headed for the door. It wasn't until he stepped through the door and closed it behind him that Anna dropped the smile from her face and allowed her ragged breathing to return. As she felt her panic rise to a level out of her control, she threw the covers off and began pulling clothes on her shaking body.

That task complete, she shoved a few articles of clothing and her journal in a duffel bag before digging through her closet to find her motorcycle helmet. Its cold, smooth fiberglass surface felt soothing to her fingers, and she closed her eyes and sighed, already feeling somewhat better.

She tucked it under her arm, scooped a pair of keys off a pegboard in the kitchen, and locked up her apartment. Anna allowed her feet to carry her to the motorcycle parked in a secluded spot in the parking lot. The moment the engine roared to life, Anna popped the helmet on her head and left, taking the quickest route possible to get her to HWY 64 and the secluded portion of Virginia Beach that always pulled her into its grasp.

Over the next two hours, Anna tried to get her mind to focus on the road, the sun, and the beach. She remained successful except for the handful of times when the negative thoughts crept back into her mind and took her breath away. Those moments created a need for her to pull to the side of the highway and wait until the panic passed before she continued her journey.

While it took longer than it should have, Anna eventually drove through the small beach town and turned onto the road that took her to her final stop. When her feet felt sand beneath them, she sighed and sank to the ground, content to listen to the roaring waves and the chatter of the surfers nearby. She pulled out her journal and ignored the other pages already filled with her writing and flipped to a blank page.

Anna let her pen hover over the page for several seconds before her hand began to move across the crisp white page, her thoughts and fears spilling out on the pages like tears falling from her soul. Around her, the sun shined, the beach bent and changed with the waves, and the water rushed back and forth from the sea, and Anna wrote, letting the comfort and safety of the beach take her fears away.

Chapter 11

Sunday - 8:00 AM - Joe

JOE'S EYES FOLLOWED Marie as she paced around his living room, her cellphone clutched to her ear. It was the fifth time in fifteen minutes that she'd waited without an answer. This time, she left a message.

"Anna, don't make me worry about you," Marie whispered. "We don't have time for this right now."

Joe's ears perked up at the sound of Anna's name, and he watched Marie closer than before. Her frenzied pacing caused his heart to quicken, and he soon felt a touch of worry gnawing at his stomach. He glared at his brother, who was busy sorting through papers at the desk Anna had taken over yesterday and not noticing Marie's distress.

When Marie glanced at her watch, sighed, and started tapping the screen of her phone again, Joe sat back in his chair and crossed his arms, no longer willing to hide the fact that he was watching Marie. This time when she pulled the phone to her ear, she sighed when someone answered her call. Joe could listen to only one side of the conversation and did his best to fill in the rest in his mind.

Marie turned her back to him and whispered, "Alex, is Anna with you? I can't find her."

Joe tried to peer around her to capture a glimpse of her face, but she rubbed her forehead, her arm obscuring his view of her. Frustrated, Joe tapped his foot on the floor and waited for her to finish the conversation.

"I stayed over at Eddie's last night," Marie said. "I stopped by the apartment this morning and she wasn't there."

Marie grew silent again and nodded as she listened to whatever Alex was telling her.

"Frankie and Claire have her car, so she had to take her bike," Marie said. "And, I checked for her journal and it's gone, too."

Marie shook her head when Alex continued talking.

"It's not your fault," she said. "How were you supposed to know? It's not like she ever says anything. Please don't worry about her. I'll keep trying to call her and will let you know when I hear from her."

After hanging up, Marie began pacing again, this time a little faster. By this time, her concern for her sister had captured both Joe's and Bryant's attention.

"What's going on?" Joe demanded when she failed to stop pacing.

Marie sighed and stopped pacing.

"I can't find Anna."

When a confused look passed between the two brothers, Marie shook her head and sat on the couch facing them both.

"Anna takes off from time to time."

"Anna just leaves?" Joe asked. "Where does she go?"

"Well, if I knew that, we wouldn't be having this conversation, now would we?"

Marie put her head in her hands and sighed. Joe frowned and pondered the situation. He thought back to the moments yesterday when Anna had seemed off.

"What does she do when she leaves?" he asked. "How long does she stay gone?"

"It depends," Marie said, her head still bowed. "Sometimes she comes back within a few hours and others she calls me to pull her out of jail. I don't know how it will turn out until she shows up."

Joe raised his eyebrows. "How often do you have to pull her out of jail?"

Marie sighed. "It's been a while. I'm hoping she doesn't restart that trend now."

Joe sat back in the chair and allowed his thoughts to take over. Before he could reach any solution, however, Marie jumped up and waved off the conversation.

"It doesn't matter," she said. "She always shows back up. We have other things to worry about."

"Why does she take off?" Joe pressed, not ready to put the topic to the side.

"Joe, really," Marie said. "It's not that big of a deal. I'm sure she'll be back this afternoon. It's fine."

"So, you would just prefer to worry about her all day?"

"What choice do I have?"

"Maybe if you tell us what's going on, we can think of a solution to the problem?" Joe said.

"Well, if you didn't gather, she deals with a bit of PTSD. But, NATURALLY, she thinks she can handle it on her own."

"And, taking off is her way of taking care of it?"

"That and writing in her journal," Marie grumbled. "You would think she could stay here to write in that thing, but nope. She has to worry everyone first."

Ignoring her sarcasm, Joe continued to press for more information.

"And you don't have a clue where she goes?"

"Trust me. I've tried to find her. We all have; Alex, Claire, all of us. We just aren't capable of finding her until she's ready to let us find her."

"So, you and Alex just keep calling her until she shows up?"

"Ugh," Marie growled. "We don't have time for this! We've got to work on this case!"

Joe thought for a minute.

"How about you and Bryant work on the case, and you let me find Anna?"

"How are you going to find her? She's been doing this for years. She's an expert at hiding," Marie said.

"Oh, I can find her," Joe assured. "She's not as sneaky as she thinks she is. But, if you'd rather I didn't, you can go back to worrying about her and not getting anything done."

Marie thought for a minute before conceding.

"She's going to kill me," she said, "but do it. Bryant and I have to get this case together for tomorrow, and I can't spend the entire day worrying about her."

Joe had already turned back to his computer and was typing on the keyboard.

"I have to let this algorithm run today anyway, so I have some time to kill."

"Marie, how about you and I head back to the office and try to finish this up?" Bryant suggested. "Joe has our number, and he can call us the minute he finds her."

Marie nodded and gathered the paperwork she had been working on and followed Bryant outside. Joe waved his hand at them as they were leaving. As he typed, his computer spun into action and he smiled when he located her phone's signal.

"Ha!"

He watched her location flicker along the map on his screen for a moment in confusion.

"Where are you headed?" he mused.

After a few moments, he saw her turn on a familiar highway and smiled.

"Gotcha," he said before closing his laptop and grabbing a few things for the road.

It took two hours for him to catch up to where she'd parked herself at the beach. Catching sight of a small black motorcycle along the road, he pulled in behind it and looked around, spotting Anna.

She had dug her feet into the sand and was busy watching the surfers tackle the large waves off the coast. He watched her for a moment from his jeep before sending off a quick text to Bryant to put Marie's mind at ease.

Bryant texted back, *"Where did you find her?"*

Joe shook his head and typed, *"Nope. I told Marie I would find her, not tell her WHERE I found her. My job is over. Have a good day at work."*

With that, he popped his phone in his glove box, locked up his jeep, and set off across the beach in Anna's direction. He could almost feel her surprise when she realized he had chased her down. He sensed she was trying to keep her face impassive as she watched him approach.

"Looks like I need to find another hiding spot," she grumbled when he pulled a chair up next to hers and sat down.

"Nah, I won't rat you out," he said.

Still not looking at him, Anna said, "If you were expecting some big conversation about this, you'll wind up disappointed."

"Nope," he said, not looking at her. "I just wanted to make sure you are all right. You worried your sister."

"She's always worried," Anna grumbled and turned her attention back to the surfers.

Joe watched her out of the corner of his eye, not sure what else to say. She crossed her arms across a white tank top, which did nothing to hide the bright colors of the bikini she wore underneath.

After several minutes of silence, Joe took a chance and asked, "Do you do that?"

"Do what?" Anna asked, sounding confused by his new tactic.

"Surf?" He pointed at the surfers.

Anna frowned at him.

"I do," she hesitated.

Joe glanced over at a stand near the water, saw a stack of surfboards for rent, and smiled at her.

"Let's see what you've got," he grinned.

"Are you challenging me?" Anna stammered.

Joe pulled off his t-shirt and rose to his feet without another word and began walking towards the surfboard stand. Anna's surprised eyes followed him, and it relieved him when she stood to her feet and took off after him.

"Wait," she said. "How did you know how to find me?"

"I have a computer program that follows cellphone signals. There's basically only one reason to take that highway, so I took a chance."

He looked back over his shoulder at her. "I would have brought my board, but I wasn't positive about surfing. Now, are we going to do this or not?"

"Fine," she said, pulling off her t-shirt and shorts and tossing them back toward her chair and other belongings. "It's your funeral."

Anna and Joe spent the next few hours trying to top each other's surfing skills. When it was all said and done, neither would concede to the other. After one more difficult ride, Anna straddled her board and floated in the water, a smile on her face. Joe looked back at her relieved to see her easy-going personality return.

"How about we call it a day?" Joe asked.

"Sure," she said. "I'm sure we have work to do at this point."

"If I let you ride your own bike back," Joe said, "will you come back, or are you going to give me the slip and make me chase you again?"

Anna laughed a bit before replying.

"I'll come back. I promise."

"Well, at least you know I can find you now," Joe said with a grin.

"Yeah, well, I must do something about that," she said, semi-glaring at him.

He laughed and began paddling back to shore, Anna close behind him. After they'd returned their rented boards, Anna and Joe walked back to their chairs to retrieve their belongings. Joe tried to ignore the looks thrown at Anna from a few guys they passed on their way. It didn't surprise Joe when she didn't notice the attention she was receiving.

"All right," he said when they'd walked back to his jeep and her bike. "You promise you won't take off on me now?"

"Yeah," she sighed. "I promise."

Joe shook his head and opened the door to his jeep, but Anna stopped him from climbing inside.

"Hey," she said. "Thank you for coming after me today."

"I figured you needed a friend."

"I did," she said with a smile. "Thanks."

Joe smiled and climbed into the jeep and watched her rev the bike's engine and pop on her helmet. He led her out on the highway, his eyes flitting from the road to his rearview mirror until he was certain she would keep her promise to him. Relieved, he settled in for the drive but soon felt something tugging at his mind. After a few miles, he sighed and opened the phone app on his jeep's dashboard and instructed it to call home.

"Mom?" he asked when his mother had picked up the line. "I take it you and dad are back from his chemo treatment. How did everything go?"

"Hey, Joe!" she said, excited to hear her son's voice. "Everything went fine! Where are you and Bryant at?"

"That's a long story," he groaned. "I'll fill you in on the details when I get home. But, mom, I need to talk to you for a minute."

"All right," she said.

Joe flinched when he heard the concern float through his mother's voice.

"Is everything ok?"

"Yeah, everything's fine," Joe said glancing in his rearview mirror at Anna again. "I just need to tell you something. But I need you not to get all worked up about it, all right?"

"Well, I'll try," she laughed. "But with you, I can't make any promises."

"Yeah, but I need you to try this time, mom," Joe sighed.

"Just tell me already, Joe," his mother chided.

"I'm bringing a girl home with me," he said.

"OK."

Joe tried to ignore the sliver of hope he heard already creeping into her voice.

"But, she's not my girl. She's just a friend. We are working together on something for Bryant."

"Why are you telling me this?"

"Because she's pretty, and you'll love her," Joe said. "But she's had a rough couple of days and doesn't need to deal with any matchmaking mischiefs you might have up your sleeve."

"I'll be on my best behavior," his mother said.

"I'm serious, mom," Joe insisted. "She has a boyfriend, and this is just a work thing. I need you to not make a big deal about this. Can you do that?"

"I'll try," she said. "But you've played her up a lot and made me curious about her now."

Joe groaned.

"Please, don't do anything crazy when I get there, mom," he said. "She's been through some stuff like I have, and I'd like to think I could help her. But that won't work if you have it in your head that we are anything more than friends."

"All right, all right," his mother protested. "You've made your point, Joe. I'll make sure I imply nothing. I won't even make the cookies I thought about making when we first started this conversation."

"Oh, you can make the cookies," he laughed. "Even friends deserve your cookies."

Chapter 12

Sunday 4:00 PM

ANNA'S EYES LURCHED open when she heard the unmistakable sound of car doors slamming. She looked around, still confused after just waking up. After reminding herself that she was in Joe's room, she threw the blanket off her and tiptoed to the door. She cringed when she could hear her sister's angry voice floating down the hall as she tried to get information from Joe.

"Where is she?" Marie demanded.

Anna strained to hear Marie's voice and cracked the door so she could listen in on the conversation.

"Jeez," she heard Joe reply. "How about you warn me next time you come in here like that?"

"Where is she, Joe?"

"Relax," he said. "She's asleep. I made her call Alex, fed her, and now I'm making her rest. Everything's fine."

"Everything is NOT fine!"

Anna sighed and hung her head as she took in her sister's anger from afar. She hesitated to venture from the bedroom, not wanting to argue with her sister just yet. Instead, she stood with her ear to the door, straining to hear Marie's continued argument with Joe.

"Marie, calm down," Joe said. "Yesterday was hard on her. Why don't you give her a break?"

Anna smiled, grateful for his defense of her. Silence filled the house and Anna imagined Marie and Joe were staring off with one another. Sighing, she opened the door a little further but stopped when her sister continued arguing with Joe.

"Can you at least tell me where she was?"

"No," Joe said. "I can't."

Marie sighed, "Why not?"

"Because I told her I wouldn't."

"After everything she's put me through, I deserve to know where I can find her when she takes off."

"Well, if she wanted you to know, she would tell you herself. It's not my place..."

"I guess I'll just have to call you the next time she disappears and make you go get her," Marie interrupted.

"Sounds like it."

Anna sighed, opened the door, and walked down the hallway. Before she could reach the room, however, she heard Bryant's voice.

"Where's Anna?" he asked.

"Don't start that again," Joe grumbled.

"She's sleeping," Marie said.

Anna rounded the corner and saw Joe turn back to his computer and end his participation in the conversation. Bryant looked to Marie with raised eyebrows.

"Where?" Bryant asked, turning back to his brother.

"Where do you think, Bryant?" Joe asked, spinning around in his chair. "I didn't have anywhere else to put her?"

Anna cleared her throat, causing all three of their heads to snap to the living room's doorway. She avoided looking in Marie's direction and ignored her critical examination. Whatever Marie saw in her countenance relaxed her, however, because Anna saw her give Joe a grateful look.

"Any results from that algorithm yet?" Anna asked, avoiding the elephant in the room.

Marie sighed but didn't start arguing with her. Joe glanced back at the computer screen and leaned forward to type a few keys on the keyboard after realizing the algorithm had run its course. Pages started spewing out of his printer. As they came out, Marie began picking them up, confused by their content.

"What is all this, Joe?"

"Those are all the businesses with a connection between your friend Lindsay's boyfriend and your nemesis Haskell."

"Wow," Marie said as the pages continued to print.

"Yep, it will take some time to sort through everything," he said.

"What are we looking for?" Marie flipped through the pages.

Joe shrugged. "A money trail or illegal connection between the holding company and Haskell, I guess."

"This is a lot to go through," Marie complained.

"Well, I guess we'd better get to work," Anna said, looking in her sister's direction.

When Marie gave Anna a chastising look, Joe swept in between them and started handing out pages before she could speak. Anna sat down on the couch and began looking through the pile he had given her. The rest of the group followed suit, and the room fell silent for several minutes until Bryant and Joe's mom walked in, carrying a plate of cookies.

"Well, I see both of my boys brought girls home with them," she said.

Anna looked up just in time to catch the glare Joe sent his mother's way.

"Mom, this is Marie. Marie, this is our mother, Beth," Bryant said. "I'm assuming you've already met Anna."

Beth smiled. "It's lovely to meet you, Marie! I thought you all could use a little snack. And don't worry about dinner. That will be ready soon."

"Oh, goodness!" Marie said. "You didn't have to worry about feeding us!"

"I love cooking," Beth said. "It's no trouble at all."

Before they could protest further, she disappeared back into the kitchen. Anna couldn't help but notice how she caught Joe's eye before making her escape. He rolled his eyes when his mother grinned at him and gave her a warning look. Knowing Joe hadn't intended her to see the exchange, Anna returned her attention to the paperwork in front of her and lost herself in the data. When she spotted something strange, a frown passed across her face.

"Hey guys," she said. "Do you know any reason a shopping center would need to spend $200,000 on delivery vans?"

"Maybe they deliver orders or something?" Bryant suggested.

Anna looked up at Marie. "If that's the case, we need to fill Claire in on this development, so she'll quit making me go to the mall with her."

"Let me see," Marie said, taking the papers out of Anna's hand. "Joe, can you look up what type of shopping center this is? It's called Kinship Plaza over on 2nd Street."

"Hmm," Joe said after pulling up the center's website. "Looks like a generic shopping center. It has a retail store, a salon, a takeout restaurant, and it looks like an accounting firm is in there. I don't see a business that would need a delivery van, though."

"Looks like we might be onto how they are laundering their money, at least," Marie shrugged.

"Let's look in that direction," Bryant said

The pile grew to include a dozen businesses. A pizza company that had bought $150,000 worth of computer equipment, a beauty salon that somehow needed to remodel their kitchen to the sum of $250,000 and even a clothing store that had invested $500,000 in a watch company even though they didn't sell watches in their store quickly made their way to the pile.

"How are they getting away with this?" Anna asked after adding a third company to the pile.

"Shady accounting," Bryant said. "Happens all the time."

Marie nodded. "This is the reason forensic accountants get paid so well. These companies bury this stuff so far in their tax returns even the IRS has a difficult time noticing it."

"On the surface, they seem like legitimate charges," Bryant continued. "The government doesn't have time to nickel and dime all these businesses."

"Half a million dollars seems like a significant amount of money," Joe said.

"Not when you're talking about holding companies who turn in multibillion-dollar tax returns every year," Marie said. "Unless they devote a team of people to sift through the financial statements like we are, they will miss some of this smaller stuff."

"And, if there are hundreds of holding companies out there doing the same thing," Anna said.

"Exactly," Marie and Bryant said in unison.

The group went back to shuffling through papers again, and silence filled the air. It was so quiet, in fact, that the sound of Anna's phone ringing made everyone jump in surprise.

Chapter 13

STILL LOOKING AT THE paper in her hand, Anna scooped up her phone and answered, her voice taking on a distracted tone.

"Well, hello to you, too," the voice on the other end of the line said.

"Oh, Claire!" Anna said, remembering the ruined weekend for the first time all day. "Are you and Frankie headed back?"

"Yep," Claire said. "And I bought you a present."

Anna groaned but laughed a little at the same time.

"Please tell me you didn't buy me something ugly again," she said.

"I'm offended," Claire said, feigning annoyance. "You just don't know good taste when it hits you in the face."

Anna laughed. "I'm kidding. Where are you guys at?"

"Oh, about two hours away," Claire said with a curious tone to her voice. "Are you still hanging out with those handsome brothers?"

Anna glanced up at Joe embarrassed, hoping he couldn't hear Claire on the other end of the line. He frowned back at her, intrigued by her sudden attention. Anna's cheeks warmed, and she jerked her eyes away from him. Her reaction to their short exchange left her feeling confused.

"Yeah," she said to Claire. "We're still here."

"Oh, goody!" Claire said.

Anna heard her clap her hands and prayed Frankie was behind the wheel of her car instead of Claire.

"I wanted to make sure where we needed to bring your car before we got too close," Claire continued. "I'm super excited to get to know your new friends better."

Anna couldn't find the words to respond to her friend.

"Anna?" Claire asked, sounding concerned.

"Um, yeah," Anna said, shaking her head to clear it. "That's fine. But I have my bike here, so I'll just follow you back home when you get here."

"Why did you hesitate just now?" Claire asked.

"I, um, didn't," Anna lied.

"Anna," Claire reprimanded. "I know you. You hesitated."

Before Anna had to answer, Beth waltzed back into the room.

"All right, my little detectives," she grinned. "That's enough work for tonight. Dinner is on the table."

"Sorry, Claire," Anna whispered. "I've got to go. See you when you get here."

"Don't think I'm dropping this conversation," Claire said.

Anna cringed at the annoyed tone she heard in her friend's voice but hung up without addressing it. Bryant and Marie were already planning out the next day before Anna even had time to hang up with Claire, but she was thankful for the distraction.

"We'll file our continuance first thing in the morning," Bryant said while he and Marie gathered up the paperwork and documents strewn across the coffee table.

"Yep, and we'll be in court all afternoon," Marie groaned.

"So, what are we supposed to do tomorrow?" Joe asked.

"I don't know about you," Anna said. "But I have class. I have a final tomorrow morning, and my professor will have my head if I don't make it in to take it."

Joe laughed. "So, after class, then. What are we doing?"

"I guess," Bryant said before Anna could reply, "you two could keep at this. We've got to find some connections and get some evidence rolling in."

"All right," Beth said, folding her arms across her chest with authority. "Now that you've settled things for tomorrow, let's get some dinner inside you before it gets cold. And, I'm sure you ladies need to get home before it gets too dark out."

Bryant and Joe looked at each other and rolled their eyes as they followed their mother into the dining room. Anna and Marie gasped at the spread she had laid out for them.

"Mrs. Malone!" Marie said after seeing all the dishes on the table. "You did not have to go to all this trouble!"

"Oh, don't be silly," Beth said. "We all had to eat. And I told you I love to cook. These boys have grown accustomed to it, so they don't appreciate it like others do. It's nice to have some new faces to cook for."

"Uh, we don't take it for granted!" Bryant kissed his mom on top of her head.

Joe, already popping a piece of a dinner roll in his mouth, nodded in agreement and gave his mom a squeeze around the shoulders.

"Well, we appreciate it," Anna said.

"You are welcome," Beth said, taking her hand in hers and leading her to a chair. "Now, eat, everyone! I need to get a plate to my husband. He's still feeling under the weather from his last chemo treatment, so he won't be at the table tonight."

The group didn't waste any time getting to work on the delicious food Beth had prepared for them. After two long days of legwork, a good, home-cooked meal tasted even better. It wasn't long before the dishes began to empty, and everyone looked as though they had their fill. Just as they finished the last few bites of the meal, Beth popped into the kitchen and brought back a chocolate pie. Bryant rolled his eyes and looked at his brother, who was eyeing the pie with renewed hunger.

"I always knew she likes you more than me," Bryant joked.

"Nah," Joe said. "She's still trying to bribe me to be good."

Anna shook her head and tried to hide her grin by sliding a bite of her piece of pie into her mouth. She hadn't caught her smile quick enough to hide it from Joe, however. He slid his hand across the table and tried to steal her plate. She glared at him, jerked the plate away, and popped another bite of the pie in her mouth.

"Stop that," his mother warned as she put a plate down in front of him. "There's plenty for everyone."

Bryant glared at his brother and shook his head. "You're a child."

Joe ignored him and eyed his pie instead.

"I know," he said as he put a bite of the pie in his mouth and closed his eyes to savor the taste.

The pie didn't last long on anyone's plates, and before long, the group began clearing the table and cleaning the empty dishes in the kitchen, much to Beth's dismay.

"I can get those!" she insisted as everyone pitched in to clean up the dining table and kitchen. "There is no need for you to do all this!"

"Don't be silly, mom," Bryant said. "You go back to dad. You have had a long day. Get some rest. We've got this!"

Beth was still shaking her head when they shooed her out of her own kitchen. Just as the group was finishing up the task, Anna heard a familiar sound outside as Claire and Frankie pulled into the driveway in her car. Anna went to check on her friends by meeting them in the driveway with Marie close behind her.

"I feel so relaxed!" Claire said as she exited the passenger side door of Anna's car.

Frankie handed Anna her keys and rolled her eyes.

"How do you deal with her all the time?" she whispered. "She's relentless! I had to carry soooo many shopping bags for her this weekend I think I need to go back to the spa just to take care of the muscle kinks she caused me!"

Anna laughed and looked over at her friend, amused. Claire ignored the conversation about her and swept up to her friend with a big shopping bag clutched in her hand.

"As promised," she grinned, "your gift."

Anna looked at the bag in Claire's hand and shook her head the moment Claire pulled out a huge floppy hat. A huge smile passed across Claire's face as she held it up for Anna to examine.

"You love it," she squealed, "Don't you?!"

"Uh, is it a bowl?" Anna asked. "Cause if you think I'm wearing it as a hat, you're mistaken."

Claire, ignoring Anna's dislike for the new treasure, attempted to plop it on her head while saying, "It's a BEAUTIFUL hat, and it will look fantastic on you. See, it's PERFECT!"

Claire jumped back, clapped her hands in delight and reached forward to make a few adjustments to how the hat was sitting on Anna's head.

"Uh, am I supposed to be able to see?" Anna asked.

She picked her chin up a bit and tried to gaze at her friend in amusement.

"If you two are quite done," Marie said while carrying the belongings she had brought with her to her car, "we need to get home. I want to see Eddie. Bryant and I have a big day together tomorrow, and I'm sure you and Alex need to have a chat."

"Crap," Anna said under her breath. "I forgot about Alex."

"How did you forget about Alex?" Claire asked, eyeing her friend.

"It's a long story," Anna said, "we aren't talking about it right now."

Claire glanced at Bryant and Joe, who were watching the proceedings take place from the porch and frowned at Anna. Anna ignored her and breezed past the brothers into the house to retrieve her belongings.

"See you ladies tomorrow," Bryant said when Anna had returned. "Marie, should we meet at the office around 6?"

"Sounds good to me," she said. "See you then."

Marie opened her driver's door and climbed inside, and Frankie plopped down in the passenger seat beside her.

Before closing the door and turning the ignition, Marie caught her sister's attention and said, "I'll take Frankie home. You can deal with all of Claire's shopping mess and take her home."

Anna looked over at her friend, who was sorting through shopping bags in Anna's trunk. Claire lifted her head out from amongst the packages and shrugged her shoulders.

"Oh, and I don't want in the middle of whatever argument you and Alex are about to have, so I'm staying at Eddie's tonight," Marie continued. "I'll see you tomorrow."

Anna rolled her eyes but nodded in acknowledgment to her sister and turned to face Joe.

"I'll text you tomorrow after class so we can come up with a game plan for the afternoon," Anna said.

"Sounds good, Mary," Joe said, a smile playing out on his face.

Anna chuckled and said, "Until then, John."

Anna ignored Claire's inquisitive glance as she watched the exchange between Anna and Joe. After the brothers disappeared inside, Anna reached inside the trunk to help her friend sort through her new belongings. Claire grabbed Anna's arm and gave her a stern look.

"Anna, please don't tell me something's going on there," she hissed.

Anna looked at her, surprised, "What in the world would be going on?"

"What the crap was that? Something's happened this weekend. You have an inside joke with him for crying out loud. And I know you. You hesitated earlier when you were on the phone with me."

"You're being silly," Anna said before slamming the trunk shut. "Nothing's going on. We have some things in common, that's all."

"Really," Claire said.

She glared at her friend and put her hands on her hips unconvinced.

"Just friends. I promise."

Anna stared back at her friend and began to feel exasperation build up inside her the longer Claire refused to believe her. To escape the uncomfortable conversation, Anna popped her helmet on her head and strode back to her bike. When Claire shook her head and climbed into the car, Anna sighed, revved the engine, and disappeared down the road.

Chapter 14

Sunday 7:00 PM - Anna

"OH, YOU ARE IN TROUBLE," Claire whispered to Anna after she had parked a few spots away from Anna's apartment.

Anna allowed her gaze to sweep over her front door and to the chair on her small porch. Seeing her boyfriend sitting there would normally bring her excitement, but today his angered expression made her stomach lurch.

She and Claire watched him for a second as he pulled French fries out of the container he held and put them in his mouth. Claire and Anna exchanged a look when he ignored their presence.

"You want me to drive you back home?" Anna asked.

"And, delay you getting to deal with that?" Claire said. "No, thank you. Besides, I'm just around the corner. I can walk."

"Thanks, Claire," Anna said.

Claire paused and wrapped her arms around her friend.

"Call me and tell me how it goes," she said.

"Well, if all goes well," Anna smiled. "I won't be calling you tonight."

Claire laughed and waved Anna off, shooing her toward Alex. Anna hung her head and took her walk of shame to her boyfriend, who still refused to look at her.

"Hey," she whispered.

"Nice of you to show up," Alex grumbled, looking up into Anna's eyes. She met them with hers for a moment, but the anger in his dark eyes caused her to look down at her shoes. As silence filled the warm night air, Anna searched her mind for something to make things right again.

"I'm sorry," she whispered.

Her eyes filled with tears and she avoided looking at him. She couldn't hide her tears from him, however. He sighed and reached out to take her hand. With little effort, he convinced her to let him pull her into his lap.

"I just worry about you when you disappear on me," he murmured. "I'm not angry with you."

Still not meeting his eyes, Anna felt him watch her profile for a second. A few tears escaped down her cheek and he caught them with his thumb. She closed her eyes, his touch bringing comfort to her tired mind.

"Can you at least tell me where you went?"

Anna was silent for a moment. She let a few more tears fall from her eyes, and they fell unhindered down her cheeks while Alex waited for her answer. She shook her head in response, cringing when he sighed.

"I wish you would talk to me about it," he said. "You know you can talk to me about anything, right?"

Anna hated the sadness she heard in his voice but couldn't explain her need to leave him behind sometimes.

"I know," she said, still not looking at him. "I just, can't."

Anna examined her hands, sensing he had something else to say to her. She let him watch her, wanting to reassure him she was all right while knowing she couldn't. He wrapped her up in his arms and pressed his cheek against her forehead.

"I need to ask you something," he hesitated.

"Okay."

"Please don't take it the wrong way."

"I'll try."

"Do we have a problem?" he asked.

Anna could hear the hesitation dripping through his voice, which was an emotion that confused her. When she didn't answer, he captured her chin with his hand and pulled her face up until her eyes met his.

"Anna?"

"I don't know what you mean," she said.

"I've never had another guy bring you home before," he said.

Anna frowned as he examined her eyes.

"Should I be worried about that?"

Anna pulled away from him so she could turn her body to face him. She placed her knees beside his hips and wrapped her arms around his neck and sat back on his knees.

"Have I ever given you a reason to doubt me?" she asked

Wanting to reassure him, she maintained eye contact. The uncertain look in his eye was like a dagger to her heart.

"Why did you come back with him?"

"I didn't have a choice, did I? That was Marie's doing. She sent him after me."

"You can talk to him, but not me?"

"Just because Joe found where I was, and I came back doesn't mean we talked about anything."

Looking unconvinced, Alex continued searching her eyes for a few more moments before relenting.

"I promise you can trust me with this," Anna insisted.

"You know I trust you," he relented. "If you say there isn't a problem, there isn't a problem."

Relieved to know she still held his trust, Anna smiled at him. Reaching up with both his hands, Alex pulled her face to his and claimed her mouth. When he finished with her, he picked her up in his arms and carried her inside the apartment.

"Let's go to bed," he said. "I want to remind you who you belong to."

Sunday 11:00 PM - Alex

ANNA'S SKIN FELT COOL under Alex's touch. He rubbed her arm with his thumb, watching her doze off to sleep. She always seemed to fall asleep with ease when she was in his arms, and restlessness was not something he suffered from when she was there either. However, tonight, he couldn't curb the thoughts rattling around in his mind and the uneasiness she had left him with.

He felt her sigh and pull away from him. She found her way to her own pillow, turned her back to him, and pulled the covers tighter around her. Her long blonde hair billowed out around her head, and the moonlight outside slipped in through a break in the window's blinds, casting a glow on it and causing it to shine. Her messy beauty always took his breath away, and Alex smiled as he watched her sleeping, oblivious to it.

His carefree happiness didn't last long. Even though he pressed his eyes closed and willed himself to fall asleep, the negative thoughts he fought all night began swimming through his mind again. Watching Anna for a few moments until he knew she was sleeping, Alex cursed himself for the millionth time, knowing he was about to betray her trust again. He slipped out of bed and tiptoed to the living room. He flipped on a lamp and pulled Anna's journal out of the bag she had dropped by the front door.

For but a moment, he resisted the urge to flip through the crisp white pages filled with Anna's familiar handwriting, but his uncertainty got the best of him. Glancing again at the bedroom door, he flipped to the most recent entry and scanned over the words she had written earlier:

Today, mom would have been 51. We would have had lunch, maybe talked about Marie's predicament. Who knows? Perhaps we would both be doing something else instead of Marie choosing to become a lawyer and me going into criminology. I still have a hard time believing my sister would want to defend criminals.

Today's feelings: Sad—I miss having her around. I miss her excitement, her bedtime stories, and her brownies. I miss everything I didn't get to have with her and everything I did. I need her comfort and wisdom. I just didn't have it long enough for it to matter.

Anger—anger at the fact I'm living life without her. She's missed so much of my life already, and there's still a ton she will continue to miss. Anger at myself for always letting everyone down and not being able to control this. I'm such a screw-up it's amazing anyone wants to deal with me sometimes.

Guilty–For our outing resulting in her death. I feel like I will never stop feeling guilty, even though there wasn't anything I could have done about any of it. But if I could just go back and realize what was happening, maybe I would have gotten out, and it wouldn't have happened.

It's not fair. I need her back. I need her for the good times and the bad. I need her for the sad and the angry.

What I wouldn't give for just a few more hours with her to ask her a handful of the questions I need to know. Why did she have to leave us? I feel like it all happened yesterday, but that it was a lifetime ago at the same time. Will I ever stop feeling so horrible about it?

Alex sighed after reading the entry. He wanted nothing more than to scoop her up and keep her safe. If he could take those feelings away from her, he would. He flipped through the other pages in the journal – ones he had read before. They contained more entries that made him hurt for Anna.

She had once told him she wrote to forget. Instead of keeping the feelings, she wrote them down. He couldn't help but notice, however, she hadn't mentioned her encounter with Joe. To him it meant that it wasn't a memory she felt the need, or the want, to forget.

Still trying to decide if it was better or not he knew how she had felt when she left, he returned the journal to its rightful place in her bag and slipped back into the bedroom, sliding under the covers and putting his arm around Anna's sleeping body. She smiled a bit in her sleep and pulled his arm tighter around her making all the feelings of rejection and jealousy disappear from his mind.

Chapter 15

Monday 6:00 AM - Anna

"GOOD MORNING," ALEX said.

Anna attempted to rub the sleep from her eyes as she made her way into the kitchen. She grumbled when she looked at the clock and realized how early it was. Alex's bright eyes and cheery demeanor made her feel even worse. She watched him spoon eggs onto a plate for her and glared at him with a playful smile, all the while wishing she were still in bed.

"How do you do that?" she asked.

Her eyes followed him around her kitchen. He stopped and looked at her, a look of confusion on his face.

"Do what?" he asked, looking at her amused. "Cook breakfast?"

"Wake up and do stuff in the morning instead of crawl to the coffee pot?"

Alex laughed as he slid her a cup of coffee. "Here. Already made you a cup."

"Well, aren't you proud of yourself," Anna joked.

She took a sip and closed her eyes in appreciation.

"Thanks."

"And, breakfast," he said and sat a plate in front of her. "You need the energy for your test.

"Oh, come on," she said. "You know I don't like to eat this much when I first get up!"

"Eat it," he said as he spooned a bite of eggs into his own mouth. "Energy. Test."

She tilted her head at him, annoyed, shook her head, and took a bite of the eggs.

"Happy?" she asked before taking another bite.

Alex's laugh filled the kitchen, and he sat back and smiled at her. He put his finger in the jelly on his toast and stuck a dab on the end of her nose.

"You think that's funny?" she asked, wrinkling her jelly-covered nose at him.

"Yes, yes, I do," he said before putting his hand behind her neck and pulling her in for a kiss.

Anna pushed her plate away and pulled him closer.

When he pulled away from her, she locked eyes with him and said, "You know, I don't HAVE to take the final to pass the class. We could take this back to the bedroom instead."

Alex sat back down and resumed eating his breakfast.

"Eat," he asserted. "You know I'm not letting you skip your class."

Anna pouted.

"Besides," he said. "It'll give you something to look forward to."

Anna smiled back at him before stealing a piece of toast off his plate and taking a bite.

"ANNA," A VOICE BEHIND her whispered, causing Anna to lift her head and glance at the professor at the front of the room. She tapped her pencil on her desk but didn't turn around.

"Why do you have a different test than me?" the voice continued, even though she didn't turn around. She looked at the professor again and rolled her eyes when she realized he was noticing the whispers.

"Because," another voice whispered, "you like to cheat off her."

"I do not!" growled the original voice as the professor marched up the aisle to address the troublemaker.

He gave Anna a look when he walked by and whispered, "Nice of you to show up today."

To the whisperer behind her, he said in a louder whisper, "You most certainly do cheat off her, and I would like to know what your skillset is because I already know what hers is."

Anna laughed to herself and went back to typing on her computer. She tried to ignore her professor but had a difficult time doing so since he was now watching her work. She paused and looked up at him.

"What?"

He scowled back at her. "You finished at least ten minutes ago. What are you doing?"

Anna shrugged. "Extra credit?"

Her professor shook his head and gave her an annoyed but impressed look. He leaned in and whispered in her ear, "Submit it, already."

"But," she said. "I just need to do one more thing."

"Submit it," he insisted. "Let me put an A on it, so you can be on your way to annoy your next professor."

"Fine," Anna whispered before clicking a few keys on her laptop.

She slid it into her backpack, stood up from her desk, and cocked her head at him.

"But, I have you again next semester."

"Greaaat," he said, but smiled at her. "Have a good summer, Anna."

"See you, Professor Fischer," she said over her shoulder as she breezed out of the class.

The rest of her classmates looked up at her in surprise as she walked by.

"You all still have plenty of time," Professor Fischer said aloud to the now worried class. "Get back to work."

Anna breathed a sigh of relief and made a beeline to the exit. Outside, she turned her face to the summer sun and took a deep breath of the fresh air. She popped her sunglasses on the end of her nose and looked around the parking lot. Anna caught sight of Alex's car and smiled at him as he leaned against it. When Alex crossed his arms across his chest and glared back at her, Anna's smile faded to confusion. Alex rolled his eyes and pointed to the vehicle next to him.

Anna groaned as her eyes flew from Alex to Joe's jeep next to him. Sweeping her eyes across the campus, she soon found him lounging in the grass nearby. Anna rolled her eyes as a handful of her female classmates gawked at him while walking to class.

Joe seemed oblivious to the attention. Instead, he had earbuds in his ears and was busy soaking up the sun from his spot on the grass. He had his leg propped on his knee, arms behind his head and foot swinging to the beat of whatever song he was listening to. Anna shook her head in annoyance and watched him, her hands on her hips.

Anna caught Alex's eye as she marched across the grass and tried not to let her annoyance at them both invade her senses too much. Joe never noticed her approach and jumped in surprise when she kicked his swinging foot.

"Are you stalking me now?" she asked.

"What?"

He removed the earbuds and squinted up at her. When he tried to move under her shadow so he could see her better, she moved to ensure the sun glared back in his eyes.

"Ow!" he said and covered his eyes with his arm.

"What are you doing here? I said I would text you when I finished."

"I know," he said. "But I got bored. And I found something."

"How about we go get a cup of coffee and talk it over," Alex said.

He had swept up behind Anna and put an arm around her waist.

"I'm hanging out with you guys for the day."

"Oh, for crying out loud," Anna muttered under her breath.

"Cool," Joe said. "The more, the merrier!"

"You've got to chill out," Anna hissed at Alex.

She swatted his arm with her hand but couldn't help but smile at the tinge of jealousy she saw in his eyes. He grumbled to himself the entire drive to the campus coffee shop and still looked sour when they pulled into a parking spot. After walking inside, Anna caught Alex's eyes, raised her eyebrows at him, and gave him a look that caused him to hang his head.

"I'm sorry," he mouthed to her.

She rolled her eyes but gave him a soft smile and waited for her order. When it was ready, they sat at a table for three in the corner and took a few sips of the drinks before starting their conversation. Much to Anna's dismay, Alex seemed determined to learn more about Joe than was necessary.

"So, does Joe have a girlfriend?" he asked.

Anna glared at him, but Joe smiled and played along.

"No, Joe does not," came the reply. "And, much to my mother's frustration, Joe does not want one."

To Anna's relief, Alex seemed to relax a little.

"Not interested in women, huh?" Alex laughed.

"Well, I didn't say that," Joe smirked. "Just not the kind you bring home to meet your mother."

"Well, it looks like you might have options in here," Alex said.

He picked up Joe's coffee cup and spun it around to show him the phone number the barista had jotted on the side.

Joe laughed and pointed at Alex's cup with the same number written on it, "She's keeping her options open."

Alex groaned and said, "Oh, no."

Anna picked up his coffee cup and turned it around to glare at the number.

Joe laughed. "It appears our lovely barista wasn't sure what the situation here was, so she took her chances."

"Hmmm." Anna continued glaring at the phone number on her boyfriend's coffee cup.

"Anna," Alex said with a warning tone in his voice.

She glared at him, picked up the cup, and marched back up to the counter. Joe grinned and jerked around in his chair to watch the drama unfold as Alex grimaced.

"I need a new cup," Anna said to the frightened barista.

When presented with the new cup, Anna poured Alex's drink into the new number-free version and set the offending vessel back on the counter with a snap.

"There," she said with an unfriendly smile. "That should clear things up for you."

"That was unnecessary," Alex whispered once she had returned his drink and sat down in the chair next to him.

"Oh, you want to talk about unnecessary?" she hissed. "A lot of things you are doing are unnecessary, but here we are."

"Now that all the housekeeping stuff is taken care of," Joe also whispered. "Can we get to what I found on the case?"

Anna and Alex looked at each other, both embarrassed.

"Sorry," Anna said. "What did you find?"

"Well, I realized we didn't need to find any more illegal activity with the businesses," he said. "We already had enough evidence."

"Makes sense," Anna said.

"I got to thinking," he continued. "What we want to know is how the guy Picture Girl is seeing is connected."

"I agree." Anna nodded.

"So, I switched focus last night and started researching him," Joe said.

Joe pulled a file out of the bag he had carried in with him and slid it across to Anna.

"This is a lot," Anna said, as she thumbed through the pages. "How long did this take you?"

"I had some free time," Joe said.

"This would have taken hours," Alex whispered in Anna's ear.

He peered over her shoulder at the documents and looked at them through his police officer experience lens. To Joe, he asked, "Do you ever sleep?"

"When I have to," he said, taking another drink of his coffee.

Joe stayed quiet for a few minutes and allowed Anna to finish going through the papers.

"Looks like you've even been able to track his movements over the past few weeks," she said and examined one page a little closer than the others.

"Mostly," he agreed.

"So, what's he been up to today?" she asked. "What is he up to now?"

"I don't know," Joe said.

"What?"

Joe shrugged, "It's like he disappeared."

"How is it possible you can't find him?" Anna asked perplexed.

"I know where he was at this morning," Joe said. "Then, the trail goes cold. It's like he has evaporated off the planet."

"Sounds like we need to go check it out," Anna said. "Where is it?"

"That's the problem," Joe said. "All maps in the area are hazy."

"Why don't we just go drive by and find out for ourselves?" Anna asked.

"That sounds super dangerous," Alex said.

"Besides," Joe said. "It's two hours away."

"You two have something better to do with your time?" Anna asked. "What harm could there be in driving by?"

Joe and Alex looked at each other.

"You're the law enforcement at this table," Joe said.

Alex looked at his girlfriend.

"I think we'd better go along with it, or Anna might just go without us."

"Better hit the road," Joe said.

Before they could even get to Alex's car, Anna's phone started to ring.

"Hey, Claire," Anna said when she'd answered.

Anna glanced at Joe and realized he still held the empty coffee cup in his hand. She pulled the phone away from her ear for a second and said, "Please tell me you aren't keeping that."

"Why not?" Joe shrugged. Anna looked at Alex and rolled her eyes and turned her attention back to Claire.

"Sorry, sorry," she said. "What did you...? Claire, slow down."

Anna listened to Claire's voice on the other end of the line for a moment. The confused look grew on her face with each passing second.

"Wait, what?" she asked when Claire took a breath between her sentences. "You're where?"

Alex and Joe looked at her with a mixture of concern and confusion on their faces. Anna started laughing.

"You've got to be kidding me," she said between giggles. "I'm sorry. No, I'm not laughing at you. OK, yes, I'm laughing at you."

"What is going on?" Joe asked Alex, who shrugged and looked at Anna for answers.

She pulled the phone away from her ear for a minute and said, "Claire has found herself in a bit of a pickle and needs our help."

When Claire realized someone else now knew about her struggles, she yelled loud enough for Alex, Joe, and Anna all to hear her. Anna grimaced and tried to calm her friend.

"Claire, calm down," she said. "I have to get someone else to help too. I can't do it by myself unless you want me to call a tow truck for you."

Anna looked relieved when her friend agreed to let the guys help with the situation.

"Good, now tell me where you are," Anna said. "Just sit tight. We'll be there soon."

After she hung up, Anna turned to Alex and Joe and said, "Sorry, guys. We need to make a detour on this road trip of ours. Joe, how do you feel about getting someone out of the mud with your jeep?"

Monday 11:00 AM

"HOW DID THIS HAPPEN?" Anna asked from the side of the road.

"There was a squirrel," Claire said on the verge of tears. "It came out of nowhere! I swear I just moved over a little, but my tire slipped off the edge, and I got stuck and couldn't get back out again."

"You will have to come out of there before I can tow your car out," Joe said.

"What?!" Claire said, even closer to tears. "I'll get muddy! Can't I just stay in here and you tow me out to dry land?"

"Sorry," Joe shook his head. "If your car slips, it could roll down the hill. It's not safe for you to stay in there."

Claire eyed the hill. Anna shook her head in dismay and put her hands on her hips.

"Is it that hard of a decision?" she asked. "Just come out of there!"

"You know I don't enjoy getting dirty!"

Anna sighed and began walking through the mud to Claire's car. "Just hang on. I'll come get you."

"But we'll both get dirty!" Claire said.

"Someone has to put the tow cables on your car and guide it back to the road anyway," Anna said. "I don't suspect you want to do that, do you?"

Claire groaned and opened her driver's door and revealed the high heel pumps on her feet.

"Oh no," Anna said. "You don't have any other shoes to wear, do you?"

"No," Claire said, tears building up in her eyes. "And these are brand new too!"

"Here," Anna said and pulled Claire's arms around her neck. "Just hold on. I'll carry you out."

Claire looked relieved when Anna could pull her up on her back to keep her safe from the mud. But after just a few steps, her shoes slipped close to the ground. Claire shrieked at the thought of her new shoes getting ruined and jerked her feet back from the mud. The sudden movement caused Anna to lose her balance. Before either could react, both found themselves toppled over in the mud. Claire somehow kept her shoes from becoming soiled, but her clothes were drenched in mud.

"Well, at least your shoes didn't get dirty," Joe said, somehow keeping a straight face.

Alex tried to cover his laugh with his hand but wasn't successful. Anna couldn't control her laughter at all and began laughing even harder when Claire picked up a fistful of mud and dumped it on her head.

"I hate you all," Claire grumbled as she crawled the rest of the way to the dry road, still determined to protect her new shoes.

Chapter 16

Monday 9:00 AM - Bryant and Marie

BRYANT'S EYES SNAPPED up when his boss, Wallace Snyder, knocked on the door. Without waiting for an invitation, he heaved his hulking frame inside the office and threw the door shut behind him. Bryant attempted to keep his face impassive and watched as Wallace maneuvered his body into a chair and threw his long legs out in front of him.

As he sat, Wallace unbuttoned the coat of his suit and flattened his tie, smoothed out his pants, and straightened his collar a bit. Only then did he bother to give Bryant any of his attention. Not falling for Wallace's intimidation tactics, Bryant waited for him to get settled before addressing him, all the while ignoring the arrogance oozing out of the older man.

"What can I do for you, Mr. Snyder?" he asked when Wallace looked his direction.

"I just heard about what happened over the weekend," he said. "I wanted to make sure you and our lady attorney are all right."

"Marie," Bryant said, supplying Wallace with Marie's name. "We're doing all right. Just trying to get this case together."

"Ah, yes," Wallace said. "I understand you are filing a continuance on it. I thought it was an open and shut case?"

"There have been a few developments we need to address," Bryant said, trying to stay as vague as possible.

"I see. The partners and I worry a misstep might put the firm in a bad light."

"That's our highest priority," Bryant said, trying to keep the annoyed tone out of his voice.

"Good!" Wallace said with a smile before standing up and adjusting his outfit again.

Just as fast as he had swept into Bryant's office, he swept back out again, leaving behind the subtle scent of his cologne and a few negative feelings for Bryant. Marie crept into Bryant's office not long after.

"What was that all about?" she asked.

"Basically," Bryant said, rubbing his temples, "we need to tread carefully with this."

"I suspected as much," Marie nodded. "Do you think he's involved?"

"I don't know," Bryant said. "Have you gotten to talk to Lindsay yet this morning?"

"No," Marie said and leaned forward. "Word around the office is she called in today."

"Well, that's just great," Bryant said, shaking his head. "How are we going to talk to her now?"

"I don't know," Marie said with a defeated shrug. "I know we have to get to court, or they will go along with this case without us."

Monday 10:00 AM

"I'M SORRY, YOUR HONOR. We are ready to proceed with the trial as planned."

Bryant glared across the neighboring council table at the other attorney before turning his attention back to the judge.

"With all due respect to fellow counsel Mr. Kolb, but these are extenuating circumstances, Your Honor," Bryant said. "Our colleague passed away this weekend, and he worked with us on this case. We are only asking for additional time to reallocate his duties and attend his memorial service that is tomorrow."

"Your Honor," Mr. Kolb said, "we believe counsel is attempting to delay the case to further tamper with OUR witness testimony!"

"That's absurd, and you know it!" Marie rose from her seat at the counsel table and glared at Kolb. Bryant jerked around to give her a warning look, but the judge had already heard enough.

"Council will meet me in my chambers, NOW!" He struck his gavel and rose from his seat. The audience in the gallery jerked to their feet.

"Counsel?" Jasper Kolb said as he walked by Marie and Bryant while adjusting the cuffs on his expensive suit. "I believe the judge issued an order."

"Five minutes," Marie whispered to Bryant. "That's all I need. Five minutes will be enough time to tell him what I think and sock him in the nose."

"You need to calm down," Bryant said, watching the prosecution team enter the judge's chambers in front of them. He tried to read their expressions but couldn't judge from their faces whether the turn of events surprised them.

"I would like to know who gave you clowns the permission to make a mockery of my courtroom," the judge said once they were all behind his chamber doors.

"Your Honor," Jasper Kolb said. "They've been trying to sabotage our case!"

"Why would we be trying to sabotage the case?" Bryant asked. "The case is in our favor!"

"Why don't you ask your little sweetheart over there?" Jasper sneered, pointing in Marie's direction. "The FBI's been investigating her for a week now. Or didn't you know already?"

"I did," Bryant retorted. "And, if you knew anything, you would know they cleared that up already."

"I thought these were my chambers," the judge said, interrupting the argument.

"I apologize for speaking out of turn, Judge Toland," Bryant said while Jasper lowered his eyes.

"Now that I have control again," Judge Toland said, looking each of them in the eye. "Let's start at the top. Mr. Malone, please allow Mr. Kolb to speak his case."

"Thank you, Judge Toland," Jasper said. "For the past two weeks, Ms. Hartman has been tampering with our witnesses."

Marie made a move to interject, but a stern look from Judge Toland silenced her.

Clearing his throat, Jasper continued, "I apologize, evidence has shown this to be the case."

"What purpose would that serve?" Judge Toland asked.

"It would make for a hefty paycheck."

"Sounds like grounds for a mistrial to me," Judge Toland mused. "Mr. Malone?"

"If you speak to FBI agents Kamera and Hoage, you will find there is no evidence of any witness tampering," Bryant said. "It's a rumor that was started to cause problems."

"I see," Judge Toland said. "But, Mr. Kolb, you cannot corroborate Mr. Malone's statement?"

"No, sir, uh Your Honor," Jasper said. "I'm unaware of these findings."

"At this point," Judge Toland said after thinking things over for a few moments, "I feel as though I have no other choice than to delay this hearing for a continuance until I have time to confer with the agents in charge of this investigation. In the meantime, I would suggest the lot of you rediscover what it means to be attorneys of the court and make sure you have all your ducks in a row before we proceed. Are we clear?"

The attorneys each nodded when Judge Toland looked them in the eye, knowing he had all the power over the case in his hand.

"Oh, and if any of you try to pull a stunt like what I saw in my courtroom today again, so help me God, I'll have you disbarred."

Chastised, the attorneys left the judge's chambers, and Marie and Bryant headed back to the office to come up with a plan. When they arrived, Bryant and Marie swept through the building and attempted to avoid Wallace Snyder's attention again. They hurried down the hall when they noticed him in the business law partner's office having a heated conversation. Before they could escape into their offices, he stuck his head out the door.

"You two," Wallace said, pointing at Marie while looking at Bryant, "Get in here."

Marie and Bryant shared a sheepish look as they followed Wallace into Devin Waggner's office. Looking about as happy as Wallace, Devin gestured toward the pair of chairs in front of his desk. Wallace closed the door behind them with a snap, shut the blinds, and walked behind the desk to stand behind Devin with his arms crossed over his chest.

"Which one of you want to tell us what happened today?" Devin demanded.

"The prosecution made some outlandish claims, and we had to defend ourselves," Bryant began after glancing at Marie.

"Judge Toland was not happy about your outburst in his courtroom," Wallace said.

His eyes glowered at Marie, and Bryant could feel her anger bubbling back up. Before she could create an even bigger issue for herself, he tried to catch her eye, but she ignored him.

"With all due respect," he said before she could open her mouth. "If someone accused me of witness tampering, I would have a negative reaction myself."

"As would I," Devin agreed after mulling it over for a moment. "That isn't something we promote at our practice."

"And, any such dealings will reflect negatively on the firm," Wallace said, letting his eyes stray from Marie and back to Bryant.

"Precisely," Bryant agreed. "Which is one reason we wanted a continuance. We didn't want any unfounded rumors to cloud the case."

"There is no truth to the allegations," Marie grumbled. "It's just a tactic to draw attention from the crimes of the defendant and open up the door to doubt."

"We could always remove you from this case," Wallace said, again glaring at Marie.

"If they are trying to create doubt, it doesn't matter who's on the case," Bryant said. "They will still cause problems."

Devin and Wallace looked at each other for a minute. Devin shrugged.

"Fine," Wallace said.

He turned back to Bryant and ignored Marie altogether.

"Go reassure the client but keep it subtle. We don't want him getting wind of this drama and causing us trouble."

Nodding, Marie and Bryant lowered their eyes and escaped the office, praying they could make their client understand the delay, all the while trying to ignore the inquisitive looks being shot their way by their coworkers.

Monday Noon

"I NEED TO GET OUT OF here!" Dominique Shaw said with obvious fear floating through his voice.

"We understand your concern, Mr. Shaw," Bryant said, trying to reassure him, "but we promise we have everything under control."

"We only need to delay the case so we can get everything back in order after Callen's death," Marie added.

"But what if the deal falls through?" Dominique asked. "I'll be a sitting duck in here if I have to stay!"

"Your safety is our top concern," Bryant said. "That's why we've requested to have you moved to a more secure location during the trial process."

"They aren't even going to be using your real name," Marie said. "Nobody will even know you are there."

"So, the plan is to keep me safe until this is all over, and then I can start a new life?" Dominique asked.

Bryant and Marie both nodded.

"I guess I can live with that," Dominique said, seeming somewhat more relaxed.

He buried his head in his hands, his shoulders sagging under the weight of everything he was going through. Marie looked at Bryant and sat down across from Dominique, waiting until he was ready to continue the conversation.

"You know," he said after a minute, looking up at her, "I never wanted this life. I wanted to be a banker. But, where I'm from, you don't have too many options. Haskell scooped me up because I was weak. You do just one thing for the guy, and he's got you. You know?"

Marie nodded, even though she didn't understand at all.

"He owns you." Dominique continued staring off into space, his eyes glassing over. "It's like a demon is following you through life. You can't get away from him. Nobody can."

His head dipped again, and he grew silent.

"You did a brave thing coming forward and arranging all of this," Marie said. "Getting a man like him off the streets will help so many people."

"I'm not so sure anymore," Dominique said, looking at his large hands. "There will always be crime. There will always be someone there to organize it. There is always someone looking to make a quick buck."

With nothing left to discuss, Bryant alerted the guards after a few minutes of silence, and he and Marie watched as their client walked away.

"We'll get through this," Bryant said, trying to comfort Marie.

"We hope, at least," Marie said, grimacing at Bryant.

Chapter 17

Monday 10:00 AM - Agents Hoage and Kamera
"SHE WAS A PRETTY ONE," Renato said, looking at the corpse at his feet.

"Damn shame," Carver agreed.

He looked at the woman at his feet and shook his head. She would have looked serene, with her arms laid out beside her, and her brown hair fanned out around her, had it not been for the way her legs bent at a strange angle and the puddle of blood flowing out from her body.

Carver wondered if she knew she would die when she got dressed this morning. She had chosen a black pencil skirt and a white silk blouse. Now, one high-heeled pump was still attached to her foot. The other had fallen off in her descent and lay on the ground beside her, visible scuffs marring its previously pristine glossy finish.

Carver and Renato stared at the woman for several moments, trying to make sense of what had happened. The woman's youthful looks kept her looking alive, even in death, and Carver couldn't help but feel sorrow over the life she no longer could live. Before his emotions could take control of the situation, he turned from gazing at the woman and began searching for answers.

"Do we know how she died?" Carver asked a police officer who walked by his location.

The officer shrugged. "Looks like a suicide. The boyfriend came home from a work meeting and found her. He said a friend of hers at work had just died and she was shaken about it. Didn't want to go into the office this morning."

"So, she was a jumper?" Renato asked, looking up above him at the second-floor balcony and calculating the distance from the ledge to where their victim now lay.

"Appears, so," the officer said before walking off to process more of the scene.

Renato glanced down at the ID he held in its evidence bag and said her name aloud, "Lindsay Sprout."

When the call came saying another member of Bryant and Marie's legal office had died, Carver thought it was a joke. As they came to find out after arriving at the scene, the call was no joke.

He hadn't even bothered arguing about jurisdiction when he arrived. Carver and Renato had shown up, flashed their badges, and got to work being an extra set of eyes. He couldn't help but notice, however, how the officers gazed over at them as they made their rounds through the scene.

"What are the odds," Carver asked as Renato took a few pictures of the scene, "that this lady would die so soon after someone gunned down one of her coworkers?"

"Seems odd," Renato said, "but not unlikely. Maybe they were having an affair. Or, she just liked the guy or something. You never know with people these days."

"Hmm, something doesn't sit well with me on this," Carver said, shaking his head.

"Oh no," Renato groaned. "Not that gut feeling of yours again."

"Yep," Carver said. "I say we go talk to the boyfriend. See what he has to say about all this."

Inside, Carver and Renato found the boyfriend sitting on a couch in the living room. He looked distressed and kept glancing out the back window at the officers looking for evidence in his backyard.

Carver took in his appearance in an instant. He was a good-looking man. Tall, dark hair, dark eyes, chiseled chin, sharp dresser; all the checks in the right boxes for being what the women would call 'a catch.' So, why was his girlfriend now lying on his back patio after having plunged to her death from his bedroom balcony?

"Mr. Walker," Carver said. "We are so sorry for your loss. Do you mind if we chat for a few moments?"

"I've already told the officers everything I know," he said. "Do I need to go through everything again?"

"We don't want to rehash old details," Carver said. "We were just hoping you might shed some light on Lindsay's state of mind for us so we can piece together some reasons she wanted to hurt herself."

"Did Lindsay have any other family around?" Renato asked.

"Please, call me Audrick," he said, his eyes darkening a bit. "Yes, she has parents. But they aren't a big part of her life. They live a few states over, and I haven't been able to reach them yet."

"Did it seem to bother Lindsay that she didn't have immediate family close by?" Carver continued.

"No," Audrick said with a short shake of his head. "She didn't get along with her parents and didn't hear from them much. A few calls here and there and that was about it."

"What about her job?" Carver asked without missing a beat. "Did she have any issues there? Lindsay get along with everyone at the office?"

"She loved her job," Audrick said. "Lindsay was an attorney. Family law. But she wasn't much of the social type. She always preferred to hang around the house and such."

"So, she didn't have any close friends other than yourself?" Renato asked.

"Not really," Audrick said. "I guess I never noticed it before. We always shared everything together, but you're right. She had no friends of her own except for some girls from college she talked to online a few times a year."

"Would you say she seemed lonely?"

"Maybe," Audrick said, his brow furrowing. "Why didn't I ever see that before?"

Audrick put his head in his hands, trying to contain his emotions. Renato looked over at Carver, who gave him a look before sitting down on the couch beside Audrick and placing a hand on the young man's shoulder.

"Sometimes, the people we love don't want us to know they are hurting," he told him. "And, when they don't ask for help, there isn't anything we can do."

Audrick shook his head and seemed to be at a loss for words. The two agents thanked him for his time and rose to leave him in peace. But, before they could go, Audrick had one more thing to say.

"Do you know how much longer they will be out there?"

"Shouldn't be much longer," Carver said. "I saw the coroner pull up the same time we did."

"Good," Audrick said, looking relieved and glancing at the backyard through his picturesque windows again. "I just need to get out of here for a bit."

"That's understandable," Renato said. "I would need a bit of time to myself after something like this happened too."

"There's a business obligation I have to get to," Audrick said. "I'll be out of pocket for a bit."

"What about the young lady's arrangements?"

"Oh," Audrick said. "I'll have my assistant take care of everything. A cremation seems best considering the circumstances. And my assistant will notify her parents in case they want to plan their own memorial."

"Hmm," Carver said, looking back into Audrick's dark, cold eyes. "How about we leave you our card so you can contact us if you have any other information to share?"

Carver laid his card down on the glass coffee table in front of Audrick and walked away without another word.

"Sorry for your loss," Renato added before following his partner outside.

"Anything about that seem suspicious?" Carver asked Renato when they were out of earshot.

"Maybe," Renato said. "But, let's see what the coroner has to say before we let that gut of yours get out of control."

Nodding to a few of the officers still milling about the scene, the agents strode over to the coroner. Distracted, he jumped in surprise when they approached. The agents let him work and watched him walk around the body while glancing up at the balcony several times.

"What's the verdict?" Carver asked, after a moment.

The coroner shook his head and looked again from the dead woman at his feet to the balcony above.

"We must get her back to the morgue for an autopsy," he said in a bit of a whisper. "But I don't know how this could be a suicide."

"What?" Carver and Renato said in unison.

The coroner flinched and shushed them.

"The height isn't right," he said. "At most, jumping from that height would have broken her legs. She would've had to land on her head for any real damage, and I'm not seeing evidence of that right now."

"Now my gut's humming," Renato said to his partner.

Thanking the coroner for his help, the agents walked back to their vehicle.

"All right, so what are we looking at?" Carver asked when they were alone.

"Well, we have a dead paralegal and a dead lawyer from the same office," Renato said.

"Not to mention all that evidence fabrication on a case sitting on the desks of two other attorneys at the SAME firm," Carver added.

"Odds are, this is all contained in that office."

"Or at least there are others there who know what's going on," Carver agreed.

"Maybe Bryant and Marie can help shed some light on who is behind it?"

"I think it's time we had a new chat with our favorite legal pair," Carver mused.

"But first," Renato said. "Let's get something to eat. I'm starving!"

Chapter 18

CARVER SHOOK HIS HEAD at Renato and groaned.

"He didn't answer," he said.

"Oh well," Renato said and dug a burger out of the greasy sack beside him. "You left a message. They'll show up."

"I suppose," Carver said.

He took off his suit jacket, loosened his tie, and rolled up his sleeves before digging his own burger out of the bag. For several minutes, the two agents ate in silence savoring the taste of the burgers and doing their best to avoid dripping grease from the wrapping on their shoes.

They were about halfway finished with the burgers when they saw Marie and Bryant strolling up the walk outside the office.

"Told ya," Renato said, his mouth still filled with food.

Carver nodded in greeting to the two attorneys and went back to devouring his burger. It took but a few moments for the men to finish up and address Marie and Bryant aloud. Carver and Renato then led Bryant and Marie to a small conference room and sat down across from them at the table.

"We have some rather disturbing news," Carver started.

"What could be more disturbing than what we've already been through?" Marie asked.

"Another of your co-workers was found dead today," Renato said. "A Lindsay Sprout."

Marie gasped, and her hands flew to cover her mouth.

"Are you sure?" Bryant asked. "What happened?"

"It's too early to say, but the coroner is performing an autopsy as we speak."

Marie began blinking back tears. She glanced over at Bryant who appeared equally shocked to hear the news. Carver let them both gather their thoughts for a few moments before allowing the conversation to continue.

"What can you tell us?" Marie asked after she had wiped a few tears from her cheeks.

"We were hoping you could tell us something. It seems unlikely that all this death in the same office is unrelated."

Carver felt his gut hum again as a strange look passed between Marie and Bryant.

"You seem suspicious," Renato said.

When neither Marie nor Bryant began talking, Carver let his frustration boil over.

"Look," he said. "You two have some information here. We need to hear what it is. People are dropping like flies around this thing. It's got to stop!"

Bryant and Marie looked at each other again, and Marie sighed and shrugged her shoulders.

All right, fine," Bryant said. "We ran across some information while we were trying to clear Marie's name."

"What sort of information?" Carver asked and leaned toward him.

"Information that could implicate Lindsay's boyfriend, Audrick, in a money-laundering scheme."

"Really?" Renato asked.

"Yes," Marie added. "We noticed some irregularities on several of the balance sheets of companies owned by his holding company."

"What does this have to do with you two?" Carver asked.

"We can't give you that information," Bryant said.

The agents looked at each other and rolled their eyes. Carver remained silent for a moment looking back and forth from Marie to Bryant.

"I will venture to assume it's related to the case we've all been investigating," he said.

He looked Bryant in the eye, but Bryant refused to back down.

"You can assume what you want, but I cannot validate it."

"Where do we go from here?" Marie asked.

"Well, I suppose we go on our merry way and see where we meet up down the road again," Renato said.

Before the agents could see them out, both Marie and Bryant's phones buzzed. No one was surprised to learn that their office had set up a 4 o'clock mandatory company meeting.

"Looks like your office has gotten wind of Lindsay's death," Carver said. "You two need to make no reference to this little meeting of ours."

"If someone is trying to cause trouble in your office, Renato continued, "you two won't be safe if they know you are working with us."

Bryant and Marie nodded in agreement and allowed the agents to show them out the building and back to their vehicle. The agents stood in the parking lot watching as Marie and Bryant drove away without revealing enough information to them yet again.

"Are you sure we can trust those two?" Renato asked when their vehicle was out of sight.

"I guess we will find out," Carver said.

"How about we go see if that fella their siblings brought to us is ready to talk yet?" Renato suggested.

"Yeah." Carver nodded. "What, he's spent a little over a day in General with the rumor going around that he's a squealer? His tongue should be good and loosened up by now."

Renato grinned and followed his partner to their unmarked car and proceeded to the local jail. After flashing their badges, personnel ushered them into a secluded, windowless room and soon dragged in the man the agents had fished out of Joe's jeep.

"Ahh, Mr. Ashton," Renato said. "Lukas, isn't it? Can we call you Luke?'

"Man, Kamera," Carver whistled, taking a long look at the man's battered face. "Those guys sure did a number on him."

"I'd hate to see how bad it winds up if he goes back in there again," he said.

"Maybe we could let them know he's cooperating, and it will be better for him?" Carver shrugged.

"God, please, no!" Lukas sputtered. "Please, don't put me back in there!"

"You gotta give us something," Carver said.

"I already told you everything I know," Lukas pleaded.

"Bullshit!" Renato put his finger in the prisoner's face. "You don't just go taking jobs to knock off random people!"

"Besides, from what you told us the last time we visited, you know what's going on," Carver added.

Lukas's eyes bounced from one agent to the next as though watching a tennis match. His resolve broke down, and he sighed.

"What do you want to know?" he asked, looking down at the table.

"That's the spirit!" Carver slapped his leg. "You'll be looking like your old ugly self again before you know it!"

"How about we start at the beginning," Renato said.

He ignored his partner and sat down in front of the prisoner instead. He pulled out a notebook and looked up at the man.

"As I told you, I was sent to scare those two snoopers off."

"Can you be more specific?"

"Those kids!" he yelled. "I don't even know their names. They were snooping around, going through internet files and shit. They stuffed me in the back of that jeep?"

"Oh, those two!" Carver said, fake enthusiasm dripping from his voice. "Continue."

"That's it," he said. "They told me to scare them off, so I showed up with a gun and..."

"And, it didn't turn out that great for you, did it?"

"No, not at all."

"What else?"

"What do you mean, what else?"

"Now, Luke..." Carver started. "The guards are right outside the door right there."

"Ugh," Lukas groaned. "I'm a dead man."

"Chances are you will live a little longer if you help us out rather than if we throw you back out there," Renato said.

He leaned back in his chair and waited for Lukas to continue.

Lukas glared at him, but opened his mouth to speak, "I don't know a lot of the details. But, there's this businessman, Haskell."

"Yes, yes," Carver said. "King of the underworld. We're up to speed. Continue."

"Well, he's had a guy turn on him," Lukas continued.

"You haven't told us anything we didn't already know yet," Renato said.

When Lukas noticed the impatience in the agent's voice, he gulped and started stammering.

"Will you calm down and let me finish?" Lukas begged. "Haskell wasn't too excited to learn one of his people flipped. And, it just so happens it's someone he trusted with information."

"Everybody trying to hit pay dirt these days," Renato said with a shake of his head.

"Something like that," Lukas said. "The guy realized the Feds were coming down hard on them and saw a way out, so he took it."

"But Haskell won't stand for that, will he?" Carver asked.

"No," Lukas continued. "He's already tried to have the guy killed three times. Was almost successful once. They've moved him five times now."

"Get to the juicy stuff," Renato demanded.

"So, now, Haskell wants to keep his own ass out of jail," Lukas continued, gulping as Carver looked at the door to the room and yawned. "He's got some people to pay people off and blackmail them and shit so they will turn the case in his favor."

"What kind of people?" Renato asked.

Carter turned his attention back to the conversation and started becoming more interested in what Lukas was saying.

"All kinds of people," Lukas continued, feeding off the excitement he was seeing in the agents' eyes.

"He paid off the snitch's attorneys?"

"No, no," Lukas said, holding up his hands. "This was too high-profile to go big. Someone would get suspicious. He's been working in the back kitchen on this one. Staying as far from the action while still getting shit done."

"So, do you know who he's been paying off?" Renato asked.

"Not a clue," Lukas said with a slight shrug. "That's just the word on the street."

"We need names," Carver said.

"I already told you I don't have names!" Lukas said. "I just know there's a bunch of them involved, and if you don't protect me, I'm dead."

"Nah," Carver said, rising to his feet. "We'll make sure they won't kill you."

"Yeah," Renato agreed. "You can just head off with Haskell's snitch when he gets done testifying, and both of you can be in Witness Protection together!"

"Hey, it will be one big happy snitch family!" Carver laughed.

"What now?" Lukas groaned. "You gonna put me back in there with those guys again?"

"We'll move you somewhere secure," Renato said.

He slid his notebook over to Lukas so he could sign his name under the statement he had just given them.

"We'll be able to find you again if we need you."

Carver motioned the guards and gave them instructions before turning back to Lukas and saying, "All right, you enjoy your stay now. We'll see you again real soon."

Renato stayed in his seat as the guards unchained Lukas and pulled him from the room. Carver smiled as he listened to Lukas's sneakers squeak on the floor when he didn't move fast enough, and the guards dragged him along.

Chapter 19

Monday 4 PM – Marie and Bryant

MARIE SUCKED IN A DEEP breath of the energized air that hit her the moment she stepped off the elevator. It wasn't every day the entire office gathered for an impromptu meeting, so nervous energy filled the crowded space. Marie tried to ignore the chattering of conversation as she moved to the front of the room and found the sign-in sheet. It had been posted by the conference room and added an air of formality to the meeting.

Bryant and Marie signed in, trying to ignore the blank space beside Lindsay's name. They tried to slide into the background and not draw attention to themselves. But before they could escape scrutiny, another member of their criminal law team approached.

"What do you think is going on?" the woman asked.

"I don't know, Autumn," Marie said. "It can't be good, though, considering everyone in the office is here."

"Well, not everyone," Autumn added. "Callen's gone."

Marie ducked her head and said, "You're right. It's still hard to believe he's gone."

"I'll miss him," Autumn said before turning her attention to the front of the room.

A hush fell over the gathering as the firm's five partners walked up in front of the group. Quinn Heron, the firm's family law partner and Lindsay's direct supervisor, looked distressed. Madison Kimbley, the personal injury partner, rubbed his back to comfort him.

Wallace Snyder and Devin Waggner took control of the meeting, leaving Luke Roland, the partner in charge of bankruptcy, to look over the sign-in sheet.

"We have some rather sad news to share," Wallace Snyder said after Luke confirmed everyone was present and accounted for. "Lindsay Sprout, one of our family law attorneys, died earlier today."

"We know this is upsetting news," Devin Waggner thundered over the murmurs. "We are still grappling with the loss of a member of our paralegal team, Callen, and now we've lost another valuable member of our family."

"As your leaders," Wallace Snyder continued, "we want to make sure you have all the resources available to deal with these losses. So, we will have counselors on-site for the next few days in case anyone wants to talk to them. We also want to encourage everyone to attend Callen's memorial tomorrow afternoon. If anyone needs the information for the memorial, I will post it on the company bulletin board in the kitchen."

As Wallace's voice faded and the crowd began dispersing, murmurs again started flittering through the office. Concern, confusion, and curiosity seemed to be the dominant trend of the conversations taking place around them.

Glancing around the room, Marie caught sight of Wallace and Devin deep in conversation. Both glanced her direction and looked away when they realized she was watching them. It wasn't long before the pair separated and walked away from each other.

"We need to go talk to Wallace," Bryant whispered.

"Why?" Marie hissed back at him. "Won't that just draw attention to ourselves?"

"I think it will draw even more attention if we don't go and a least see what they are doing with our case," he said.

Traversing the room, Marie and Bryant soon found themselves in front of Wallace's closed office door. Taking a deep breath, Bryant knocked. The door swung open and Wallace Snyder stared back at them. The immaculate suit Wallace typically addressed them in hung disheveled on his body. Marie couldn't help but notice the tired look on his face. He sighed, ushered them both inside, and closed the door behind them.

"Scotch?" he asked, pouring himself a double in a tumbler he pulled from a drawer in his desk.

"No thanks," Bryant said.

"I suppose you two are here about that case you are working on," Wallace said after taking a sip from the glass and closing his eyes. Without paying attention to them, he sat down at his desk and rubbed his temples before taking another large sip from his glass.

"We just wanted to know if the judge had ruled to continue our trial or not," Bryant said.

"Yes, yes," Wallace nodded. "The judge cleared you two of any tampering and agreed to move it based on everything going on."

"What's our new court date?" Bryant asked.

"He gave you until Friday," Wallace said. "I expect you two to be ready this time."

"Yes, sir," Bryant nodded. "We will be ready."

"And by ready," Wallace continued, "I mean ready to complete the deal as we have already set it up. I want no more surprises going on with this case. Understood?"

"We'll get everything ironed out before Friday, sir," Bryant said as Marie nodded in agreement.

After leaving Wallace's office, Marie once again felt her eyes gravitating toward Quinn. She couldn't help but notice how distraught he seemed and how Madison continued to stick by his side. She started to feel suspicion grow in her stomach and decided she shouldn't ignore her gut instincts any longer.

"Hey, you go ahead," she said to Bryant. "I want to pay my respects to Lindsay's boss."

Bryant gave her a funny look but didn't question her motives and padded back to his office. Marie strode up to Quinn and Madison, who were still whispering in the corner.

"I just wanted to say how sorry I am about Lindsay's passing," Marie said to Quinn.

"Thank you," he said. "We will miss her around here."

"Is there anything I can do to help?" Marie pushed. "Does her family need anything? Are there any arrangements in place yet?"

While she was talking, Quinn shook his head.

"No," he said. "Her boyfriend is handling everything. Her parents live out of state, so any memorial service will be up there with them."

"What about casework or anything your department could need?" Marie asked, still fishing for information. "I just feel like there's something I could do to help bridge the gap or something."

Quinn's eyes softened a bit at her, and he said, "Thank you so much for the offer. If there is anything I can think of, I'll let you know. I'm sure it will be a while before we get everything sorted out. My mother has been in the hospital battling cancer, so I've been in and out. The rest of my team has been holding down the fort. Lindsay was a big part of it, but now it looks like Reid, Stella, and Carter will all have to pitch in more for now."

Marie nodded, "I wish there was something I could do to make things easier on you guys. I didn't know Lindsay that well, but she always seemed nice. After our team just losing Callen the way we did, I know you guys have to be hurting."

"Just tragic," Quinn said.

"Please let me know if you think of anything I can do to help your team," Marie said before saying her goodbyes to Quinn and retracing her steps to Bryant's office.

"You learn anything?" he asked.

"I found out Quinn has a sick mother in the hospital," she said. "Other than that, nothing."

"That's a good motive for needing cash from an organized crime boss," Bryant said.

Marie glanced over at Quinn, who was already back in the clutches of Madison. She took Quinn's arm in hers and patted it with her hand before leaning in close and whispering something in his ear.

"Very strange," Bryant said, also gazing their direction. "But not proof of anything at this point."

"Seems like the only thing we can do at this point is hope Joe and Anna have found something by now," Marie sighed.

Chapter 20

Monday Noon - Joe and Anna

ANNA GAZED OUT THE window and ignored the scowls Claire threw her way every few seconds. She also did her best to ignore her sullen boyfriend, but that was proving difficult. When the four of them had piled into Joe's jeep to head out on their trek to find Audrick, Anna had elected to ride in the backseat with Claire. She'd hoped to make things less awkward, but Alex was making that impossible.

She let her eyes roam to the front of the jeep, but the moment she caught sight of Alex's deep scowl, she jerked her attention back outside the vehicle again. The atmosphere in the vehicle differed from the day before when it was just her and Joe, and she knew Joe had to notice the difference.

She allowed her eyes to stray again, this time to the rearview mirror and Joe's reflection in it. He noticed her attention and caught her eye in the mirror. When Joe's sudden change in posture caught Alex's attention, Anna deflected her attention to Claire.

"I think my jeans are ruined, Claire."

Claire ignored Anna's forced smile and frowned at her.

"I can't believe you dropped me," Claire said.

173

"I can't believe after pulling your car out of the ditch, we STILL had to call a tow truck," Joe said.

He looked back at her in the rearview mirror and grinned. Claire's cheeks grew red, and she sank back into her seat with an angry huff.

"Didn't you know you had flooded your engine?" Anna asked.

"No, I did not!" Claire said.

She found a piece of mud in her hair and threw it at Anna before turning her attention to Joe.

"I apologize for all the mud we are getting in your jeep, Joe. I'll make sure Anna cleans it out later."

Joe raised his eyebrows and said, "It's seen worse. Trust me. Not a big deal at all."

"You should have seen it Saturday," Anna said, her voice just above a whisper.

Joe's playful eyes pivoted from Claire to Anna and he glared at her reflection in the rearview mirror.

"How about we don't worry about the mud," Alex said. "Distractions are the last thing we need at the moment."

"Great," Anna thought. *"Mr. Uncomfortable is back."*

Anna ignored the look Claire shot her way after Alex's comment and tried to draw attention away from the tension he'd created.

"What is our plan?"

"Let's just drive by and see what we see," Joe said. "We can go from there."

"How much further?" Claire groaned. "We've been driving forever, and I need to go to the bathroom."

"We're about 30 minutes away," Joe said. "But there is a gas station coming up if you want me to stop."

"Yes, please!" Claire said.

Joe pulled the jeep into the gas station's parking lot and both Anna and Claire escaped inside. The moment Anna entered the store, Claire shoved a t-shirt into her hand.

"Here. I'm done being muddy for the day."

They made their purchases, changed shirts in the bathroom, and headed back outside to find Alex and Joe waiting for them in the jeep. Joe was munching on a bag of chips.

"Didn't we just eat?" Anna asked him when they were back inside the jeep.

"Yeah," Alex said, his arms crossed over his chest. "Like fifteen minutes ago."

"These are the best!" Joe said.

He ignored Alex and held the open bag in Anna's direction.

"I haven't seen a bag of them in YEARS! Couldn't pass them up."

Anna raised an eyebrow at him but took a chip from his bag and put it in her mouth.

"Hey, those ARE good!" she said.

"Told you."

"Can we go now?" Alex asked.

"Aye, aye, captain," Joe said.

Anna hung her head and went back to staring out the window as Joe put the jeep in drive and headed for the highway. She ignored Claire's gaze again, closed her eyes, and allowed the silence in the jeep to engulf her.

The outside road noise flooding the vehicle was a welcome distraction from the task at hand. Before long, Joe pulled off the highway and followed his GPS to the address. Anna felt her head sway from side to side as Joe took turn after turn. The distinct crunch of gravel under the tires caused her eyes to jerk open.

"Are we close?" she asked.

"Yep, it's just around this bend here on the right," Joe said. "I will drive as slow as I can."

Anna pulled out her phone and snapped a few pictures of the small house tucked into a thick forest as they passed by. Her eyes swept across the property, looking for signs of life, but the only interesting aspect was the blue sedan double-parked behind a gray BMW in the driveway.

"Well, someone's home," Joe said as he drove past.

Anna flipped back through the pictures she had taken while glancing up at the road in front of them.

"Hey," she said and pointed to a small opening in the woods. "Pull in there for a minute."

"What are we doing?" Alex asked. "I thought we were just going to drive by."

"We need a closer look," Anna said.

She hopped out of the jeep before he could protest.

"I'll be gone two minutes."

As she walked around the jeep, she heard Alex's passenger window buzz down and felt his eyes following her. When he didn't call out or follow her, Anna sighed and continued her trek. Joe's voice made her hesitate, however.

"So, you aren't going with her, then?" Joe asked.

Anna cringed when she realized he was talking to Alex.

"I'm a police officer," Alex said. "I'll lose my badge if I'm caught trespassing!"

"Well, glad to know you've got your priorities straight at least," Joe said.

Anna stopped and turned back when she heard Joe's door open and shut. Before he followed her, he turned back to Alex again.

"Would you mind sitting over here in case we need a quick getaway? I take it driving isn't against your code of ethics."

"Um, guys," Claire said. "Could one of you please go make sure Anna doesn't get killed, please?"

Anna shot her friend a grateful glance when the distraction was just enough to keep Joe and Alex from completely losing control of their tempers. Without another word, Alex slid across the seat to take Joe's place behind the wheel. When Joe caught up with Anna, he motioned for her to follow him.

"Looks like the windows are all covered," he whispered. "But, there's one by the back of the house that looks like it might be open. Maybe we can see something inside."

Joe and Anna crept across the small backyard, their eyes darting from one side to the next in search of company. When they approached the open window, voices began floating out to reach their ears. Anna took a chance and slid up the wall to peer inside the window.

"I don't want to hear your excuses, Audrick," said one voice.

Anna's eyes swept the room behind the open window. She could just make out a pair of men in the room. She pulled out her phone and took a few pictures.

"I'm sorry, I'm sorry!"

Anna assumed the groveling man on the floor was Audrick. He had visible sweat on the back of his dress shirt, and he sat on his knees in front of the other man. He peered up at the man, who glared down at him with his hands on his hips. Audrick turned his face to the ground again and continued pleading with him.

"She was going to the FBI. I didn't have a choice."

"Audrick," the larger man said.

His tone caused Audrick to sink further than Anna thought was possible. She watched his shoulders tremble.

"What do you think the police will think about this?" the standing man continued. "It's like you're standing outside that law firm with a huge red flag and saying, 'look at me!'"

"I know."

Anna watched as Audrick wiped tears from his cheeks. He placed his hands on his head and leaned forward until his forehead rested on the other man's shoes.

"Please, forgive me."

"Between those FBI jokers and those other two lawyers getting in our way, we can't be making mistakes like this."

Audrick's lost his ability to form logical sentences, so he stayed at the man's feet, sobs wracking through his broad shoulders. The sound of a car door slamming caused Anna to jump, and she felt Joe's hand grip her forearm before he jerked her down below the window and out of sight of those inside. He put his arm across her chest, pinning her to the side of the house, using his own body to protect her.

Anna's eyes swept across the yard in front of them and picked out the fastest escape route. It wasn't long before Anna and Joe began hearing a third, female voice drift through the open window. Anna went to look through the window a second time, but Joe pulled her back down and shook his head at her.

He pulled out his phone and raised his head to peer in the window. Anna strained her ears to make out the argument that was occurring inside.

"You're an idiot, you know," the woman said.

"I know," Audrick said. "I'm so sorry. I'll do better. Please, just let me fix this!"

"Tell me what happened."

"She didn't want to do it anymore," Audrick said. "Said she wanted out."

"Was she going to the police?"

"I was trying to convince her not to," Audrick said, "but with everything she knew, I didn't think we could take the risk."

"How much did she know?"

"I tried to keep her in the dark as much as possible. She knew we would take pictures of her with those men and blackmail them, but she didn't know why."

"But you know why," the woman said. "You know exactly why."

"Please!"

Anna closed her eyes at the sound of his growing desperation.

"You know I'm solid," Audrick said. "I would never compromise anything. I can fix this mistake."

"That chance for reconciliation ended the moment you took that girl's life."

Anna watched Joe continue to take pictures while a sick feeling grew in her stomach. Before they could get much deeper into the drama, Joe dipped his head back below the window and leaned in close to Anna's ear.

"We need to get out of here. Now," he said.

Anna nodded and led him back across the yard. She followed the escape path she had mapped out in her head earlier. The way back to the jeep seemed longer than before, and they both did their best to make as little noise as possible. The sudden sound of a gunshot took them both by surprise.

Joe reacted by wrapping his arms around Anna's waist, sweeping her feet out from under her, and pulling her to the ground underneath him. For several moments, he kept them in that position, trying to look around to survey their surroundings. Anna couldn't help but gaze up into his cool blue eyes that were brimming with both concern and focus.

Once he decided they were in the clear, Joe looked down at Anna. When his eyes landed on hers, he hesitated for a few seconds before letting her up.

"Sorry," he said.

He helped her to her feet and they both dusted the leaves and grass off their clothes.

"We need to get out of here."

Anna followed him the rest of the way back to the jeep, the whole time trying to ignore the magnetism she had just felt. When they emerged unscathed from the forest, Alex and Claire both looked relieved to see them.

"Thank God!" Claire said. "Let's go! I'm not sitting here another moment!"

Alex slid back over in his seat to allow Joe back into the driver's seat and glanced back at Anna, who was attempting to avoid his gaze. She looked through the pictures in her phone of the men and shot a few off to her sister.

"Joe, you need to send some pictures to Bryant, so he and Marie can see if they recognize that woman," she said.

Joe complied before maneuvering his jeep back onto the road. Before the tires threw up a mile of gravel, Anna's phone began ringing.

Before she could get a greeting out of her mouth, Marie was screaming at her.

"Where are you two? You need to get out of there right now!"

"Why? What's wrong?" Anna asked. "We're already back in the jeep and driving."

"That's Haskell's attorney!" she said.

"The other man was Audrick," Anna said.

"Anna!" Marie said. "I thought you said wouldn't take any risks!"

"We were just looking in a window," Anna said.

"Go wait for us somewhere. Send me the address of wherever you end up. Just make sure it is far from those people and that you're safe!"

"We can do that. But, there's one more thing you need to know."

Joe caught her eye in the rearview mirror and grimaced.

"We heard a gunshot as we were leaving," Anna said. "From the conversation we overheard, I wouldn't hold out hope Audrick will still be around to answer questions when you get here."

The anger Anna felt shooting her direction from Alex and through the phone from Marie was palpable. Trying to avoid Alex's gaze, Anna turned her eyes back to her lap. After what seemed like an eternity, Marie addressed the situation further.

"I'm calling the agents. You just send me the address."

"A gunshot?" Alex asked when she had ended the call with her sister. "You two stuck around long enough for a gunshot to happen? What's the matter with you?"

"We were safe," Anna said. "We had a way out the whole time."

"Where are we going?" Claire asked Joe.

Anna was grateful for her presence and her continued attempts to change the atmosphere in the jeep. She caught Claire's eye and smiled at her.

"Well, I saw a go-kart place a few miles back."

"You want to drive go-karts?" Alex asked. "At a time like this?"

"I figured we could all use a little destressing time. Might be fun?"

Alex grumbled under his breath but didn't argue.

"I don't like go-karts!" Claire said.

"That's because you can't drive!" Anna said.

She hoped her gentle teasing would shut down the angry feelings emanating out of Alex.

"I can too drive," Claire said with a pout.

Joe turned to glance at her before shaking his head and turning back to face the road.

"Our earlier experience and all the mud still in your hair would say otherwise," he said.

To Anna's relief, Alex allowed a small laugh to escape his lips at Joe's remark. When they parked, he walked to her side of the car and pulled her away from Joe and Claire.

"Don't do that to me again," he said.

"I'm sorry," she said and looked at her feet.

Alex cupped her chin in his hand and pulled her eyes back up to his.

"Anna," he said. "I love you. Having you in that dangerous of a situation is too much for me to deal with. They could have hurt you!"

Anna gave him a kiss on his lips. She gazed up into his worry-filled eyes and tried to put his mind at ease.

"I promise you we were being safe," she said. "Besides, Joe was there to protect me."

The look in his eyes made her want to suck the words back into her mouth. He pulled away from her and walked toward the go-kart track. Anna caught up with Claire and tried to ignore the negative feelings rumbling around inside of her.

"I can't believe you are making me do this," Claire said.

"Oh, come on, Claire," Anna said.

Anna began walking backward in front of her friend and forced a smile on her face.

"This will be fun!"

"Yeah," Claire said. "The last time you said that we were seven and I ended up with a broken arm, remember?"

"You're exaggerating."

"Uh, no, I'm not," Claire said. "Mom kept the cast. There are pictures. It was my birthday for crying out loud!"

"Well, I promise not to break your arm this time."

"Yeah, looking at how fast those things are going around the track, I'll wind up with a broken neck this time."

Anna stopped and put her arm around her friend's shoulder.

"You can drive as fast or as slow as you want to," Anna said. "I promise you won't get hurt."

"Whatever," Claire said.

Claire jerked out from underneath Anna's arm and grinned at her.

"I'm not going to just let you beat me."

Anna laughed until tears rolled down her cheeks.

"What's so funny?"

"You think you can beat me!"

Claire glared at her and put her hands on her hips as Anna tried to catch her breath.

"If you didn't cheat all the time!"

"I don't cheat," Anna said.

Anna threw her hands up and looked at Alex for support. When their eyes met, he sighed, and Anna could tell that his anger was dissolving.

"Yes," he said. "You cheat."

Joe started to laugh, and Anna glared at him and punched him in the arm.

Chapter 21

Monday 4:00 PM

ALEX'S EYES FOLLOWED Anna's go-kart around the track for what seemed like the hundredth time. Claire's quiet sigh from beside him broke the cycle. Rolling her eyes when he looked at her, Claire turned to the track, pursed her lips, and then dove back into the game she was playing on her phone.

Trying to stay attentive to Anna's interests, Alex checked the time on his watch, noted how slow the past three hours had passed, and averted his eyes back to the track.

Three laps into what Alex hoped would be their last race, his ears caught the sound of gravel behind him. He turned, relieved to see Bryant and Marie pulling into the parking lot. Claire put her phone in her pocket and watched them approach.

"Who's winning?" Marie asked.

"God, I've lost track," Alex said. "They both keep saying they are tied, and they need one more race for a tie-breaker."

"Please make them stop," Claire said.

"Where did you come from?" Marie said, noticing Claire for the first time. "And, why are you covered in mud."

"It's a long story," Claire said.

Before she could go into more detail, all their eyes snapped to the racetrack as Joe's front tire caught Anna's back tire, causing her to spin out of control. He sped by as her kart rolled to a stop. He crossed the finish line as her kart sat on the track backward.

Anna ripped her helmet off and yelled at him, "You cheated!"

"Oh, please," Joe said with an amused grin. "You know you jumped the line when we started."

"Only because you jumped it the last race," Anna said.

Joe laughed before noticing his brother for the first time.

"Oh, hey Bryant!" he said as Bryant shook his head.

Ignoring his brother, Bryant turned to Marie instead.

"I'm sorry," he told her. "I didn't know you lived with the female version of my brother. I feel for you."

Joe and Anna both glared at their siblings before driving their go-karts back to the holding area.

"You owe me a rematch."

Joe leaned in close to her and whispered, "You're just mad because you know you can't beat me fair and square."

He grinned when she shot him an annoyed look.

"If you two are quite done," Bryant said and crossed his arms.

"Can someone please tell me who's idea it was to come out here?" Marie asked.

"Well, we were waiting for you guys, and this track was nearby, so we thought we would stop..." Anna said.

"Not here, dummy!" Marie rolled her eyes. "Whose idea was it to track down Audrick."

"And, take pictures?" Bryant asked.

"And almost get shot?"

"We didn't almost get shot," Anna said.

"We were supposed to just drive by and see what was here," Alex interjected. "That was the plan. But someone wanted a closer look."

Anna looked at the ground.

"And someone stayed in the car and let her go alone," Joe said.

Sensing rising tempers, Bryant stepped in between his brother and Alex to defuse the situation.

"All right," he said. "Calm down. It's all over and done with now. No sense blaming anyone for anything. Let's just drop it and get on with things."

"The FBI agents are on their way," Marie said. "So, we need to talk before they get here."

"Are you kidding me?" Alex said. "I'm so going to lose my badge. What have you gotten me into, Anna?"

Anna's eyes shot up from the ground and darkened into a cold glare at Alex's words. Without replying, she pulled out her phone and started tapping on the screen.

"What are you doing?" Alex asked.

Anna ignored the exasperation in his voice and continued typing on her phone without looking at him.

"I'm calling you and Claire an Uber."

Anna's fingers tapped her phone, her face twisted into a scowl. Denying Alex's attempt to take her hand and avoiding the awkward faces of the rest of the group, Anna shoved her phone back in her pocket and stormed away from the group.

She only stopped when Alex caught up with her and grabbed her elbow, pulling her to a stop.

"I can't believe you are mad at me," he said.

"Are you kidding me?" Anna said. "You just asked what I got you into. I didn't get you into anything. I didn't ask you to come today."

"You don't want me here?"

"We both know WHY you came today," Anna hissed.

Anna's eyes shone with fury as Alex couldn't help but glance over at Joe. Before he could get any wild ideas, she jerked his attention back to her.

"You need to get over yourself."

"I can't help the way I feel about it," Alex said. "But I'll leave you here to do whatever."

Anna jerked away from him and stormed back to the group, grateful he didn't follow her again.

"So, what happened?" Marie asked when her sister returned.

"We followed Audrick out here to a house," Anna said. "He was here with that man we sent you a picture of, and they were arguing. The woman showed up, they argued more, and we left."

"What did they argue about?" Bryant asked.

"They were blaming him for that girl's death," Joe said. "Lindsay, I guess?"

"The woman said something about him taking her life," Anna said.

"Wow," Bryant said. "That's something. But doesn't give us any proof of how she was involved."

Anna and Joe looked at each other and grimaced.

"There's more. They discussed what Lindsay knew. Audrick said Lindsay was sleeping with men so they could take pictures and blackmail them, but he'd never told her why."

"With Haskell involved, I imagine it wasn't for anything good," Marie said. "That's still nothing we can prove though."

Anna let the others continue to muse over the case but checked out of the conversation, letting her sullen mood take over while attempting to ignore Claire's concerned looks. When the Uber arrived, however, Claire didn't give her any more opportunities to ignore her.

Claire pulled her into a tight hug, and whispered in Anna's ear, "Are you all right?"

"I'm fine," Anna said. "Sorry we didn't have time to take you home first, and you had to come along today."

"Oh, please," Claire said. "And miss out on all this fun we've had today? I don't think so!"

Anna smiled at her friend and pulled her back in for another hug. "I'm so glad you are my best friend."

"Speaking of best friends," Claire said and turned to peek at Joe. "Don't let that dummy over there steal mine while I'm gone."

Anna laughed. "Now you are getting jealous too?"

"No, I just think he's pretty cool."

"Whatever," Anna said.

Claire grinned. "He's not bad to look at either. I wouldn't mind seeing him around more if you know what I mean."

Anna glanced at Joe and back at Claire before trying to force a smile on her face.

"Yeah, I guess so," she said.

"You did it again," Claire said. "You hesitated."

"Will you quit telling me that? I didn't hesitate!"

"Fine," Claire said. "I'm going to go ask him to dinner right now. How about that?"

Anna sighed and said, "No, don't do that."

"Well, you know our deal," Claire said. "You have your one boyfriend block. If you want to use it on Joe, then have at it."

"Fine," Anna said. "Consider him blocked."

"Anna!" Claire gasped. "Are you kidding me right now?"

"No, I'm not, Claire. Just leave him alone."

"Want to tell me why?"

"I just don't think he's able to handle being pursued by you. That's all."

"This has nothing to do with your feelings about him?"

"Of course not," Anna said. "I'm with Alex, remember."

"So, you just used your block on a guy you aren't interested in just because you're trying to be a good friend?"

"I guess so?"

"Well, that's just the most adorable thing ever. Almost adorable enough to give you back your block. But not quite."

Anna laughed before letting her eyes stray from Claire to Alex. She sighed and walked over to him, stood on her tiptoes, and kissed him, ignoring the surprised look in his eyes.

"I'm still mad at you," she said, but let a small smile play on her lips. "But I still love you."

Before he could reply, Anna marched back over to Claire, just in time to watch a sedan pull into the parking lot. "Uh, oh. It looks like you need to get out of here. Our FBI friends are here."

After saying goodbye to Marie, Claire grinned at Anna before telling Joe, "Thanks for pulling me out of the ditch. See you around, BB."

Anna glared at her as she sped toward the waiting car Alex had already hopped into.

Joe watched her go, a look of confusion crossing his face before turning to Anna and whispering, "Why did she call me BB?"

"She's crazy," Anna said. "Don't worry about it."

She ducked her head and hoped her cheeks didn't reveal her embarrassment. Joe raised an eyebrow at her but dropped the subject when the agents approached the group.

"Your friends in a hurry to get out of here?" Carver asked.

"Just had something to get back to," Anna said.

"Mmm, hmm," Carver said.

"So, which one of you two want to explain to us why we are all the way out here in no man's land," Renato said.

He took turns glaring at Joe and Anna while waiting for one of them to answer.

"Right to the point," Joe mumbled.

He looked at his shoes and glanced at Anna before answering for them.

"It's my fault. I did a little snooping on the boyfriend of the girl from their law firm and traced him here."

"No," Anna said. "It isn't your fault. I said we should drive by."

Joe looked at Anna, arguing with her directly, "Yeah, but I would have gone by myself if you hadn't said it first."

"But who got out of the car, huh?" she asked, putting her hands on her hips.

Before Joe could respond, Carver held his hands up.

"Stop it," he said. "We've established you are both idiots. Great. Can we just agree not to do something like this again?"

Anna and Joe both looked at the ground this time, avoiding the angry gaze of the agents and their siblings.

"Can you just tell us what happened?" Renato asked.

"I was looking for that Audrick guy," Joe said. "His phone pinged at the house we visited and then it disappeared. It's like he took it offline."

"How do you know that?" Carver asked.

The guilty look on Joe's face made him hold up his hands.

"Never mind, I DON'T want to know. Continue."

"So, we drove by to see what was here," Anna said.

"We couldn't see much from the road, so we took a closer look," Joe said.

"Seems like the logical next step," Carver said.

"All we did was look in the window," Anna said. "We saw Audrick and some guy arguing. A woman showed up and yelled at him more, and we left."

"On the way back, we heard a single gunshot," Joe said.

Anna locked eyes with him for a split second before jerking her attention back to the agents. Much to their relief, the agents turned their attention away from Anna and Joe and focused on Marie and Bryant instead. Anna glanced down at the ground and ignored Joe's attempts to catch her eye again.

"And you say the woman is someone who works in your office, and the other guy is an attorney at another firm?"

Bryant nodded.

"Anything else you need to tell us before we send you on your way?"

"You had us drive all the way out here just to send us back home?" Bryant asked.

"Well, maybe you can convince your siblings to avoid any wild-goose chases, so you keep miles off your vehicles," Renato said, already walking away from them.

Joe grabbed Anna by the elbow and whispered in her ear, "Unless you want to hear an earful for the next two hours, I would suggest you get in my jeep right now."

The pair were already walking away before Bryant and Marie could even say a word to them. Anna cringed as she overheard their conversation before getting in Joe's jeep.

"Do you think they just woke up, got coffee, and said, 'Hey, what stupid things do you think we should do today?'" Bryant asked.

"I don't know," Marie said. "But I will kill them when I get my hands on them."

"At least I can blame you for introducing them to each other," Bryant said.

Marie glared at him and said, "Just get us back home so I can kill my sister, please."

Chapter 22

CARVER AND RENATO WATCHED as the group pulled out of the parking lot. When they'd disappeared out of sight, Carver looked at Renato and shook his head.

"It's hard to believe they can accomplish this much intel as civilians," Renato said.

"Oh, I imagine they have access to just about everything we do," Carver said.

"We need to think about putting a stop to that."

"Yep," Carver said, and shook his head again. "You want to go check out this address they sent us?"

"Well, we have come all this way," Renato said. "Why not?"

The pair remained quiet on the ride to the abandoned house. Both knew they were likely to find an unpleasant scene and tried their best to prepare their minds for the shock of whatever they were about to come across.

When they pulled up, only one car remained in the driveway. Renato pulled his gun and checked out the car before turning his attention to the house in front of them. Carver followed suit. He covered his partner and watched the windows and the surrounding woods, his nerves tingling.

When he reached the door, Renato tried the door handle and found it unlocked. The two pushed forward into the darkened house. The stench that met them was almost unbearable, and the men covered their noses with their hands in disgust.

"Looks like someone had an awesome party in here," Renato said.

"College kids," Carver groaned and swept his eyes across the broken furniture, beer bottles, and rotting food strewn around the family room.

They moved through the house and cleared each room as they went. Their search ended when they reached a small bedroom at the back of the home.

"Damn," Renato said under his breath as he took in the sight of Audrick Walker lying on the floor, a puddle of blood spread out around him.

Carver circled the body and assessed the situation. "Gun's still in his hand. All the signs of suicide."

"Yeah, but we know better, don't we?"

"Yep," Carver said, looking for any evidence to lead them down the correct path instead of this fabricated one.

"I'll call it in."

Carver ignored him, still searching around the body, doing his best not to disturb anything. To his surprise, he saw a scrap of paper sticking out of the corner of Audrick's shoe.

"Bingo," he said.

He took a few pictures of the man's shoe on his cellphone and of the card lodged there before pulling out a pair of gloves and an evidence bag. He pulled the piece of paper loose and shook his head when he saw it was a business card belonging to Madison Kimbley, the woman Joe and Anna had taken a photo of earlier.

"You won't believe this," Carver said on his partner's return to the scene. "Our buddy Audrick here made sure we had a clue."

"Well, well, well," Renato said with a sound of surprise floating through his voice. "Looks like we have a reason to give Miss Kimbley a visit."

"I wonder what she'll say about this," Carver said.

Sirens began to fill the air and the agents went outside to greet the approaching squad cars. Already, police officers were piling out of cars and seeking information from the agents. After giving them the details of what was going on, the agents made the long trek back home.

When they reached Madison's home, she was already in her pajamas and answered the door in a huff when they continued ringing the bell.

"Do you mind?" she growled. "I have children who are sleeping!"

"We apologize for the late call, Ms. Kimbley," Renato said after showing her his badge. "But this can't wait."

Madison stared at the men, a look of horror passing through her eyes when she realized they were FBI agents. However, she regained her composure. Without acknowledging his apology, she strapped her arms across her chest and glared at them, not daring to invite them inside.

"What's this about?" she asked.

"We found your business card on the body of a dead man."

"What? What dead man?"

"He's the boyfriend of one of your junior attorneys who committed suicide today, Audrick Walker."

"I'm sorry, I don't know him," Madison said, feigning confusion. "Are you talking about Lindsay's boyfriend? I barely knew the girl. Don't get me wrong. It was tragic, but I wasn't really acquainted."

"So, how did Audrick get your business card?"

"A lot of people have my business card."

"How about we take a trip to our office, and you can tell us more about your non-relationship with Audrick."

"How about I'm not going anywhere without a warrant," she said.

"Great!" Carver said. "We'll be back tomorrow to pick you up. I'd suggest you don't go anywhere in the meantime."

Chapter 23

Monday 7:00 PM – Anna and Marie

"I CAN'T BELIEVE YOU did something that STUPID!" Marie fumed as she followed her sister around their apartment.

Anna's attempt at ignoring her while tidying up wasn't keeping her sister from chastising her. But Anna kept moving, avoiding her sister's eyes at all costs, stopping only a few times to roll her eyes at something Marie growled at her.

"I mean, really, Anna," Marie said, running out of things to yell at her about. "What were you thinking?"

Anna spun on her heels and glared at her sister.

"I was thinking, gee, I would love for my sister not to go to jail," she fumed. "Maybe I can see what's going on in here, and it will get us somewhere considering nothing else seems to be working."

"But it was so dangerous!"

"Marie, I was well aware of the dangers," Anna said before returning to cleaning their apartment. "I just figured the evidence was more important. Plus, it's not like I went out of my way to get caught or anything. Joe was there..."

"And, that's another thing," Marie said, remembering the other half of the equation. "What in the world were you doing with him today? Why did he go with you and not Alex?"

"You'll have to ask Alex about that," Anna retorted, pausing for a second to look down at the throw blanket she held in her hands. "I didn't invite either of them on my little adventure. I figured they would both wait in the car."

"Why was Alex even there in the first place?"

"Oh, don't get me started on that," Anna growled before tossing the blanket into a basket by the couch and sweeping up a glass sitting on the coffee table with so much force the entire table shook. "We are NOT discussing that."

Marie stood in the middle of the living room, watching her sister bustle around the apartment. Anna ignored her and continued tidying up. She couldn't measure her relief when Marie ran out of things to yell at her about. Sighing, Marie sat down on the couch and put her head in her hands.

"I could use a glass of wine," she said. "How about you?"

"It'll be all right," Anna said after a moment, appearing by her sister's side with the requested glass of wine in her hand. "We will figure all of this out."

"I already feel my career circling the drain," Marie sighed. "All those years of school and all those hours of studying for the bar wasted."

"You need to stop worrying so much and focus on finding a solution," Anna said. "We've got this. I promise! We're right there. I can feel it."

Marie reached over and took her sister's hand and squeezed it. Before she could counter her sister's positivity, they heard a knock on their door. Marie leaned back and closed her eyes as Anna went to answer the door. Anna opened it and peered outside in surprise when she found Alex standing on their doorstep with a massive flower bouquet.

"What are you doing here?" Anna asked, still annoyed even though her heart leaped a bit when she saw the sad, guilty look in his eyes.

"Did you know there are thirteen flower shops in this town?" he asked, ignoring her question.

"Thirteen, huh," Anna said, eyeing the flowers in his hand and the lavender lilacs sprouting among the baby's breath.

Alex pulled the bouquet up in front of his face so only his eyes were visible to her. Anna traced the flowers with her eyes until she was staring back into his dark eyes. Although she glared at him, she couldn't help but feel her resolve breaking already.

"You brought lilacs," she stated while trying to keep an even tone to her voice.

"Your favorites," he said. "Apparently, they are out of season, but one shop still had them."

"Hmmm," Anna said, not impressed.

"I owe you an apology," he said with a sigh.

"You think?" Anna said before taking the flowers out of his hand and turning away from him to put them on the kitchen counter. He followed behind her.

"You know, Claire gave me an earful all the way home," Alex said, rubbing his head with his hand. "She thought I was a jerk today."

"She's not the only one," Anna mumbled.

"She got me thinking," Alex continued, ignoring her comment. "I haven't given you the benefit of the doubt in all of this."

Anna busied herself with putting the flowers in a vase, fluffing them up, and making sure they had the proper amount of water while trying to ignore her boyfriend.

"Anna," he said and took her hand. "Can we please talk?" When she didn't pull away from him, he pulled her around to face him, putting his free hand on her cheek.

"I'm really, REALLY sorry," he said. "Can we go get some dinner?"

Anna felt a small smile form on her lips, and he pounced on the situation by leaning in to give her a kiss. Her eyes fluttered closed as she let him envelop her with his embrace for a moment, but she pulled away and addressed her sister who was still sitting on the couch nursing her glass of wine.

"Marie," she said. "Will you be all right tonight if I go out?"

Marie held up her glass of wine and pointed to the bottle on the counter.

"I'm all set," she said. "I plan to take a bath and go to bed soon anyway."

"OK, I'll see you tomorrow," Anna said, turning her attention back to Alex.

"Why don't you pack an overnight bag," he whispered after leaning in and kissing her on the neck.

"I'll bring one," Anna said, gazing back into his eyes and brushing her lips against his but denying him the kiss he was expecting. "But you must earn that right back over dinner."

She pulled away with a sly smile and headed to her bedroom to pack. Calling back to him over her shoulder, she said, "And I expect dessert."

Chapter 24

Tuesday 8:00 AM - Marie

"YOU SEEM LOST IN THOUGHT," Marie heard a voice say.

Glancing around, Marie stood in the kitchen at the law firm, stirring creamer into a cup of coffee. Looking down, she realized the mug no longer warmed her hand as it had when she first poured it. Shaking her head, she looked up to see her co-worker, Autumn, smiling at her.

"Sorry," Marie said. "I guess I'm a little out of it today."

"There's been a lot going on lately," Autumn said. "So, that's understandable."

Marie poured her mug of coffee in the sink as she realized she was no longer in the mood to drink it. "First Callen and now Lindsay."

"Yeah, I can't believe they are both gone," Autumn whispered before remarking a little louder. "Hey, have you met the new paralegal?"

"No!" Marie said. "I didn't realize we had already replaced Callen!"

"Yep," Autumn said with a shake of her head. "Started today. I guess the show must go on."

"Hmm," Marie said. "Well, I guess I should go meet her."

"She seems nice," Autumn said and started to leave the kitchen. She stopped when she passed the bulletin board. "Are you coming to Callen's memorial this afternoon?"

Marie looked at the handwritten note and nodded, a lump forming in her throat. "Yes, I'll be there."

"Such a sad thing," Autumn said before disappearing out of the kitchen.

Marie followed Autumn out the door and allowed her eyes to sweep over the office before resting her attention on the new paralegal, who was chatting with Bryant. Continuing her visual tour of the office, Marie let her eyes float by each office until she saw Maddison and Quinn shut up in his talking. Maddison's hands were waving around as she talked.

Avoiding Bryant's gaze, she began walking across the office. Feeling him watching her, she knocked on Quinn's door and waited for a response before she entered. After a moment of hesitation, Madison came to the door and stuck her head out.

"We're in the middle of something Marie," she stated. "Can this wait?"

"No," Marie said. "I need to talk to you both about some concerns I have."

"You can't talk to Wallace about this?"

"I'm afraid not," Marie said. "And it can't wait."

"Fine," Madison said, after staring in her eyes for a moment. "Come right in."

Marie glanced back at Bryant, who shook his head at her in desperation. Ignoring him, she followed Madison inside Quinn's office and shut the door behind her.

"What can we do for you, Marie?" Quinn asked.

"A few pieces of evidence I discovered earlier this week are causing some concern," Marie said.

"What type of evidence would that be?" Madison asked.

"Well," Marie continued. "I believe someone is tampering with some of my witnesses."

The silence in the office was palpable, and Marie tried her best to keep her composure while Madison and Quinn mulled over her comments. The look that passed between them was deadly.

"What would give you that impression?" Madison asked after a moment, her eyes on Marie's.

"As I said," Marie said, her gaze not wavering. "I have evidence."

"Hmmm," Quinn said. "That's a significant accusation."

"Who do you believe to be involved in this alleged tampering?" Madison asked.

"I believe Lindsay was, which is why I'm alerting you to the situation."

"But, other than that?"

Marie shrugged her shoulders and said, "I'm assuming there are others involved within the firm, but I haven't narrowed it down far enough yet. I'm close, though."

"Could you share the evidence with us so we can do our own investigation?"

"That's not possible at the moment," Marie said. "I don't have it on site."

"Well, we appreciate you bringing this to our attention."

"I just want to save the firm from an embarrassing situation."

"Yes, as do we," Quinn said.

"Thank you for letting me speak my mind," Marie said before stepping out of the office.

Closing the door behind her with a snap, Marie met Bryant's eyes for the first time that morning, his confusion and anger distinct even from across the room. Walking past where he stood at the paralegal's desk, she looked at him and made her way back to the kitchen. After a moment she heard him turn to follow her.

"What are you doing?" he hissed when they were in the confines of the kitchen.

"I'm sick of playing this game," she whispered. "I'm tired of waiting around wondering if someone in this office will do something to me."

"Please tell me you didn't do something stupid," he hissed. "We are both in this together, and we need to talk about these things before you go AWOL."

"I guess that depends on your definition of stupid," Marie said. "They already assumed I knew something, so I just confirmed it. Now we'll see how the cards fall."

"Please tell me you didn't," Bryant said.

"I told them I had evidence of witness tampering and I wanted them to know about it because I thought Lindsey was involved."

"Marie," Bryant said. "That's putting us at risk! What were you thinking?"

"Well, I at least didn't bring you into it," she said, "So if anything goes down, it will be on me and not you. I got us into this mess anyway. I might as well finish it."

Bryant shook his head in disbelief and started to leave the kitchen in disgust.

"You need to be careful," he said over his shoulder.

"I guess we'll just have to see what happens next," Marie said, following him. "The ball's in their court now."

"Well, while we wait for them to do something, come meet our new paralegal."

"I can't believe they replaced him so soon."

Marie followed him to Callen's old desk despite her hard feelings about the situation. The young woman stopped arranging things on her desk the moment Marie and Bryant approached. Standing, she brushed her fingers through her bangs, resetting a strand of auburn hair that had strayed from its clip. After resting her green eyes on Bryant for a moment, she turned to Marie for an introduction.

"Hi, I'm Allison," she said with a dazzling smile. "But most people call me Allie."

"It's nice to meet you, Allie," Marie said returning her smile. "My name is Marie. Are you settling in well?"

Allie nodded and said, "Just fine, thank you. Bryant here has made sure I knew where everything was and helped me find the supplies I needed to get started today."

"I'm glad he's been so helpful," Marie said, giving Bryant a suspicious look. He didn't look back at her as he hadn't taken his eyes off Allie since they had arrived at her desk moments ago.

"Please let me know if there's anything I can get started on for any of your cases," Allie said. "I'm excited to get to work with the team."

"We are excited to get to work with you too," Bryant said, flashing her a debonair smile before glancing at a picture on her desk. "Hey, is that Denali?"

Allie looked from his surprised face to the picture behind her and smiled a little before replying.

"Yep," she said. "That was a great trip. Tough, but so fun. It took me six months to get ready for it. Do you climb mountains, too?"

"I do!" Bryant said. "I've never made it out to Denali, though. That's impressive."

"My brother and I are planning to hit up Mont Blanc," she said with a smile. "But, that's a much bigger endeavor than either of us have attempted, so we aren't rushing into anything."

Bryant nodded. "I hiked that one a few years back. It was beautiful."

"I'll bet," Allie said, her eyes shining as Bryant became a lot more interesting to her.

"We'd better let you get back to settling in," Bryant said, smiling back at her. "Please let us know if we can help you."

"It was nice to meet you," Marie said.

After not finding a reason to linger any longer at Allie's desk, Bryant followed Marie back to their portion of the office. Marie grinned at him as he couldn't help but steal looks back in Allie's direction.

"Finding yourself distracted?" she asked.

"Hmm, what?" he asked, jumping a bit.

"I said, are you having a hard time concentrating?"

"Sorry," Bryant said, shaking his head. "I don't know what's the matter with me. Guess it's all the stress."

"Sure," Marie said, a playful smile forming on her lips. "I'm sure that's it."

Bryant glared at her but glanced back at Allie one more time before settling down at his desk. Shaking her head, Marie made her way back to her own office. Sinking into her chair, she sighed and ran both her hands across her face in tired frustration. Kicking her heels off under her desk, she reached into her file cabinet for the familiar documents related to the Haskell case and began pouring back over them again.

Sadness seeped into her mind every time she noticed Callen's familiar handwriting, but she tried her best to push those thoughts away from her. After reading each witness statement three times, she began to realize they would not give her any insight into the situation she found herself in and placed them to the side.

She began flipping through the remaining pages in the file, only stopping when she felt her finger catch on something on the back of one of them. Frowning, Marie turned the page over, finding herself both surprised and confused by a sticky note attached with an address written on it. Frowning, she looked at the address, trying to remember what significance it had to the case.

Deciding to have Anna and Joe check out the address online later, she pulled her phone out and took a quick picture of the note for future reference and continued her search through the file. However, before she could finish, she looked up just in time to see Carver Hoage and Renato Kamera stroll into their office.

They avoided eye contact with both Marie and Bryant as they made a beeline for Madison's office and presented some papers to her. After arguing with the men for several minutes, she ultimately exited the office looking both perplexed and furious. Marie didn't miss the death stare Madison sent her way as the agents followed her to the elevator.

Chapter 25

Tuesday 8:30 – Agents Hoage and Kamera

CARVER SWEPT INTO THE law firm with Renato on his heels. Avoiding the curious gazes of everyone in the building, including Bryant and Marie, they entered Madison Kimbley's office and tossed some papers onto her desk.

The surprise he saw on her face was satisfying and caused him to smirk a bit. He couldn't believe the limited amount of hearsay evidence he had was enough for a judge to issue a warrant, but it had worked, so Carver was going with it. The warrants were limited, but her personal property and desk were fair game.

While he didn't expect to find much, Carver hoped the noise they made was enough to scare others enough to make a mistake. Both Carver and Kamera monitored the faces that gazed their direction. While it was natural for the employees to show some interest in the action, they were looking for anyone who seemed overly attentive.

Before rifling through the papers, Madison argued with the agents for several minutes, her voice raising several octaves throughout their conversation. Staying calm, the agents waited for her to tire herself out. She sighed and picked up the papers they had given her and looked through them, her face growing pale.

Eventually, she rose from her chair while other agents began rifling through her desk drawers. She stepped over to her file cabinets and secured them. Carver and Renato then led her out of the office while trying to minimize the stares of her coworkers. The trio didn't stop moving until they had reached the parking lot and the agents' vehicle.

"All right, Ms. Kimbley," Carver said when they had the woman secured in the backseat of their car. "You made us play this game, so I hope you will cooperate with us now."

"I have nothing to say to you," Madison said. "You can speak to my attorney. Should I call him now or when we get to your office?"

"Oh, that's fine," Carver said as he put the car in drive. "Renato and I have plenty of things to chat about when we get you to the interview room, so you can wait a few hours to call your attorney."

"You can't do that!" Madison said. "I demand to have my attorney present!"

"We aren't arresting you," Renato said. "And, we aren't questioning you. We're holding you while we execute our search warrants."

"Warrants?" Madison said in obvious distress. "There are more?"

"Shouldn't there be?" Carver asked, looking at the woman in his rearview mirror. "We have agents at your office and your home as well as your mother's home and the storage unit you thought no one knew about."

"We've got plenty of time to chat with you," Renato said, leaning back in his seat and closing his eyes.

As Madison started to argue with them again, Carver chuckled and pulled the divider glass between them closed, shutting off the sound of her voice.

"That's effective." Renato laughed and kept his eyes closed.

The car remained silent on the rest of the trip back to the office. Inside, Carver led the frantic Madison into an interview room before joining Renato back outside so they could let her stew a bit.

"What do you think?" Renato asked. "Is she going to give us anything?"

"She doesn't seem like she's the one in charge of all this if you ask me," Carver said, thinking out loud.

Before the agents could muse over the situation anymore, Carver's phone rang. He glanced down and groaned when he realized it was Marie.

"What do you want now?" he asked when he accepted the call. "We're in the middle of something here."

Shaking his head, Carver looked at his partner in exasperation as he listened to Marie on the other end of the line.

"Listen, just like you can't ever tell us anything," he said, "we can't tell you anything."

Marie started talking again, and Carver groaned and pulled the phone away from his ear.

Renato grinned at him. "You have to admire her determination."

"Yeah, whatever," Carver said as he put the phone back to his ear and interrupted Marie again. "Again...we aren't telling you anything. I'm hanging up now. But first, I want to make sure you know we need you and Bryant and your team of misfits to back off. You're kids. Go on a date or something. Quit getting involved in this. Let us do our jobs!"

Marie was still protesting as he ended the call.

"Those kids will give me gray hair!" Carver shook his head.

"What are you talking about?" Renato joked. "You barely have any hair left as it is!"

"Ha ha...very funny," Carver said, glaring at him. "Let's go see what Ms. Kimbley has to say about things, shall we?"

Addressing Madison as they entered the room, he said, "Ms. Kimbley! I didn't realize you were still waiting for that lawyer of yours to show up. Did you get hold of him yet?"

Madison did nothing but glare back at him.

"The way I see it, me and my partner here will just have a nice conversation and keep you company while we wait on your lawyer to arrive. How about that?"

When she didn't respond, Carver turned to Renato and started laying out some photos on the table in between them and Madison.

"What do you think, Kamera?" he mused. "Do you think both these folks offed themselves in a matter of hours?"

"Hmm, I don't know," Renato said, feigning confusion. "I guess it could have happened that way."

"Or, could it be the people our witnesses placed in that abandoned building had something to do with this one's death?"

The agents both noticed when Madison became a little more interested in what they were saying. However, she still did not respond to their comments.

"Well," Carver said. "I guess we will just have to talk to the other guy and see what he has to say about the whole deal. Didn't you pick him up already?"

"Yep," Renato said. "Tony and Mitch are bringing him in right now. They say he's already singing a loud tune."

Madison started laughing at this point. "I see what you are doing, you know."

"What would that be?" Carver asked her.

"You're trying to trick me into telling you something," she scoffed. "It won't work. I have nothing to tell you, so you might as well go bug someone else."

"Is that so?"

"Yes, that is so," Madison said. "Now, if you don't get out of here and get my lawyer, I will sue."

"Well, you don't have to be so snotty about it," Carver said before scooping up the images and stuffing them back into his folder.

Renato followed him from the room but turned back to Madison before leaving and said, "Now, if there's anything we can do to make your stay more comfortable, please don't call us. I'm sure your attorney will be along any hour now."

Madison flipped him off, causing Renato to chuckle before letting the door slam behind him.

"Hopefully, that will at least get her thinking about her life choices," Carver said to his partner.

"Yeah, but we won't be able to hold her for long," Renato said. "Just long enough for her to get worried."

"I will go see what forensics has for us. Should have something on my desk by now about both the deaths we're dealing with," Carver said, already heading to his office.

"I will go get some coffee," Renato said with a yawn. "I'll catch up with you soon."

Carver nodded and began rifling through the first of the two large files forensics had left for him. Most of the pages were glossy images of Audrick's dead body. Carver began laying them out on the desk in front of him, examining the various angles, trying to find anything amiss. But everything appeared just as suicide should.

"You find anything?" Renato asked as he came back with his cup of coffee.

"Nope," Carver said. "No sign of trauma, other than the gunshot to his head. Nothing seems amiss at all."

"Do we know why he was at that house?"

"Yep," Carver said. "He'd just purchased it to flip. He was working on it with his girlfriend, but we all know how that wound up."

"What about the girlfriend? Any word on her cause of death, yet?"

"Yep," Carver said after picking up the second file and peeling back the cover. "M.E. says she died of strangulation. My guess is Audrick murdered her and then threw her off that balcony to cover it up."

"With Audrick dead too, this could wind up being classified as a murder-suicide thing."

"They have a big argument, he gets mad and strangles her, tries to cover it up but can't take it, so bam..." Carver shook his head.

"Throws a big wrench in our evidence."

Carver went back to examining crime scene photos and documents, his anger seeping through into his work. Renato began flipping through the papers in frustration, too, while his partner began pacing around the office letting his thoughts consume him. When a huge grin spread across Renato's face, Carver stopped walking and looked at him.

"What?" Carver asked. "You found something, didn't you?"

Renato cleared his throat.

"According to Audrick's medical history, he was suffering from myositis. Apparently, it was a bad case."

"You're going to have to elaborate on that because I don't know what that means."

"It's muscle weakness," Renato said, still grinning. "Specifically, muscle weakness in the fingers."

"No, shit?" Carver said.

"Yep," Renato said. "He couldn't have pulled a trigger even if he wanted to."

"Thank God, we got a break," Carver said.

"Now, let's go see if we can break Madison."

The agents made their way back to the interview room, where Madison was busy discussing the situation with her attorney. Both looked up when they walked in, and the conversation ended.

"I see you found that attorney of yours, Ms. Kimbley." Renato grinned at her.

"Yes, and my client will leave now," the curt response came. "You have no reason to hold her."

"Actually, we do," Carver said, noting the look of surprise on Madison's face. "We believe a murder we are investigating involves your client."

"Well, two of them, actually," Renato added.

"That's preposterous!" Madison fumed. "TWO murders? What murder are you talking about?"

"Murders," Carver corrected her. "Well, for starters that fella we found your business card on."

"And, that girl at your office too," Renato added.

"I th...thought," Madison stammered. "I thought she committed suicide."

"M.E.'s report says otherwise," Carver said, leaning back and crossing his arms. "And we have photographic evidence you were at the scene of Audrick's murder just a few hours before we found him dead."

Carver watched the color drain from her face and waited as the wheels turned in her head.

After a few moments of thinking through her options, Madison sighed and whispered, "What do you want to know?"

"Well, for starters," Carver said, talking over her attorney as he attempted to stop her. "What the hell is going on?"

"If you think I'm just going to give you everything you want to know without getting something in return, you're mistaken."

"You've got to give me something before we even consider a plea deal," Carver said, crossing his arms and leaning back in his chair.

"We have you on two murders, witness tampering, and a whole slew of other charges," Renato continued. "Plus, we haven't even seen what evidence they've found at your house and other properties."

Madison put her head in her hands, pressing her palms against her temples.

"They will hurt my kids," she said. "I don't know what to do."

"Who will hurt your kids?"

"Haskell's people," she said, tears coming to her eyes. "They said if I didn't help them out, they would hurt my kids."

"What did they have you do?"

"I'm in charge of organizing the blackmail operation," she said. "Lindsay was the one who did all the work, and I organized the blackmail."

"What do you mean, Lindsay, did all the work?"

"You know," Madison said. "...In the bedroom."

"She was sleeping with men, and you were blackmailing them? Who?"

"All sorts of people that could get the verdict changed."

"So, let me make sure I'm following the narrative," Carver said after thinking things over for a second. "Lindsay was sleeping with lawyers, judges, and whoever the hell you told her to. Someone in your clan took pictures. Then you blackmailed the men she slept with?"

Madison nodded and said, "We didn't have a choice. I was to help Haskell get off, or they would kill my kids."

Carver and Renato shared a look of concern, and Renato stepped out of the room.

"Where's he going?" Madison asked.

"We will pick up your kids and put them in protective custody,"

"What about me? What will happen to me?"

Carver looked back into her tear-filled eyes, trying to find the right words to say that wouldn't lock up any more of the information she had inside her.

"We'll talk to the D.A. and see what kind of deal we can get for you," he said. "But this situation is bigger than yourself, and there are more people in danger than just your kids. We need your help to make sure everyone stays safe."

Madison sighed, looked at her attorney, and said, "You need to go."

Chapter 26

Tuesday 9 AM – Bryant and Marie

"WHAT DID HE SAY?" BRYANT whispered as Marie hung up her phone.

"He said we're kids," Marie said with an incredulous look on her face, "and that we should go on a date."

"Carver wants us to date each other?" Bryant asked, confused.

"I don't think he cares," Marie said. "He just wants us to leave him alone."

"Well, we aren't giving him all the information we have either," Bryant mused.

Bryant thought back to the photographs of Lindsay and the extra information Anna and Joe had gathered they'd left out when discussing the case with the agents. Still not able to grasp the entire situation in his own mind, he wasn't sure how to even begin to derive an explanation.

"How about we work separately for a bit," he suggested when he couldn't come up with the next logical step. "I have some other cases I need to deal with. Do you have time to look through those photos a little closer and see if we can find a connection between our case and those men?"

"I have some free time before Callen's memorial," Marie said with a nod. "But I don't feel comfortable doing it here. I'll take it all home with me. Anna would help me with it, but she has a few more finals this afternoon."

"I'll cover for you," Bryant said. "And I will get Joe to work on tying Audrick a little tighter to our case. I'm not sure what he will find more than he already has, but I don't know where else to start."

Bryant tossed the information they'd gathered around in his brain for a moment, which only made him more distressed than he already was.

"What are we going to do, Bryant?" Marie asked drawing him from his thoughts.

"You know what?" Bryant said, a strange smile growing on his face. "I think we do what Agent Hoage suggested."

"You mean go on a date?" Marie asked. "Have you lost your mind? We can't go on a date now!"

"Why not?" Bryant shrugged. "This isn't the only case we will ever work on that will go a little south."

"Well, it won't be for you, at least," Marie said. "I will be in jail!"

"No, you won't." Bryant waved her off. "My point is, we've grown too close to it all. There's something we're missing."

"And going on a date will help us figure out what that is?"

"It'll let us step back for a minute and clear our minds," he said. "I bet we think clearer once we take a break for the evening."

"I suppose."

"Good!" Bryant said. "Now, I'm assuming you don't have any plans tonight? Maybe we could catch a movie?"

"Umm...you aren't suggesting that we...as in you and me...go on a date? I don't think Eddie would approve."

Now it was Bryant's turn to look annoyed.

"Don't be ridiculous," he said. "I was planning to ask Allie. But I figured it would be much better if it were a group thing instead of a one on one thing. At least at first."

"I see," Marie said, laughing a little to herself. "She made an impression on you."

"Do you think Anna and Alex would want to come too?" he asked before rolling his eyes. "I already know Joe is in. He can always find a date last minute."

"Any excuse to snuggle up with Alex is Anna's idea of a good time," Marie said. "But I'll ask her when I talk to her at lunch."

"Great!" Bryant said and rubbed his hands together excitedly. "Now to go seal the deal with Allie!"

Marie shook her head, and Bryant let Marie's door close behind him, already turning his attention to Allie. She smiled at him when he approached her desk, causing him to lose his resolve a bit.

"Um, hey Allie," he hesitated.

"Hello, again," she said, raising her eyebrows at him and grinning a bit.

"Listen," he said, running a hand through his hair. "I have a few documents I need to have filed at the courthouse. They are all ready to go but do you mind filing them for me, so they are ready for in the morning?"

"Sure, Bryant," she said. "I don't mind at all."

"Thanks!" he said before standing awkwardly in front of her desk.

Allie waited for a moment before somewhat whispering, "Was that all you needed, Bryant?"

Coming out of his daze, Bryant stammered, "Oh, I'm sorry! No, I was wondering...I mean a group of us are going to see a movie later, and I thought maybe you would want to come with me...er us."

"Are you asking me on a date?" Allie asked, an amused smile forming on her face.

"Um, well," Bryant hesitated. "It's a group of couples, so...Marie is coming!"

Allie laughed. "Yes, I will go to the movies with you and your group."

"Great!" Bryant said, relieved he didn't have to continue the conversation. "We could grab a bite to eat after work and meet up with everyone else at the movie theater. Most of the office will be gone this afternoon for Callen's memorial, but I could swing by afterward and pick you up?"

"Sounds good to me," Allie said, her lips still smiling.

"Cool," Bryant said, trying to sound casual. "I'll see you after work."

"Um, Bryant?" Allie asked. "Did you have papers you needed me to file?"

"Oh, right. Hang on just a second," Bryant said before speeding off to his office and coming back with a small stack of papers. "Here you go!"

"I'll get them filed this afternoon and get you a copy in the morning," Allie said, already paging through the papers.

Not knowing what else to say, Bryant walked back to Marie's office and sat down in the chair in front of her desk with an anguished look on his face. Marie looked at him, amused.

"Everything go ok?" she asked.

"Sometimes I would kill to be my brother," he said, loosening his tie a bit. "He doesn't have one problem with women. All I did was ask Allie to go to a movie with a group of friends, and now she probably thinks I'm a lunatic."

"Well, did she agree to go, at least?" Marie asked.

"Yeah," Bryant said. "But I'm surprised she did, considering I acted like an idiot."

"I'm sure you were a charming idiot." Marie laughed.

"You aren't helping!"

Chapter 27

Tuesday 11 AM - Marie

MARIE LET THE SILENCE soothe her when she walked into her apartment. She was tempted to turn out the lights, pour herself a glass of wine, and tumble into bed, but pushed away the procrastination and pulled out the file of photographs she'd found in Callen's desk instead.

Sighing, she flipped through each picture, making notes of the men she recognized and making a pile of those she didn't. Soon the picture of the situation started to become a little clearer. After a few quick internet searches, she found most of the men were judges, lawyers and other officials who had been a part of cases involving Haskell.

"Looks like Anna and Joe aren't the only ones who can figure stuff out," she said before calling Bryant to fill him in on what she'd learned.

While the newfound information excited both Marie and Bryant, the added stress of making the situation even more complicated was challenging to handle. Plus, Joe's research wound up further muddying the water.

"Joe didn't like the information he discovered," Bryant said after they'd discussed Marie's findings. "With keeping the blackmail information in mind, he did a little more digging and found a whole slew of transactions. It appears Audrick was Haskell's money man and moved around money so often there's no way we can sort everything out."

"I knew you would say that," Marie sighed. "Nothing is simple, is it?"

"Nope. Now we have witness tampering, blackmail, money laundering, and who knows what else tied up in this case."

"We've got to get some of these wrinkles ironed out instead of just getting more of them in our case file!" Marie complained.

"Let's revisit everything tomorrow," Bryant said, sounding defeated. "Hopefully this date night will be just the refresh we need to see things clearer than before."

"I sure hope so," Marie said. "I'm finishing up here and heading out to Callen's memorial."

"Yeah, most of the office is also packing it up. Afterward, I must pick up my new car at the dealership and then Allie and I are planning to have dinner, so I'll meet you guys at the movie theater."

"I just hope you can keep this one intact," Marie said with a tired laugh.

"I FIRST WANT TO THANK you all for coming," a small woman said into a microphone. "My Callen would have loved this turnout."

Marie looked down at her lap as the woman collected her thoughts. She felt tears welling up inside her when she saw Callen's face on the memorial paper in her hand. She looked back up when the woman continued.

"Callen was always a good son," she said. "He worked hard and made sure we were all taken care of. His family loved him. One of my favorite memories of him was the time when he was about ten years old..."

Marie glanced over at Bryant as Callen's mother continued reminiscing about Callen. He looked back at her with a sad expression on his face. Marie looked around at their other coworkers in the room. Callen's mother was right. There was a good turnout for his memorial. Most everyone held tissues and would dab tears from their eyes as the service progressed.

Eventually, someone said a prayer, Callen's family left the room, and the others were left to their own devices. Many headed to the parking lot, but a few stayed around for refreshments and to reminisce. Marie met up with Bryant in the reception hall and looked around at the others still milling around.

"It's crazy to think this is it for Callen," Marie said in a hushed tone. "After today, life will go on, and we probably won't talk about him in the office again."

"Death is a strange thing," Bryant said. "I sure hope his mother will be all right after this. You shouldn't have to lose your children."

"I know," Marie said. "I'm going to go pay my respects to her and then head out to get ready for this evening."

"I'm right behind you," Bryant said. "I still need to go pick up my new car before the dealership closes and swing by to pick up Allie for dinner."

"Can you keep your cool with her when you pick her up and not sound like an idiot this time?" Marie said, shooting him a quick grin.

He glared back at her. "Shut up!"

Chapter 28

Tuesday 6 PM

FOR THE THIRD TIME since they arrived at the movies, Anna glared at Joe as he sat three rows in front of her and Alex with the barista from the coffee shop. She couldn't believe he had the nerve to bring her after Anna had so successfully put her in her place. The smug look on that girl's face when she showed up on Joe's arm was almost enough to make smoke come out of Anna's ears.

Out of spite, Anna pulled a piece of popcorn from the bucket Alex was holding and threw it at the back of Joe's head. She grinned in success when it bounced off the top of his head, causing him to turn around and look at her.

"You need to chill out," Alex whispered.

Joe shook his head at her, before turning around and giving his attention back to his date.

"I need to chill out?" Anna hissed. "He brought that stupid girl with him. Remember her? She wouldn't care if she was on a date with you or him right now."

"Well, you don't have to worry about her from my perspective," Alex laughed.

"I want to punch her in the nose," Anna said, ignoring what he said.

Alex sighed and put his arm around her before pulling her body closer to him.

"Maybe you will get your chance at some point," he said, letting his fingers run through her hair. "How about you ignore this stupid movie and focus on me instead?"

Anna gazed up into his eyes for a second before smiling at him and giving him a quick kiss on his lips.

"That's all you get," she whispered. "I like this movie."

"Yeah, right," he said before putting both his hands in her hair and pulling her face closer and capturing her lips with his.

Anna gave him a few more soft kisses before smiling at him and moving the armrest out of her way so she could snuggle down in his arms more. Leaning her body across his, she rested her head on the shoulder opposite of her, relishing the feel of his strength as he supported her weight with his arms.

She sighed and looked up at him, her soft cheek grazing his. She kissed his chin, ignoring the prickly hairs from the beard already starting to grow back from this morning's shave that tickled her lips. Alex looked down at her and moved a strand of hair out of her eyes with his fingers.

"Don't you fall asleep this time," he teased.

"I do NOT fall asleep in movies," Anna said.

"We'll see."

He smiled at her and went back to watching the movie. It wasn't long before Anna's body started to relax in his arms, and her breathing became even and soft. He looked down at her and shook his head amused. He guided her sleeping head down until she was using his forearm as a pillow.

Just as Alex's arm was falling asleep, a loud noise from the movie caused Anna to jerk awake with a squeal, toppling the popcorn bucket and causing the entire group to look at her in confusion.

"I told you, you would fall asleep," Alex said with a grin on his face.

"Oh, shut up," Anna said, before breaking into a smile of her own and kissing him on the lips. Noticing Joe was looking back at her with a grin on his face, she glared at him and threw another piece of popcorn his way before turning her attention back to the movie.

Before long, Anna noticed movement out of the corner of her eye as Bryant bolted from his seat and headed out into the lobby. Joe watched his brother leave, obvious concern on his face. Just as he was about to follow him, Bryant stuck his head back in the theater and motioned to his brother.

"What's going on?" Anna asked, leaning across Alex to whisper to her sister.

"I don't know," Marie whispered back. "It looked like he got a call or something."

"Should we go check on them?" Anna asked.

"Well, you two aren't watching the movie, so let's go," Eddie piped in from beside his fiancé.

Bryant and Joe were talking to each other when they reached the lobby.

"What's going on?" Anna asked.

"Dad had a bad reaction to the chemo this week," Joe said. "Mom had to rush him to the hospital."

"What are we going to do?" Bryant asked. "I've got to get Allie home, and you've got that girl with you."

Anna looked at Alex.

"Yeah, yeah," he said. "I know."

"Alex can take them home," Anna said.

"Thank you so much," Bryant said to Alex before turning his attention to Allie. "I'm sorry about this."

"Not a problem," she said. "Hurry and get over there to your dad. I'm sure your mom is worried sick!"

"Which hospital are they at?" Anna asked before Bryant and Joe could walk away.

"She took him to Community Hospital," Joe said. "Over on 28th."

"Let us know if you need anything."

Before they could speak any more, Joe and Bryant were speeding out of the movie theater.

"I guess the movie's ruined now, huh," Eddie said to Marie. "Come on. I'll take you home."

After bidding adieu to her sister, Anna turned to Joe's confused date for the first time and glared at her.

"All right...What's your name again?"

"Karen," she said with a glare.

"Karen," Anna said, rolling the word around in her mouth as though it left a bad taste. "MY boyfriend will take you home now. Don't get any smart ideas. In fact, why don't you ride in the back."

"Anna," Alex warned.

She looked up at him with a sheepish look in her eyes.

"I'm going to the hospital," she said. "Their mom is super nice, and I'm sure she could use some stuff. Snacks, drinks, stuff like that."

"How did I know you would say that?" he sighed before kissing her.

Behind her, Allie cleared her throat and asked, "Would you mind if I came with you?"

"Extra company is always a good thing," Anna said, turning to her with a smile. "Let's go!"

Anna and Allie made their way to Anna's car in the parking lot. Anna paused for a second to glare one more time at Karen as she got in Alex's car. Grumbling to herself, Anna watched them drive out of the parking lot before putting her own vehicle in drive and proceeding to the nearest store.

They filled their basket with snacks and drinks, and Allie grabbed a few toiletries for Bryant and Joe's mom before they made their way to the checkout. By the time Anna and Allie got everything paid for, organized and made it to the hospital with the supplies, it was well past 8.

"I just realized I don't know their dad's name," Anna said.

"Me either," Allie said, laughing a bit. "I guess we didn't think this through, did we?"

"Well," Anna said. "I guess we'll just have to wing it."

They grabbed their bags and headed inside, looking around for someone to guide them on their journey. But because of the late hour, the information desk sat empty.

"Hmm," Anna said. "I guess we'll just have to find them ourselves."

They rode the elevator up one floor at a time looking for Bryant and Joe. It wasn't until they had reached the sixth floor that they found them. Bryant spotted them first and kicked his brother's foot, nodding in their direction. Joe turned the direction his brother was staring just in time to watch Anna stride through the hospital waiting area toward them with Allie on her heels. She held up the bags and smiled at him when he noticed her.

"What in the world are you two doing here?" Joe asked, taking the bags from Anna's hands.

"Well, we thought you could use some snacks," Anna said. "And Allie thought your mom might need a few things."

"We didn't know how long you would be here," Allie said hesitating.

"Thank you," Bryant said with a tone of sincerity.

"You gonna make her hold that bag all night?" Joe whispered, causing Bryant to turn to glare at him.

"Sorry, Allie," he said, taking the bag from her hands.

"No problem," she said with a sweet smile.

Anna looked at Joe with a smile as he spotted a bag of the chips he had introduced to her and pulled them out with a grin.

"Those would be mine," he said. Laying them out of his brother's reach, he took Anna's arm and pulled her further away from his brother so Bryant and Allie could have a private chat.

"I take it this was all your idea?" he asked.

"Well, yeah," she said. "But Allie volunteered to come along on her own. I didn't ask her to."

"Mom will love this," Joe said.

"Mom will love what?" a voice asked behind them.

Anna and Joe turned to see his mom standing behind them with a look of utter joy on her face.

"Anna brought snacks," Joe said, pointing at the bags.

"And Allie," Anna said, making sure Beth was getting the whole picture.

"Who's Allie?" Beth asked.

"This is Allie," Bryant said, stepping up to introduce his mom. "She just started in our office and came to the movies with us."

"Oh," Beth said, a smile forming on her face. "It is so nice to meet you. I'm Beth!"

"It's nice to meet you, Mrs. Malone." Allie said with a smile. "I'm so sorry to hear your husband isn't feeling well."

"Please, call me Beth!" she said, taking Allie's hand in hers. "It's so nice to see some female faces around here for a change. It's a nice complement to all these boys I'm usually with!"

Anna laughed as Joe looked down at the ground and shook his head. Anna knew Allie wasn't missing the embarrassed look on Bryant's face. Joe shared a look with his brother as their mother abandoned Allie and turned to Anna instead.

"We've known you less than a week, and I'm already thinking about adopting you," she said.

"Mom!" Joe said. "Stop it!"

"Well, she is fantastic, isn't she?" Beth said, peering around Anna at her son.

"Mother!"

Anna looked down at the floor, laughing. Joe couldn't do anything but shake his head at her in embarrassment.

"We'd better let you guys get settled in," Anna said. "I'm sure you all need to go make rounds in the room."

"Yeah, we'll get out of your hair," Allie said, before turning to Bryant. "I'll get those papers filed for you and have them ready for you in the morning. If you need to sign anything, I can get them to you here."

They said their goodbyes and made their way to the elevator with the three Malone's watching their every move. As the elevator closed around them, Anna saw Beth turned to Joe and glare at him. Joe rolled his eyes, snatched his bag of chips, and popped one in his mouth.

Chapter 29

Wednesday 8 AM - Anna

TAPPING HER FOOT, ANNA let her eyes sweep across Marie's office. Each face she glanced at had the potential of being an enemy in hiding. Yawning and trying to look natural, she continued her inspection of Marie's co-workers, looking for evil intent, sighing when nothing appeared obvious.

When none of the faces she inspected turned her direction, Anna grumbled to herself and scooped up a magazine from the pile in the small waiting area and sat in a chair before flipping through the pages. In her distracted state, Anna didn't even notice Allie's approach.

"Are you getting married soon?" Allie asked, causing Anna to jump in surprise.

"What?" Anna looked up at her confused.

Grinning at her, Allie pointed to the magazine in Anna's hand and whispered, "That's a wedding magazine."

Glancing down at the magazine in shock, Anna threw it back on the table as though it were a snake, causing Allie to laugh. Feeling her cheeks warm, Anna stepped away from the pile of magazines, cleared her throat and changed the subject.

"You said you had some papers Bryant needs to sign?"

"Yep," Allie said. "Thank you for offering to take them to him. I just can't get out of the office today."

"Not a problem," Anna said. "I wanted to go check on them this morning anyway."

Allie handed her a packet and said, "Please tell Bryant I wish I could have brought these over myself."

"I'm sure he will understand," Anna said before winking at her. "Besides, I'm sure the two of you will see a lot more of each other."

This time it was Allie who was blushing.

"Oh, stop it!"

Anna grinned back at her and said, "I'll get these papers to him and back to you as soon as possible."

"Thanks, again," Allie said, smiling at her but still blushing at the same time.

Outside, the sun burned Anna's eyes, causing her to squint and pull her sunglasses back down on her nose. Being so early in the summer, it surprised Anna to see the temperatures already rising so much, but at least her time spent at the beach later this summer would feel good.

Sighing, Anna hopped in her car and cranked up the air conditioner before speeding away to the closest coffee shop. After picking up a few various options, she made her way back to the hospital and past a sleepy information desk attendant who didn't even question her presence in the hospital.

Anna found Joe and Bryant in the same waiting area where she'd left them the night before. Joe had his head propped up on his hand but opened his eyes when he heard her approach.

"You're back!" Joe said. "And you brought coffee!"

"Yes, and yes." Anna laughed. "Sorry, Bryant, I didn't know how you took your coffee, so I just got a few options."

Anna looked down at her collection of coffee cups and tugged one of them out of the carrier before handing the rest to Bryant and the single cup to Joe.

"Ah, even with the crazy barista, you remembered my order," Joe said after he took a sip.

Anna laughed, "It was the most memorable coffee shop experience I've ever had. Can't say I've ever threatened a barista before only for her to show up on a date with my friend the next night."

"Yeah, well," Joe said after taking another sip of his coffee. "What can I say? I don't let opportunities go to waste."

Anna shook her head at him and said, "You're unbelievable."

"But you do like me," Joe said with a grin.

"Not to rush you or anything," Bryant interjected, "but did you have some papers I need to sign? Allie texted to say you were bringing some over."

"Oh my gosh! I'm so sorry!" Anna said, pulling the packet out of her bag and handing it to him. "I forgot what I came here for."

Bryant got to work signing the papers Allie had prepared for him, and Anna plopped down next to Joe, who was still nursing his coffee.

"So, how did everything go last night?" she asked.

"Good," Joe said. "Dad seems to be getting better. They think he will go home tomorrow if not the next day."

"That's great!" Anna said.

Before Anna could reply, Beth strode back into the waiting room, looking tired, her face lighting up when she saw Anna.

"You're back!" she said.

"That's exactly what Joe said when she came in," Bryant joked, still signing the papers in front of him.

Ignoring him, Anna said, "I had to bring over some papers. Thought you all could use some coffee."

"Ah, coffee," Beth said and snatched one out of the holder sitting next to Bryant. She took a sip and closed her eyes before sitting down.

"Mom," Joe said, looking concerned. "Why don't you go home and get some rest?"

"Yeah," Bryant said, looking up from the papers in his hand. "Joe and I aren't going anywhere right now. We can stay with dad."

"I would love a shower," she said but looked toward her husband's room. "But I sure hate to leave your dad here."

"Mom," Joe said. "We're right here. He's not alone at all. In fact, how about I promise one of us will stay in his room at all times?"

"I guess that would work," she conceded.

"Yeah," Bryant said, beginning to stuff the papers back inside the packet. "Take a nice shower and lay down for a bit. Don't hurry back! We'll call if anything changes."

"Fine, fine," Beth said, rising to her feet. "Let me go tell your dad what I'm doing, and I'll let you boys take over."

Joe shook his head as his mom left the waiting room.

"She hates to leave him," he smiled.

Anna smiled. "That's sweet."

"Yeah, I guess. She's always taken care of him," he said. "I guess when you love someone, you make some sacrifices."

"That's how it should be, at least," Anna said, still smiling. "Everyone should have someone willing to sleep next to them in a crappy hospital chair."

Joe took another sip of his coffee to avoid having to say anything more on the subject and looked up when his mother walked back into the waiting room.

"All right," she said. "I'm all set. It thrilled your dad to hear you talked me into leaving for a bit."

"He's probably just excited he doesn't have to watch HGTV anymore for a while," Joe whispered to Anna, causing her to laugh.

"I heard that," Beth said, glaring at her son. "Bryant, make sure he behaves while he's here. Don't let him embarrass us or something."

"What did I do?" Joe asked. "I've just been sitting here minding my own business...not bothering anyone!"

"Mmmm hmmm," Beth said. "Please remember most of the nurses are MARRIED, and they are WORKING, so please leave them alone."

"I don't like what you are implying," Joe said, sounding annoyed, but still grinning at his mother.

"Mother," Bryant said. "Go home. Rest."

Handing the packet of papers to Anna, he said, "And, thank you, Anna, for bringing these and the coffee."

"You're welcome," Anna said, standing to leave. "If you guys need anything, my schedule is open at the moment since my classes are wrapping up."

"I'll walk you out," Beth said, taking her arm before glancing back at Joe again with a grin. He rolled his eyes at her.

Wednesday 11 AM – Anna and Marie

ANNA PUT HER CAR IN park outside Marie's office and gathered the papers for Allie. Not paying much attention to her surroundings, she hopped out of her car, hoping to make her stop inside the law firm a brief one.

But just as she reached the door to the building, she felt a presence approach from behind and stand a bit too close to her. Annoyed, she turned around, trying to get a look at the offending party only to find herself staring directly into the sun. Squinting, she glared at the man behind her even though she couldn't see his face well.

"You're Marie's sister, right?"

"Yeah," she said. "What do you want?"

"Can you give her something for me?"

"I guess," Anna said.

The man handed her an envelope and disappeared down the street. Anna stared after him for a moment, her eyes still hurting from the glare of the sun, before entering her sister's firm. Sighing, she rode the elevator up to the third floor and looked around for Allie, who was busy sorting through a pile of papers on her desk.

Smiling, Anna approached and said, "Here you go! Bryant said to tell you hi."

"Oh, great!" Allie said, smiling up at her with an over-whelmed look on her face. "One thing off my to-do list. How was everything at the hospital?"

"Looks like they will get to go home soon, so everything looks good!"

"That's a relief," Allie said.

"Hey, have you seen Marie? Some guy outside wanted me to give her this."

"I think she stepped into the breakroom," Allie said. "I'm sure it's fine if you go back there. Do you know the way?"

"Thanks!" Anna said. "Yeah, I've been back there be-fore."

Anna strode into the breakroom and found Marie stir-ring sugar into a cup of coffee.

"It's a little late in the day for that much caffeine, isn't it?" Anna asked with a laugh.

Marie jumped in surprise at the sound of her sister's voice.

"What?" she stammered before looking down at the cup in her hand.

"You don't normally drink coffee this late in the morn-ing," Anna mused.

"Oh, yeah, I guess it is. I got a little distracted."

"I can see that," Anna said. "Hey, I just dropped off some papers for Allie, and some guy in the parking lot wanted me to give you this."

Marie looked at the envelope in confusion.

"What did he look like?"

"Didn't get a good look at him," Anna said. "He just asked if I was your sister and asked me to give it to you."

Marie opened the envelope and pulled out a single sheet of paper. Anna watched her sister's face pale, any semblance of a smile fading away. She walked over to read the letter for herself. She gazed at the big block letters, not sure what to think about what they said.

Keep up this investigation, and you're next, Marie.

Let it go. Everything needs to play out how we have it planned.

Otherwise, the next letter won't be so friendly.

"What does this mean?" Anna asked.

"I don't know," Marie whispered. "But we need to call Agents Hoage and Kamera."

Anna and Marie were still sitting in the breakroom when the agents arrived. Having instructed Marie to not let others touch the envelope or the letter, there was little they could do while they waited. Anna spent the time watching her sister's face and noting the worry she found there. She couldn't help but be a little worried about the predicament herself.

When the agents strode into the breakroom, both Anna and Marie looked up at them, relieved. Saying little, Carver put the envelope and the letter in an evidence bag and looked at the sisters.

"We need to separate you," he said.

"Why?" they asked in unison.

"We did nothing wrong," Anna said.

Renato spoke a little softer than his partner.

"We need to question you both," he said. "And we don't want either of your stories influencing the others."

"I guess that makes sense," Anna said.

"Can you talk to Anna here, and I can go to my office?"

Nodding, Carver followed Marie back to her office, leaving Anna behind with his partner.

"So, what happened?" Renato asked when they had disappeared.

"Nothing," Anna said. "I was coming into the office, and a guy asked if I was Marie's sister."

"So, he had been watching you long enough to know who you were?"

"That seems to be accurate," Anna said. "But he could have just looked us up on social media."

"And that's all he said?" Renato continued. "He asked you to give a letter to your sister?"

"Yep."

"Nothing else?"

"Nope. It was a quick thing. Took less than a minute."

Carver came to the same conclusion as his partner and was soon leading Marie back into the kitchen. They didn't have enough information to help them out with the threat against them. Anna felt relieved to be back in the same room as her sister but sighed when she realized the agents weren't finished with them yet.

"Did you notice anyone missing from the office today?" Carver asked Marie after she'd sat back down next to Anna.

"The only person I know wasn't here was Bryant," Marie said, before glaring at Carver "Bryant had nothing to do with this letter. He's at the hospital with his dad. Anna just left him there!"

"Very convenient, don't you think?"

"No, I don't think," Marie said. "You need to drop that line of thought and focus on finding whoever is really involved!"

"Just testing the waters," Carver said.

"I still think we need to take all of you away until we figure this mess out," Renato said.

"Absolutely not," Marie said. "I've worked too hard to get my career where it is right now and too hard on this case to run away from it. I'm seeing this out."

"Even if it kills you?"

Anna frowned at the comment and looked at her sister.

"Look, Bryant and I are the only people standing between our client and someone who's trying to sabotage his chances of getting his deal and testifying against an evil man," Marie said. "If I don't stand by that, why did I even take the oath to be an attorney?"

"I just want to make sure you know you are in danger, here," Carver said.

"I think having my sister receive a threatening letter on my behalf says enough." Marie glanced at Anna as the words left her mouth.

"Any chance I could get you and Joe somewhere safe for a bit?" Carver turned his attention to Anna.

"Yeah, right," Marie said with a huff before Anna could even reply. "What do you think we tried to do when this mess got started in the first place?"

"We aren't going anywhere," Anna said, speaking for both Joe and herself.

"Well, I guess all I can say is I hope the next time I see one of the four of you it isn't on a morgue table."

"Yeah, me too," Marie said and gave her sister another worried look.

Chapter 30

Wednesday 1 PM – Anna

ANNA TOOK A SIP OF her drink and watched Alex spear a carrot on the end of his fork before popping it into his mouth. She waited for him to finish chewing so he could continue their argument.

"Anna, no," he said. "This is done. I'm NOT letting you do this anymore!"

"Alex," Anna said. "You do remember what I'm studying, right? And who suggested I go into that field?"

"Of course, I remember," he said. "But your focus is on forensic technology, NOT crime scene investigations. This is way more than what they train you to do."

"You're being ridiculous," Anna said, her cheeks growing pink with anger. "I'm not abandoning my sister. Someone threatened her life!"

"Yes," Alex said. "And used you as the proxy to threaten her. So, who were they really threatening, you or her?"

Anna sighed, not able to argue his point.

"I don't know," she conceded.

"Exactly!" Alex said and threw his hands in the air. "Who knows? Maybe the next time the guy pays you a visit, he won't be so nice."

"Alex, I promise to take better precautions," Anna said, reaching out for his hand across the table, which he jerked away from her. "I just can't...not help Marie."

Alex stopped and gazed at her. She felt his countenance softening and reached across the table for his hand again. This time he let her take it.

"I know you want to help your sister, but does that mean I have to accept the danger you are being put in?"

A small smile formed on Anna's face as she took another bite of her lunch. Their eyes met across the table and any anger between them disappeared.

"You know," Anna said, her voice taking a joking tone. "Being your girlfriend isn't a walk in the park."

"How's that?"

"You're in danger every day," Anna said. "So, that means I have to worry about you all the time."

"Hmmm. So, I guess me worrying about you for a change makes things even?"

"I guess so."

Alex reached across the table and took her hand in his, rubbing the top of it with his thumb.

"Please, be careful," he said, looking deep in her eyes.

"I promise I will."

Alex pushed his plate away and watched Anna eat for a moment. "Hey! How's Bryant and Joe's dad doing?"

Anna took another sip of her drink and said, "He's on the mend. They are sending him home tomorrow."

"That's great," Alex said with a smile before scooping up his own drink and putting the straw in his mouth. After taking a long drink, he asked, "Have you made it back up to the hospital again?"

Anna gave him a look, "What are you asking me, Alex?"

"Nothing. We're just having a conversation."

Anna narrowed her eyes at him. "Allie needed me to bring Bryant some papers this morning. That's why I was at Marie's office today."

"Hmm.

"Hmm, what?"

"Nothing Just replying."

"You know this jealous thing was cute at first, but it's getting on my nerves."

Alex gazed back at her for a few seconds watching her poke at her food with her fork, her brow furrowed. "I'm sorry. I can't really tell you what my problem is."

"Have I ever given you a reason..." Anna started, but Alex interrupted her.

"No," Alex said, looking in her eyes. "I trust you 100%. It's just...something I'm going through, I guess. I'm not used to having to share you."

"You don't have to share me, silly," Anna said. "I'm yours. 100%."

Alex smiled back at her before replying.

"How about I make a deal with you?"

"Anything," she said but raised her eyebrow at him in confusion.

"If he ever becomes a problem, I want you to tell me."

"You'll leave me alone about it?" she asked, an annoyed tone entering her voice. She sighed when he nodded in reply. "Fine. I can do that."

"Thank you," Alex said.

"Can we finish our lunch in peace now?" Anna asked before grinning at him. "And, yes, we're springing for dessert."

Wednesday 2 PM – Marie

SIGHING, MARIE'S TIRED fingers reached for another file. Closing her eyes, she laid the papers in front of her and rubbed her temples before shaking her head and attempting to make sense of something in her life. Lifting the first sheet closer to her eyes, attempting to inspect the data on the page, she grumbled when she felt something fall from the file and flit its way to the floor.

Still grumbling, Marie bent under her desk to retrieve the wayward scrap of paper, all the while considering laying down beside it for a nap. Sighing, she scooped it up and glared at the letters printed on it. She couldn't hide her surprise when she realized the small slip of paper held a familiar address, the same she'd found on the sticky note in the Haskell file.

"What in the world?" Marie asked herself, looking back at the contents of the file on her desk. "This file has nothing to do with the Haskell case."

She turned it over, trying to make sense of what she was seeing, knowing it couldn't be a coincidence she'd seen the same address on random scraps of paper twice in one day.

Marie frowned at the paper trying to gain clarity. Finding none, she turned to her computer and typed the address into her internet browser. Before the results could provide her with much information, there was a knock on the door to her office.

"Hey, Autumn," Marie said, looking up at her co-worker. "What's up?"

"You lost in thought, again!"

Marie shook her head and tried to put a smile on her face.

"Seems to be a new trend," she said. "It would be nice if something would make sense around here."

"I know what you mean," Autumn said with a shake of her head. "Hey, well, you have a visitor at the front desk."

"I do?"

"Yep, she said her name is Frankie. Something about you guys having lunch plans…"

"Oh my gosh!" Marie said, putting her things away and shutting down her computer. "I forgot!"

"Sounds like you need an assistant," Autumn laughed as she walked back to her own desk.

Marie rushed to the front desk where her friend was waiting for her.

"Frankie, I am so sorry!" she said, putting her arms around her. "I forgot about lunch."

"Well, we can do it another time," Frankie said. "No worries."

"No," Marie said, "Let's go."

Frankie followed Marie out of the office and to her car while Marie did her best to put her distracted mind to rest for a bit. They remained quiet on the trip to the restaurant, and it wasn't until after they'd ordered that Frankie struck up a conversation by giving her friend a strange look.

"What?" Marie asked with a laugh.

"You don't look so great," Frankie laughed.

"Well, thanks," Marie said. "Aren't you supposed to not tell people things like that?"

Ignoring her, Frankie continued, "I'm serious, Marie. You look super tired. Are you sleeping? When's the last time you've eaten anything?"

"Ugh," Marie said. "This case is killing me!"

"You want to talk about it?"

"I can't talk about it!" Marie complained. "Everything is confidential. Anna already knows way more than she should about it. I can't get you involved too."

"Well, I'm here if you need me," Frankie said. "You know that, right?"

"And, I'm so happy about that," Marie said before shaking her head. "No, not going to do it. This is our last work lunch together for an entire year. We're not ruining it like this. Tell me something to distract me."

"Well," Frankie said with a grin. "I have fifteen more boxes packed."

"That's great! But that doesn't cheer me up!"

"I know. Every box I pack makes me a little sadder. I wish I didn't have to go away for so long."

"It's a terrific opportunity for you. I'm so proud of you for landing that internship. It will get your career going!"

"Yeah, yeah. I know. But I have to be away from everyone I know for an entire year!"

"We'll all go visit you," Marie said. "Just make sure you don't meet someone down there and fall in love and wind up staying."

"I'll make sure that doesn't happen," Frankie laughed.

"Exactly! No dating."

After the food arrived, Frankie grew more serious.

"So, can you tell me anything about this case?" she asked. "Are you safe, at least?"

"Honestly, I have no idea," Marie said, looking even more tired. "Anna was basically threatened on my behalf today and those FBI agents from the other day are still on my case, so no, I don't feel safe at all."

"Why don't you let the FBI handle it?"

"Because that doesn't help my client," Marie said. "If I abandon him now, everything we've worked for will go to pot. And, the deal Bryant and I worked to set up will go out the window!"

"What are you going to do?"

"I will have to figure out how to get everything back in line again, I guess. I need to do it without involving Anna."

"You know Anna won't let you go it alone, right?"

"Yeah. I've already tried to get her to back off fifteen times. She won't do it. She's so darn stubborn!"

"Well, it runs in the family!" Frankie laughed.

"Hey!" Marie protested. "I'm not stubborn!"

Frankie shook her head at Marie, not sure how to help her friend deal with the situation. Before they could discuss the situation anymore, the waitress came back with drink refills, and both Frankie and Marie got back to work on their sandwiches. Marie hadn't realized just how hungry she was.

As she chewed her sandwich, she mused over the case. Starting at the beginning and traveling through the sequence of events leading her up to where she was at today, Marie circled the evidence in her mind looking for something she might have missed.

Meanwhile, Frankie ate her sandwich, giving Marie space to think. Marie was still lost in thought when the waitress came back to top off their drinks one last time, clear their plates, and drop off the check.

"I will miss this," Marie told Frankie.

"I know. Me too."

After lunch, Frankie drove Marie back to her office, but before they could go their separate ways, they gave each other a quick hug.

"Hey, Marie," Frankie said before pulling away again. "I just thought of something that could help with your case."

"Oh yeah," Marie said, squinting back at her while shielding her eyes from the sun with her hand. "What's that?"

"Me being the math nerd I am, I love patterns," she said. "There are always patterns to everything, even crimes. You hear about it all the time on TV. Criminals have patterns. So, you need to look for a pattern."

"Hmm, not sure I know what to look for, but I'll think about it," Marie said before saying goodbye and heading back inside to her office.

Marie thought about Frankie's pattern theory all afternoon, and it wasn't until she was about to close her office when she realized there was only one tiny pattern that had ever seemed to surface in all this.

Glancing back at her computer, she pulled up the address that had been floating around on scraps of paper. Nothing seemed remarkable about the property from what she saw online, but she knew she couldn't let it haunt her any longer.

Printing off directions to it, Marie looked down at her phone, wondering what she should tell Anna. Knowing her sister would become worried if she didn't show up at home soon, Marie fired off a lie to her via text before locking her files away and closing her office for the night. She exited the building determined to come back with at least some knowledge that would help her, even if it took her all night to find it.

Chapter 31

Wednesday 7 PM – Anna

ANNA SAT HER WINE GLASS down on the coffee table in front of her and picked up her phone. Reading the text from her sister, Anna sighed, knowing it meant she would sit at home alone again for the evening. Even Alex was out of pocket for the night, having signed up for an extra night shift so he could look good for his bosses. Anna glared at her phone as she reread Marie's text.

"Gonna have dinner with Eddie," it read. *"Don't wait up."*

"What am I supposed to do now?" Anna asked the empty living room. She looked around at the quiet space and groaned. "We should get a cat. I would at least have someone here to keep me company!"

Realizing she had no desire to spend her evening alone, Anna scooped up her purse and keys, threw shoes back on and headed out the door, knowing there was at least one other person out there who could use some company for the night.

When she reached the hospital, both Bryant and Joe looked up at her in surprise. She'd swung through a drive-thru on her way, and they could both smell the greasy burgers she held in a paper bag before she even entered the waiting room.

"You are an angel!" Bryant said. "We're starved, and the cafeteria closes an hour early on Wednesdays!"

"Well, you're in luck!" Anna said with a grin. "Because my Wednesdays are so boring, I thought delivering burgers to the hospital sounded dandy."

"And, you even brought extra stuff!" Joe said, already digging through the bag and finding enough food for his mother too. He pulled out a burger and a sack of fries and stuck one in his mouth.

Anna shrugged, "I didn't want to leave anyone out, so I got plenty."

Bryant jerked the bag out of his brother's hand and retrieved his own burger and set of fries.

"Thank you," he said, also getting to work on his own food. Anna watched them eat for a minute before speaking.

Grinning, she glanced at Joe and winked. "Are you and Allie going to get a makeup date, Bryant?"

Bryant shook his head, somewhat embarrassed, and said, "Yeah. I talked to her today. There will be a redo."

"Good! I liked her," Joe piped in and was promptly rewarded with a glare from his brother.

Anna laughed and let them eat for a few more minutes in silence.

"So, your dad gets to come home tomorrow?" she asked.

"Yep," Joe said between mouthfuls. "He's ready to go home now, but they let him stay tonight and rest. He'll get out of here first thing in the morning."

"That's great!" Anna said. "Bryant, when do you and Marie have to be back in court?"

"The judge gave us until Friday on this case," he said with a grimace.

"So, we have one day to wrap it up?" Joe murmured, raising his eyebrows in concern.

"And, we don't know anything at this point," Anna added.

"Pretty much," Bryant sighed. "If you guys have any ideas, I'm all ears."

Anna and Joe exchanged looks, knowing whatever idea they came up with wouldn't be super helpful. Anna just hoped there was something they could do to help the situation. She could tell Joe felt about as helpless as she did.

Looking back to his brother, Joe said, "I think we're back at trying to find connections between your co-workers and the Haskell guy."

"Yeah," Anna agreed. "I don't see a way around going through that process, either."

Bryant groaned, "That will take a bit, won't it?"

Anna and Joe looked at each other again.

"We pretty much have to do everything by hand," Joe said.

"There's not any way to make it go faster," Anna added. "We'll just have to look for a connection, whether it be family, financial or something else."

"And just hope you find something?"

"Yep."

"God, I hate asking you two to do that."

Anna leaned back and smiled, "I have a boyfriend who works all the time and an open schedule this summer, and I have a tendency to find less productive things to do when I get bored, so this is probably a good thing. Marie will be thrilled I'm not getting into trouble."

Bryant rolled his eyes and glared at his brother, who had returned to eating his burger.

"Trust me," Bryant said. "I can relate to that."

"What did I do?" Joe said, his mouth full of food.

"You gonna help or not?" Anna laughed.

"Oh, I'm going to help. But I'm doing it under duress," Joe said before mumbling under his breath, "You can relate, HA."

"I'm kidding...I'm kidding," Bryant said, holding his hands up.

Joe looked at him and grinned, "I'm kidding, too. But now you owe me a get out of jail free card for the next time you have to bail me out of trouble."

"You two are too much," Anna laughed. "Joe, you want to meet somewhere tomorrow morning, and we can work on this stuff?"

"How about I pick you up around 9, and we can go back to the library to work?"

"Sounds good," Anna said, pulling her phone out of her purse. "I'll text you my address."

"Thanks again for the burgers," Bryant called.

"Make sure your mom gets one," she said with a grin that caused them both to jump up at once as they realized they had forgotten all about their mother.

Thursday 7 AM – Anna

"MARIE?" ANNA CALLED into her quiet apartment. "You home?"

Not getting a response, Anna headed over to her sister's room and peered inside. Nothing seemed out of place, and she could tell Marie hadn't slept in the bed last night. Smiling to herself, she mused over the circumstances that had kept Marie out all night before grabbing her phone to send her a text.

"I see Eddie kept you company last night," she texted. *"Joe and I will meet up today to do some work. I hope you have a good day if you got enough sleep last night to make it into work that is."*

Anna grinned at her phone for a moment before hopping in the shower to get ready for the day. After finishing up, she glanced at her phone, surprised her sister hadn't texted her back yet.

"I guess you're still busy!" Anna said, laughing and shaking her head. "I will have nieces and nephews any day if you keep that up!"

Realizing she was running out of time, Anna sped up her getting ready process by blow-drying her hair and throwing on a casual outfit and rushing through her makeup process. Just as she was throwing a few remaining items in her bag, she heard her doorbell ring. When she opened the door, she found Joe leaning against the wall outside, holding a steaming cup of coffee.

"Ah," Anna said. "I see it was your turn to bring ME a treat. Thank you!"

Joe smiled and handed her the coffee before leading her toward his jeep.

"I had a thought last night," he said as they were getting in the vehicle. "What if we start as close to this thing as possible and work our way out?"

"That might work," Anna said. "We already know some of the people who might be involved, so how about we work that angle?"

"Exactly," Joe said, putting the jeep in reverse. "And, I also think we should focus on the rest of the criminal law team too. They would have the easiest access to Marie and Bryant and therefore stand the best opportunity for messing with their files and evidence and whatever."

While he drove, Anna looked through the paperwork they had gathered so far. Pulling out the list of names she and Joe had stolen from the HR firm, she scanned the list looking for anything that stood out.

"Other than Marie and Bryant, I think the only other lawyers on the criminal law team are Marvin and Autumn."

"And the partner guy," Joe said, glancing at the list when he stopped at a red light. "What's his name? Snyder or something."

"Yeah," Anna said, finding the man's name on the list. "Wallace Snyder. So, how about you work on looking for links between Wallace and that Madison woman the FBI picked up, and I'll try and see what these two are up to."

Inside the library, Joe and Anna gave each other a look as the same librarian glanced up at them and glared down her nose when they walked by. Joe and Anna walked past her desk and found a table in the corner where they might not make as much trouble this time and pulled out their laptops.

For a long time, neither made much noise as they searched the internet for answers. Every few moments, one or the other would write a note or two before getting back to work on the computer. It wasn't long before they could both feel annoyance and frustration building in the other.

"I think it's time for a break," Joe whispered. "Let's go outside where we can talk for a minute."

Anna sighed and followed him outside in frustration.

"I just can't find anything!" she complained when they had reached the side of the library. "How can there be nothing to find?"

"I feel like we're missing something," Joe said.

"I've checked their bank accounts, social media platforms, email accounts..." Her voice trailed off as a thought circled through her mind.

"What?" Joe asked.

"I'm an idiot," Anna said. "I've checked everything out, but I forgot one little thing."

"What's that?"

"Women get married!" Anna said, throwing her hands up. "I've been focusing so much attention on looking up information on them right now I didn't even consider the fact they might be using a different name!"

"So, you think there might be information under the women's maiden names?"

"It can't hurt to check!" Anna said, already heading back inside the library, making just slightly more noise than the librarian liked.

Joe watched as Anna pulled up the court records in their area and searched Madison and Autumn's name in the system. It didn't surprise her when she found a hit for both women.

"See," she whispered. "Madison's maiden name is Grayson. Autumn Fritzman used to be Autumn Renshaw."

"Wait," Joe said. "Did you say, Renshaw? That's Callen's last name!"

A satisfied smile formed on Anna's face, and she pointed at her screen before going back to typing. She gasped when her screen revealed a huge secret.

"They were first cousins."

"So, Autumn's first cousin works in the same legal office as her, which means they are close, but she doesn't even bat an eye when he's killed?"

"Can't be a coincidence," Anna said, already heading outside with her phone in her hand. "She has to be in on this. I'm going to call Marie."

Joe followed Anna out the doors of the library thinking through the new information while waiting for Anna to talk to Marie. But after a few moments, Anna hung up the line in frustration.

"Voicemail," she complained. "Where the crap is she?"

"She didn't tell you what she was up to today?"

"No," Anna said, shooting off a text to her sister. "She texted last night saying she was going over to Eddie's and I haven't seen her today. I figured she must have stayed over."

When Marie didn't text her back, Anna tried calling her again, but still got her voicemail.

"Ugh," she said. "I'm calling Eddie."

Anna pushed a few keys on her phone and felt relieved when Eddie picked up on the second ring.

"Eddie!" she said. "Where are you hiding, Marie?"

"I'm sorry?" he asked.

"Oh, come on, Eddie," Anna joked. "I know Marie stayed with you last night. Where's she at? She's not answering her phone, and I need to talk to her."

"Anna, I don't know what you're talking about," Eddie said. "I didn't see Marie last night."

Anna felt the smile drop from her face. She looked up into Joe's eyes, a look of concern blazing through them. Somehow being able to compose herself, Anna reassured her future brother-in-law.

"Oh, gosh, Eddie! I'm sure I was mistaken. I went out last night myself and fell asleep right when I got back. She must have slipped in the apartment when I was asleep and left before I got up."

"Should I be worried, Anna?" Eddie asked.

Glancing again at Joe, Anna tried to reassure Eddie again, "No, no...don't worry, Eddie. I'm sure she's in a meeting or something. I'll let you know when I hear from her."

She hung up the phone and sat still in shock for a few seconds.

"Anna?" Joe asked, breaking her thinking spell.

"He hasn't seen her, Joe," she said, her voice sounding dead and quiet. "He doesn't know what I'm talking about."

"If she texted you last night saying she was with Eddie," Joe said, whispering the thoughts that were already circling through Anna's head, "where the hell is she?"

Anna couldn't answer him over the lump forming in her throat.

Chapter 32

Thursday 8 AM – Bryant

BRYANT BREEZED INTO the office, smiling at Allie as he stopped by her desk. Seeing her smiling face made the situation of dealing with his dad along with the difficulty of the case he and Marie were working on a little easier.

"Good morning!" he said.

"Hey," Allie said with a smile before growing serious. "How's your dad?"

"He's doing a lot better. Thanks for asking," he said. "We got him and mom settled back at home early this morning. They are planning to rest today. He has a doctor's appointment tomorrow to go over his new chemo treatment plan."

"Well, I hope it works better than the last round!"

Bryant took a quick look around the office, frowning when he saw Marie's dark office.

"Hey, have you seen Marie this morning?" he asked.

Allie turned to also look at her office.

"Oh, Autumn said she wasn't coming in today," she said.

"Really?" Bryant asked. "Why?"

Allie shrugged. "She said something about Marie needing to work on her wedding with Eddie or something."

"What?" Bryant asked. "They aren't planning a wedding for an entire year. We just talked about it three days ago!"

"I don't know," Allie said. "That's what Autumn said."

Before Allie could say any more, Bryant was rushing away to find Autumn. He located her at her desk and began interrogating her.

"Marie called in?" he asked, skipping the pleasantries.

Autumn looked up from her desk with an annoyed look on her face.

"Well, good morning to you, too," she grumbled. "Yeah, she texted me this morning and said she wasn't coming in."

"Why?"

"I don't know, Bryant," she said. "She said something about picking out a venue for her wedding or something."

"That makes no sense," Bryant countered. "Did she say where she was going?"

Autumn seemed beyond annoyed at this point but sighed and picked up her phone.

"As a matter of fact," she said, looking down at her phone, "she texted to say she had forgotten to pick up the address of the place off her desk. She had me text it to her. Would you like it?"

"Yes, please," Bryant said, already leaving her office. "Text it to my phone."

"My pleasure," she said.

Bryant missed the subtle smile playing out on her lips.

Thursday 10 AM – Anna and Joe

JOE PICKED UP HIS OWN phone and said, "I'm calling Bryant. Maybe she's at the office and just not answering or something."

Anna sat back in her chair, a lost look on her face while waiting for Joe to connect with Bryant.

"Shit," he mumbled after a few seconds.

"What?"

"He's not answering, either," he said.

They stared at each other for a minute, not sure what their next step should be, both trying to keep their panic level from rising too much.

"I'm calling the office," Anna said, picking up her phone again. She sighed a breath of relief when Allie answered the phone.

"Allie?" she asked. "It's Anna, Marie's sister. I was wondering if you've seen her or Bryant this morning?"

"Good morning, Anna!" Allie said. "Bryant was in the office this morning, but I haven't seen Marie. It's funny, though. Bryant was confused when Marie wasn't here either. Especially after I told him Autumn said she called in sick. He rushed out of the office after talking to Autumn about it."

Anna closed her eyes, her heart racing with fear.

"Thanks, Allie," she said. "Could you get either of them to call me or Joe the second you see them again?"

After hanging up with Allie, Anna relayed the information to Joe, trying to ignore the apprehension she saw in his eyes that reflected her own. Autumn being involved was not a good sign.

"Come on," Joe said, his voice taking on a bit of a growl.

He marched back inside the library and scooped up his laptop and other belongings and stuffed them in his bag. Anna followed his lead and did the same with her own items.

After spending only seconds inside the library, she followed him back outside, rushing to keep up with him as he marched toward his jeep. "Where are we going?"

"We're going to the only other person we know we can trust," he said. "Alex."

Anna tried to focus on remaining calm as Joe drove them to the police station at a maddening pace, but her panic was brimming by the time they pulled into the parking lot. Without a word, Joe stormed inside, causing several heads to turn their way. A police officer approached them with a cautious look on his face.

"Can I help you..." he started before noticing Anna standing behind Joe. "Oh, hey, Anna."

His voice deadly quiet, Joe asked her, "Where is he?"

"That way," Anna pointed before rushing to catch back up with him again as he strode through the station and up to Alex's desk, who looked up at them in surprise as they approached.

"What's wrong?" he asked, concern passing through his eyes when Anna could no longer keep the tears from spilling down her cheeks.

"We can't find Marie," she whispered.

"Or Bryant," Joe added.

"Come into the conference room," Alex said, putting his arm around Anna and leading them to privacy.

Once inside, Anna sunk into a chair while Joe took to pacing around the room.

"All right, what's going on?" Alex asked, folding his arms across his chest.

"We found something on this Haskell case we're working on and tried to call them," Joe started.

"Woah, woah, woah," Alex said, holding his hands up and reaching over to shut the door to the conference room. "Are you saying this is about Jim Haskell?"

"We can't talk about this here," Alex hissed at them when Anna nodded. "There's a park a block to the east. Meet me there in 10 minutes."

Joe rolled his eyes but marched back out of the police station with Anna on his heels. They both remained silent as they waited for Alex to arrive. The anger Anna felt emanating from Joe was comforting and helped take her mind off the absolute terror building up inside of her.

She glanced at her watch but somehow kept herself from doing the math back to the time she had last spoken to her sister in person. Seeing Alex's car pull up beside Joe's jeep, she breathed a sigh of relief and hopped out to greet him.

"All right, we should be safe to talk here," Alex said when he, Joe, and Anna connected at the park. "Start over."

"So, Bryant and Marie are on the Haskell case," Joe said. "Someone in the office is trying to sabotage it, and we found a connection between one of their co-worker's and Haskell's organization. We assume that co-worker is behind the sabotage."

"What makes you think Bryant and Marie are in trouble?"

"Because Marie texted me last night to tell me she was with Eddie," Anna said. "But he didn't know what I was talking about when I called this morning."

"So, maybe she went somewhere else?"

Anna shook her head.

"The girl at their office we think is sabotaging the case told Bryant and Allie that she called in to work on wedding stuff with Eddie," she said.

"And, she's not starting any of that until next year," Alex said, starting to follow along.

"Now we can't get ahold of Bryant, either," Joe said. "Allie told us he talked to that same girl this morning and then rushed out of the office."

Alex stood still thinking for a minute.

"This gets a lot trickier now that Haskell is involved," he said. "We aren't supposed to go anywhere near that guy."

"We have to find Marie and Bryant," Anna pleaded. "What can we do?"

"I want you two to go wait somewhere safe," he said. "I will go back to the office and start digging around for Marie and Bryant, hopefully without tipping off any of the dirty cops."

"You want us to just go wait somewhere?" Joe said, not liking the sound of that.

"Yes, Joe," Alex said. "That's what civilians do. They wait and let the police do their jobs."

Joe glared at him but said nothing more, so Alex turned to Anna instead.

"You'll call us the minute you find something?" Anna asked, trying to defer Alex's attention away from Joe, who was glaring at him.

"I will," Alex said. "But I need to know that you are somewhere safe, Anna."

"We'll be safe," Joe said. "We'll go to Anna's apartment. I am not about to go home and worry my parents just yet."

Alex gave him a grateful look before sweeping Anna into his arms and trying to comfort her.

"We'll find her," he whispered in her ear. "I promise we'll find her."

Anna nodded, trying to keep her tears at bay before climbing back into Joe's jeep.

"Where are we going?" Anna asked as they pulled away from the park.

"We really are going back to your apartment," Joe said through gritted teeth. "But we aren't waiting around. Or at least I'm not."

"Hey," Anna said. "You and I are in this together. So, if you need to do something, I'm right there with you."

Joe nodded but remained quiet for the rest of the trip to her apartment. The moment she walked in, Anna flipped on some music to help drown out the silence permeating through the place because of her sister's absence. Both she and Joe set up their laptops on the kitchen table and got to work.

"I will try to find their phones," Joe said. "You keep working the Autumn angle and see what you can find out about that. I want to know how she is connected."

Pushing down the anxiety and fear, Anna searched through countless social media accounts, court records, and bank accounts, but kept coming up empty. Growing frustrated, she shoved away from the table and started a pot of coffee trying to refresh herself. Closing her eyes, she listened to Joe's frantic typing and mouse clicking. When he stopped, Anna opened her eyes and stared at him.

"I can't find a signal at all for Marie's phone since she texted you yesterday," he said. "Bryant's has been off-grid for at least the past hour, and the last place either phone was active was their office."

The silence grew between them as they both mulled over the situation in their minds. After several more minutes of thinking, Anna was the first to break the silence.

"Maybe Autumn told Bryant where to go?" she mused.

"But where?"

"I have no idea," Anna said.

"I'll check Marie's cloud account and see if she has Autumn's number in her phone," Joe said before his fingers began flying over the keys again.

Feeling helpless, Anna tried to keep herself busy by straightening up the apartment. She kept glancing at her phone, hoping Alex would give her an update, but that didn't appear to be happening soon. Sighing, she sat back down in front of her computer, propping her hands on her head and closing her eyes.

Trying to imagine Joe's keyboard and mouse were music instruments, she created a little tune in her head to keep herself from going crazy. It was just enough to jar something in her mind she hadn't thought of yet. Her eyes flying open, she jerked forward, causing Joe to jump a little in surprise.

"I have an idea," she said. "Callen has to have a death certificate and paperwork. Someone had to sign for his body."

"If we find out who that is," Joe said, jumping to the same conclusion she had. "Maybe they will have a connection to both Autumn and Callen."

Without another word, Anna got to work searching for the desired paperwork. Since Callen's death was one someone wanted to wrap up fast, the paperwork was already available. Anna smiled when she saw a woman's name listed as Callen's next of kin.

"Bingo," she said to herself and began gathering information on the woman who turned out to be Callen's mother. It was just a matter of time before she sat back, surprised at just how easy it was to put all the pieces together.

"So?" Joe asked, an anxious look passing across his face.

"Well, Callen's mother was the one to request access to his body," she said. "Nothing spectacular about her. But she has a sister, who I traced back to Autumn because it's her mother."

"Good job," Joe said.

"Oh, it gets better," Anna said. "Autumn's mom has a husband. He isn't Autumn's biological father, but he's been in her life for several years. He is receiving regular payments from that holding company we've been investigating."

"Let me guess," Joe said. "He doesn't work for them."

"He's an electrical contractor. The payments he's receiving are astronomical compared to the work he'd be doing.

But they are just under the limit for federal reporting regulations, so no one is even noticing."

"Hmm," Joe said. "Well, that at least gives us our connection. I'm striking out on Autumn's phone."

"Marie didn't have it in hers?"

"Oh, she did," Joe said. "But it's been off the grid since this morning too. She did something with it about the same time Bryant disappeared."

"Was she at the office last night when Marie was there?"

"Nope," Joe said. "Already checked that. Marie was there by herself. Her phone disappears after she leaves the office."

"Where the hell did she go?" Anna asked.

Joe sat, staring at his screen for a minute, churning the data through his brain. An idea flashed through him, and he started typing again.

"I just had a thought," Joe said. "If she was at the office, she was working on her computer. What if she got an email or message telling her to go somewhere or something?"

Joe continued typing while Anna walked up behind him, watching him work. Before long, he sat back from his computer and pointed at his screen. "The last thing she searched was an address."

"Let's go," Anna said, already heading for the door.

"Hold on. That's how Bryant and Marie got into trouble, remember? Rushing into things. Let's check things out a little better."

"Fine," Anna said, pulling up a chair beside him.

"All right. According to the property records, this building belongs to our friend Haskell."

"What are they using it for?"

"It looks like a warehouse."

"That can't be all it is!" Anna threw her hands in the air.

"Let's see what's been going on there the past few days," Joe said, flipping to another program.

Anna's eyes grew wide as she watched him click through various portions of the program.

"You want to tell me what THAT is?" she asked, raising an eyebrow at him.

"Oh! I haven't shown you this yet? This was the program I told you about that helped me look at cellphone signals."

He typed a few more lines on the screen, causing Anna to become even more surprised as she began to realize the magnitude of what he was doing.

"Is that doing what I think it is?" she asked.

"How do you think I found you so easily when you left the other day?" he said, still typing.

"Enlighten me, please."

Joe stopped typing altogether and sighed. "It's a program I built. It's not exactly...legal."

"I would say not! It looks like you can hack into the phone grid."

"Pretty much," Joe grinned. "I can find any phone, for the most part. If they aren't deactivated, like Marie's and Bryant's are, anyway."

"And go back in time," Anna said.

She continued to watch him, unable to hide how impressed she was.

"Yep. For example, I can see that over the past several weeks, there has been a lot of activity at this location. Most, of the cellphone numbers that have been there trace back to people with evidence of a Haskell connection."

"So, it's almost like they were using it as a base of operations or something?"

"Exactly," Joe said. "But all that changed yesterday evening. Just before Marie disappeared, most of the signals left."

"How many were there when she headed that way?"

"Three," Joe continued. "They left the area yesterday evening and returned this morning for a brief amount of time. The property is clear of any signals now."

"You think whoever was there last night took her and came back for Bryant this morning?"

"Considering the numbers are track phones, I would say yes. I'm also assuming someone was jamming her signal because her phone disappears the moment she got in her car at the office."

Anna's eyes filled with tears at the thought of her sister in the hands of Haskell's men.

"But," Joe said, trying to give her some hope. "One of the great things about people who kidnap people for a living is they aren't usually the most adept."

"Meaning?"

"Meaning," Joe said. "One of the idiots kept the track phone."

"And, you know where it is?"

"Not exactly." Joe sighed. "I didn't build old-style track phones into this program. I can tell it's still on, and I know it was at this location, but I can't figure out where it is now."

"Ugh," Anna groaned. "So, that leaves us knowing someone has Marie and Bryant, and not being able to do anything about it?"

"Actually, I can still trace the line, but only a few miles at a time."

"What do we need to do?"

"We will have to chase them down. We can start at the place we know Marie was at and follow the phone trail until we find them. I don't know how long that will take."

"Let's go," Anna said, gathering up some supplies and her electronics.

"What about Alex? Should we let him know?"

"We'll let him know when we find them," Anna said.

Joe nodded. "We need to be armed before we start this."

"Who are you, James Bond? Not going to stick with a rubber band arsenal this time?"

Grateful for the slight reprieve from the tension building up inside of her, she let a small laugh escape her lips.

Joe smiled back at her before growing serious. "Trust me. Whenever we find whoever took Marie and Bryant, they will wish I was James Bond 'cause he would be a lot nicer to them than I will be."

Chapter 33

Thursday 11 AM – Alex

ALEX SWEPT BACK INTO the police station, pausing for a second to look around at the men working at their desks. As much as he hated to do it, he divided his co-workers into two groups in his mind, those he could trust and those he couldn't. Even faster, he singled out a few of the men he felt were the most likely to be on the up and up and took his chances.

Walking up to a fellow SWAT member, Alex attempted to get some help with his problem without alerting too many onlookers. He hoped Anna and Joe's assumption that something was wrong would prove false, but he wasn't about to take any chances.

"Hey, Stafford," he said in a hushed voice. "Could I get you to do me a favor?"

"Sure, man," came the reply. "What's up?"

"Well," Alex said, laughing a bit. "My girlfriend's sister seems to have had her car stolen but didn't want me to get involved in it. Would you mind throwing a BOLO out there for me, just so we can keep an eye out for it?"

"Sure," Stafford said, already getting to work. "What kind of car is it and do you have the license plate?"

Alex gave him the information and went back to his desk to do more research. Finding the information he needed on Bryant and Marie's phones, Alex plugged them into the system to trace them. Just as Anna and Joe said, both were powered down, but it looked like the last place they both had been was their office.

Sighing, Alex got up from his desk and left the station, only relaxing when the sunshine hit his face through the windshield of his squad car. He spent the entire drive to Marie's office musing over the situation and hoping Anna didn't get the wise idea to go off looking for her sister herself.

Putting the thought out of his mind, Alex turned back to the task at hand. The more he thought about the situation, the more nervous he became. Two missing attorneys in the heat of a trial dealing with Haskell was not a good thing, especially when one of them was Anna's sister.

Trying to shake the anxiety building up inside him, Alex pulled into the parking lot of the law firm, keeping his eyes peeled for Marie's car. Driving up and down the rows of vehicles, he hoped beyond hope he would spot the familiar car, but to no avail. Sighing again, he put his car in park and stepped out.

Knowing he didn't have a warrant and not wanting to cause too many heads to turn his way, Alex knew he would need creativity to gather the information he needed. He also knew he had somewhat of an inside face to help.

Putting on a big smile, Alex strode into Marie's office and scanned the receptionist's desk. She looked up at him with a guarded smile as he approached but seemed hospitable enough.

"How can I help you, Officer?" she asked.

"Good morning, Sylvia," he said after glancing at the woman's nameplate. "My girlfriend's sister is an attorney here, and she has something that belongs to me in her office. She's not here, but she told me Allie could help me out."

"Oh! Certainly," Sylvia said, gazing up at his charming smile. "Allie is the first desk in the criminal law division. If you take a left and an immediate right, you can't miss her."

"Thanks so much, Sylvia," Alex said, smiling at her again. "I appreciate your help."

Allie looked surprised to see him but still looked at him with a look of recognition when Alex walked up to her desk.

"It's Alex, right?" she asked. "Anna's boyfriend?"

"You have a good memory." Alex smiled. "I need your help."

"It's about Marie and Bryant, isn't it?" she said. "They've been gone all day. I'm worried sick."

"So are Anna and Joe," Alex whispered. "I need to check Marie's office. Your receptionist thinks Marie has something of mine, and you are helping me get it."

"I have keys to everyone's offices, so I can get you in there."

"Great," Alex said. "I need to check Bryant's too, but I don't have a reason to go in there."

"I have some files I can go put on his desk," she said. "What are you looking for?"

"Anything that might tell me where they went. We can't start searching the place. It needs to be a quick search...something obvious."

"Gotcha," Allie said, grabbing her set of office keys and a stack of files. "I'll let you in Marie's office and I'll check Bryant's."

As Alex expected, Marie's desk was spotless. She was meticulous in her daily life, so what made him think she would leave anything out of place at work? Sighing, he sat down at her desk and opened the desk drawers. Besides general office supplies, he wasn't coming up with much of anything.

Pushing the bottom drawer shut again, Alex prepared to stand to his feet, frustrated by the lack of information he'd found when he noticed a small scrap of paper sticking out from under the bottom of Marie's desk. Frowning, he scooped it up and gazed at the handwritten address on it.

Acting on a hunch, he stuffed the note in his pocket for future reference and headed back out to find Allie at her desk.

"Did you find anything?" he asked.

Allie shook her head in disappointment.

"Yeah, I found nothing substantial either," Alex said before handing her one of his cards. "Would you call me if you hear from them?"

"Will do," Allie said, a worried look passing across her face.

Alex smiled at her and left the office. This time, he couldn't help but let the anxiety build in his stomach on his way back to the police station. Still trying to attract as little attention as possible, he strode to his desk, only stopping for a moment at Stafford's.

"Any hits on that BOLO?" Alex asked.

"Nothing yet, man," Stafford said, shaking his head.

"No worries," Alex said. "Let me know if you see anything. I'm headed out for the day here in a few minutes. I have some personal things I need to take care of. But you can call me on my cell if anything comes across."

Alex focused his gaze on his desk, ignoring the other men in his office, and sank into his chair before pulling the scrap of paper out of his pocket. Glancing around to ensure he wasn't being watched, Alex typed the address into his database before sliding the note under his keyboard to hide it.

The information on the screen wasn't beneficial. It appeared to be a warehouse of some sort but hadn't been in use in years. Frowning, Alex scrolled through screen after screen, trying to find a connection to Marie or a case she might be working on, but couldn't seem to find anything.

"Where is this place?" he mused out loud before pulling up a map of the area.

"Shit," he mumbled under his breath as he came to the one conclusion he was hoping he wouldn't reach. It was right in the middle of Haskell's territory. Marie had no way of knowing that, nor did Bryant when they both headed this direction.

Closing his eyes and rubbing his temples, Alex thought about calling Anna but decided against it. With this information, he now feared he wouldn't find either Marie or

Bryant, at least alive, anyway. But there was no way he was telling Anna that right now.

With little to go on, Alex prepared to leave the station again, knowing he would have to stop by his house and change before heading to check out this location. There was no way he was heading into Haskell's territory sporting a police uniform and driving a squad car.

Thursday 11 AM – Agents Hoage and Kamera
PACING AROUND THE CONFERENCE room, Carver glared down at the papers strung across the desk. Renato sifted through his notes, trying to find something helpful. Frustrated, Carver slunk down into a chair and threw his feet up on the table.

"Where are we at on this?" he asked.

"Somewhere between where we started and halfway to hell from what I can tell," Renato muttered.

"How can we have nothing?"

"I don't know," Renato said, glancing up at the door behind his partner. "But you better come up with an answer real quick cause here comes the boss."

Carver threw his feet to the floor and spun around just in time to see his boss sling the door to the conference room open and stride in.

"You clowns have been at this for over a week now. What do you have for me?"

Carver looked at his partner before standing up and moving around the table, gathering papers.

"We're getting there, Irving," he said. "I promise we're getting there."

"You've had three people get killed over this," Irving said. "How many more body bags am I gonna have to line up beside your desks before it's all said and done?"

"We are getting close," Renato said. "Just looking for a few more pieces of the puzzle and iron out a few wrinkles, but we're there."

"You know the brass will have all our heads if this thing gets out of hand, right?" Irving asked, folding his arms across his chest.

"That won't happen, Irving," Carver promised.

"You've got a couple more days," Irving said, "but after that, I'm pulling you two off this case."

Carver and Renato remained silent as he slammed the door shut on his way out of the conference room. Carver went back to pacing while Renato sat musing over the facts.

"What are we doing with Madison Kimbley?" he asked.

"They cut her a deal," came the reply. "She's cooperating, and I don't think she has any more information."

"They kept everything tight and divided, didn't they? She oversaw just one aspect of the case."

"Seems to be the case," Renato said, propping his head on his wrists and watching his partner continue to pace around the room. "Same as that fellow those kids brought us. He knew just enough to confuse our search for answers."

"Well, someone has to know the whole plan. Let's start with the obvious," Carver said before securing a picture of Lindsay and one of Audrick to the board in the room with a magnet. "We know these two and Kimbley were at the center of the blackmail ring."

"Not to mention the fact Audrick's holding company works with Haskell's businesses."

"True, true," Carver said, gazing at the board. "After these two, we know Haskell's attorney is involved since those kids have pictures of him in that house where we found Audrick's body."

"But we can't touch him with a ten-foot pole," Renato said.

"Can't even get a warrant to question him," Carver grumbled, sitting down in frustration.

Renato stepped back from the board, frowning at it.

"Why do I feel like we are missing something in all this?" he asked.

Carver shook his head and stared at the board with him, racking his brain for a sign. Almost simultaneously, the agents turned to each other, an enlightened expression on their faces.

"Because we are," Carver said.

"That kid! How could we have forgotten about him? Callen, wasn't it? What's his connection to all this?"

"We never found the shooter and all the forensics pointed to a professional hit, so I thought it was just a wrong place/wrong time situation. We've been working that case as if Marie and Bryant were the targets because of their work on the Haskell trial. But what if they weren't?"

"What do you say we get more information on him?" Renato asked, grabbing his phone to call his assistant.

While waiting for her to bring them the desired information, the agents sifted through their documents for any other signs of things they had missed. They were still at it when she breezed in and displayed a stapled stack of papers.

"Thanks, Alicia," Renato said, already turning his attention to the data in front of him.

"Well?" Carver asked as he watched a smile form on his partner's face.

"Callen's aunt has a daughter who also works at that damn law firm."

"Well, that doesn't say much," Carver said. "But it's a start. Let's bring her in and talk to..."

"Did I say I was finished?" Renato asked with a grin. "This young lady has a stepdad who has a slight connection to Haskell."

"Now we're cooking," Carver said, picking up his phone. "I'm calling our lawyer friends to fish for some information on her."

Renato leaned back in his chair and closed his eyes for a moment waiting for his partner to find something to dictate the next steps they would take. He only opened them after he heard Carver mumbling to himself.

"Odd," he said.

"What's wrong?"

"Nothing, necessarily," Carver frowned. "Both Marie and Bryant have their phones turned off. I'm calling their office."

Renato watched his partner as he connected with the criminal law department at the law firm.

"Allison Heiland!" a voice said in greeting. "How may I help you?"

"Ms. Heiland," he said in a sweet tone. "I'm looking for Marie Hartman."

Carver couldn't help but notice her hesitation.

"She isn't in today, sir," came the reply.

"Oh, well, I'm sure another attorney can help me in the office," Carver said. "How about Bryant Malone? Is he in?"

"Can you tell me what this is regarding?" Allie said, suddenly sounding brisk.

"Hmm, I'm afraid not," Carver said, starting to grow suspicious. "Do you know when either of them will be back?"

"No," she said. "No, I don't."

"Do you know where they are?"

She hesitated just long enough to make him uncomfortable before saying, "Perhaps I could be more helpful if you told me who you are and what you want."

"I will assume you don't know where they are," he said, looking at Renato. "Since they aren't available and you don't know where they are or what time they will be back, what about Autumn Fritzman? Is she there?"

"All right, now I must insist you tell me who you are," Allie whispered.

Carver sighed, "My name is Carver Hoage. I'm an FBI agent who's been working on a case involving Marie and Bryant and need to speak with them."

Allie was silent for several more seconds before she continued the conversation. "As I said, they aren't in. But if you give me your number, maybe I can have someone call you who might help you."

Frowning, Carver agreed and rattled off his number. Allie hung up without even telling him goodbye.

"What?" Renato asked, peering at his confused face.

"She's going to have someone call me."

Chapter 34

Thursday 1 PM – Alex

ALEX CIRCLED THE WAREHOUSE once before finding a spot to park his car. Noticing no signs of activity in or around the building on Marie's sticky note, he crept closer. Looking for any sign of Marie or Bryant, he glanced down the alleyways and sidewalks on his trek.

The sinking feeling he'd been trying to ignore all morning intensified as he took in the sight of something he was hoping not to find, Marie's car. Sighing, he pulled his sidearm out of its holster and approached. Knowing Marie had a bad habit of leaving her door unlocked, it didn't surprise him when the door swung open.

As with the rest of her life, Marie's car was clean, and he felt relief when he didn't find her inside. His gut-churning, he pushed the button to open her trunk, praying it would be as empty as the rest of her car. Holding his breath, he walked to the back of her vehicle, trained his weapon at her trunk and swung up the lid. Only after finding the trunk empty did he sigh in relief and holster his weapon.

Keeping an eye out for company, Alex returned to the front of the car and searched it for anything of substance.

Finding nothing under the seats, middle console, or glove compartment, he closed Marie's car and turned his attention back to the imposing building in front of him.

Trying to ignore the eerie stillness around him, Alex found an open door and slipped inside the warehouse, once again pulling out his weapon to defend himself. He made his way through the building, clearing each area before moving onto the next. Most of the warehouse was open and empty.

"What could she have been doing here?" he thought to himself after he circled through the building, finding no sign of her.

Letting his eyes sweep the room and windows above him, Alex frowned in confusion. Holstering his weapon a second time, Alex put his hands on his hips and looked across the warehouse, taking in the clean floor and neat over-all appearance, which were a stark difference from the damaged walls and broken windows. One such window caused the sunlight to dance across the floor, producing odd angles, making everything even more confusing, but a glimmer shining amongst all of it caught his eye.

Narrowing his eyes, Alex approached the glimmer and sighed in frustration as his fears felt confirmed. Reaching down to scoop up the offending item, Alex turned it over in his hand, took in its familiar shape, and pocketed it. He sighed again as he felt his phone ring in his pocket and tugged it out to look at it.

Looking around one more time to make sure he was still alone, Alex answered the device.

"Alex? It's Allie...from Bryant and Marie's office."

"What's up, Allie?" he asked. "Have you heard anything?"

"No, not from Bryant or Marie," she said. "But I received a call from an FBI agent who is also looking for them. An Agent Hoage. He even asked about Autumn."

"I didn't tell him about you," she continued when he didn't reply. "But I got his number and told him I would give it to someone who might call him."

"Send it over to me, would you?"

"I will," she said. "What's going on, Alex? I'm worried."

"I'm not sure yet," he said. "But I want you to keep your head down and stay safe. Try to go about your day and don't go anywhere alone if you can help it. I'm not liking this."

"Please keep me informed. Call me on this number. It's my personal cellphone."

After ending the call, Alex picked his way back to his car, still wary of his surroundings. Again, he put the thought of calling Anna out of his mind, hoping his desire to keep her in the dark wouldn't come back to bite him later.

Instead, he opened the text from Allie and called Agent Hoage's phone. It only took two rings for him to pick up the line.

"Carver Hoage," came the gruff greeting.

"My name is Alex Vega," Alex said. "Officer Vega, actually."

"What can I do for you, Officer?"

"To be frank, this isn't just a professional call. I'm Anna Hartman's boyfriend."

"Ahhh, yes," Carver said. "Yes, we are familiar with Ms. Hartman. Didn't know her boyfriend was a police officer. That must cause some interesting situations for you."

"Yeah, well, it is what it is," Alex said. "I'm calling about her sister and co-worker, Bryant."

"You're looking for them, too, aren't you?"

"I've come to a standstill," Alex admitted. "I've found Marie's car and where she was last, but I'm stuck past that point."

"Wait," Carver asked, interested in what Alex was saying. "You found her car? Where is it?"

"I found an address on a slip of paper in her office and checked it out. Her car is sitting in an alleyway nearby."

Alex pulled the object he found in the warehouse out of his pocket and looking at it again. "I also found a necklace inside the building I know is Marie's. It was her mother's, and she always wears this thing."

"You didn't find any sign of Bryant, though?"

"I didn't do an extensive search of the area, so I'm likely to have missed something, but I saw nothing obvious."

"Send me the address, and we'll be there in 30 minutes," Agent Hoage said. "And, Alex, wait there for me, please."

Thursday 2 PM – Agents Hoage and Kamera
"WE'VE GOTTA GO," CARVER said to his partner, scooping up their evidence.

"Where we going?" Renato asked, already beginning to help him.

"That was Anna Hartman's boyfriend," Carver said and raised his eyebrows, "who is a police officer."

"You don't say," Renato said with a chuckle. "How does she stay out of trouble?"

"I have no clue," Carver laughed before growing serious. "Our lawyer friends are missing. Officer Boyfriend's been looking for them all morning. He just ran across Marie's car in an alley somewhere."

"But no Marie, I take it?"

"Nope. Or Bryant. He found a necklace nearby that belongs to Marie."

Carver and Renato locked up their evidence and strode to their car. Staying silent on the drive to Alex, both agents tried to keep their minds off what might be happening to Marie and Bryant. The address wasn't too far away, however, so they didn't have long to ponder each scenario crossing their minds.

They found Alex sitting in his car down the street from the address and approached him. He eyed them just when they got out of their vehicle but said nothing to them at first.

"I think we might have some mutual friends," Carver said after nodding to Alex in greeting.

"That could be the case, but how would I know?"

"Well, I think our mutual friend lost a car around here somewhere," Carver continued. "Would you know anything about that?"

"Do you have identification?"

Carver flashed him his badge, and Alex did the same in return, both men trying to be as secretive as possible.

"This is my partner Renato Kamera."

"Nice to meet you both," Alex said. "But I wish it were under better circumstances."

"Mind if we take a look?"

"Be my guest. Maybe you can find Bryant's car."

Carver nodded, and the three started off toward the warehouse, repeating the same process Alex had gone through earlier. The agents also found nothing to note but did locate Bryant's car two alleys down from Marie's. When they found no further clues to their whereabouts, they trudged back to their own vehicles to discuss the situation further.

"Well, that settles it," Carver said while leaning against his car. "They were both here."

"But why?" Alex asked.

"Not sure. Any idea who would have tipped them off to this place?"

"Anna said a girl at their office said Marie had called in today. But the reason she gave didn't make sense. Anna thinks she's involved in all of it."

"Did Anna give you a name?"

"Autumn Fritzman," Alex said.

Carver and Renato looked at each other in amazement.

"You want to tell me how those two are always five steps ahead of us?" Carver asked, turning back to Alex.

"Anna's always been hard to keep up with, and I'm starting to realize that Joe has a lot of tricks up his sleeve too."

The agents looked at each other again and shook their heads in amazement.

"What's the next step?" Alex asked.

"Well," Carver said. "Autumn being involved in all this didn't help things."

"Why's that?"

"Can't tell you that," Renato said, looking at the ground. "You don't have clearance for that information."

"What we need you to know is Anna and Joe aren't safe," Carver said, before frowning at him. "Where are they?"

"I sent them back to her apartment. I wanted them to stay out of the way and somewhere safe."

"Well, we need to get them somewhere even safer."

"Like in protective custody?" Alex asked. "Is that what you're telling me?"

"Yeah," Carver said. "I think that's the best option. I don't like the direction this is heading."

"You and me both," Alex sighed before picking up his phone to call Anna.

Alex called Anna's cellphone and frowned when it went to voicemail.

"Hey, call me back," he said before addressing the agents. "I'm going to text her, too, but she didn't answer."

"Let's get over to her apartment," Carver said, already getting back in their vehicle.

Alex tried to shake the sickening feeling in his gut as he raced to Anna's apartment complex. The thought of her in the same situation as her sister was enough for him to go crazy, so he tried to push that out of his mind the best he could.

"Well, her car and bike are here," he said to Carver and Renato when they pulled into the parking lot and approached her apartment. "But Joe's jeep isn't."

The agents stood to the side of her door, their hands on their weapons while Alex knocked on the door in vain. When she didn't answer, Alex dug through his pocket and located his set of keys and let himself inside only to find darkness and silence.

"They aren't here," he said after circling through the rooms.

"I don't see any signs of a struggle," Renato said, glancing around.

"And with Joe's jeep being gone," Carver continued. "I would say they left on their own."

"So, where are they?" Renato asked.

"Damn it, Anna," Alex said, kicking a chair at her kitchen table.

Chapter 35

Thursday 3 PM – Marie and Bryant

MARIE ATTEMPTED TO open her eyes, but sharp needles of pain shot through her body, causing her to close them again. Confusion raced through her mind as she attempted to move her arms and legs. Panic began to set in when she found them secured.

As her senses began to return to her, she started hearing the muffled sound of voices somewhere nearby. Tentatively, she opened one eye and then another, squinting and blinking several times, attempting to clear her vision.

Her eyes floated around the room in front of her, searching for something she recognized. Tugging at her arms again, Marie felt the zip ties holding her bite painfully into her skin.

"Marie?" she heard Bryant's familiar voice say. "Are you awake?"

Marie shook her head, trying to clear it further while attempting to turn toward the sound of his voice only to find it was just out of her sight.

"Yeah."

"Are you hurt?"

"I don't think so," she said, looking down at her body. "I'm a little disoriented, though, so I'm not sure."

"Do you know where we are or how we got here?"

"No, do you?" she asked. "I don't remember much."

"Me neither," Bryant said.

"I'm so sorry I brought you into this," Marie said, tears coming to her eyes.

Before Bryant could reply, their ears began picking up the sound of footsteps coming their direction. Marie and Bryant both attempted to turn toward the sound of the steps coming their way but had to strain their necks to do so. When the faces of their captors came into view, both Bryant and Marie gasped in shock.

"Surprise!" a smug voice said.

"Callen?" Marie asked. "But we saw you die! I don't understand."

"Autumn?" Bryant said, addressing the second person in the room. "What is going on?"

"You'd be surprised at just how many cops you can buy these days with a small amount of money," Callen laughed. "Faking my death was simple actually. I had you believing it, didn't I?"

"Shut up, Callen," Autumn grumbled. "We don't have time for idle chit-chat. As soon as the team is back from preparing the dump site, we are gone."

"Yeah, yeah, yeah," Callen said. "Who are they going to go tell now anyway? Let me have my fun while we wait."

"Whatever," Autumn said before walking away and into the other room.

"I don't understand what's happening," Marie said in confusion as she watched her leave.

"Well, Marie," Callen said, stooping down in front of her and speaking to her in a childlike voice. "We will make sure the Haskell case goes how we want it to. Autumn will take over now, and that deal you worked out for ole Dominique Shaw, just isn't going to work out."

"You can't do this," Bryant muttered from behind Marie. "You won't get away with it."

"Oh, I can, and I will," Callen retorted. "And you will be dead and buried somewhere, and I'll be sipping Mai Tai's on a beach with stacks of money to keep me company."

"Please, Callen," Marie begged. "Don't do this! You're a good guy. Please!"

"Sorry, Marie," Callen smiled. "Everyone has their price. Besides, this is a family business, so I didn't have much of a choice."

When Marie didn't reply, Callen continued without her.

"You don't need to know about all that," Callen said. "Let's talk about my big acting success instead. Did I have you fooled? Did you think I died? It was dramatic, right?"

Marie could only stare back at him in confusion and anger. Likewise, Bryant didn't seem too excited to critique his horrendous performance. Autumn walked back in before Callen could press the issue.

"All right, Cuz," she said. "The crew is here. We need to get out of here. I've got to be at work tomorrow, and you need to finish packing up my apartment."

"Ah, come one," he said. "Let's hang around a bit and show them how awesome of a job we did."

Autumn folded her arms across her chest and glared at him. "Right, like how if I didn't intervene in the nonsense you created and get them both to come to headquarters so we could take care of them, they probably would have blown the lid off the whole thing?"

"Please, I've been the one successfully keeping everything under control through this whole thing!"

"Oh, do elaborate," she groaned. "Are we talking about how you caused all this mess in the first place by messing with the evidence and catching her attention?"

"I was trying to distract her!"

Marie's eyes shot back and forth between them like she was watching a tennis match. She could feel her panic level rising above her control and tried to think of a way to escape.

"Right," Autumn grumbled, jerking Marie's attention back to her. "Or how about how you brought even more attention to this thing by blowing up his car in the damn FBI's parking lot?"

"Yeah, maybe a little over the top on that one."

"I think my favorite screw up of yours was when you showed up in front of the office and handed a note to her sister."

"Oh, that was fun!" Callen said, his eyes shining with excitement before turning to Marie. "God, she's pretty, isn't she? I may have to pay her a visit before this is all said and done."

Marie couldn't stop the tears that sprang to her eyes and spilled over and down her cheeks. Callen gave her a sad look and wiped them away. Glaring at him, Marie jerked her face away from his touch, nearly knocking her chair over. Autumn shook her head and turned her attention to the other room before calling back over her shoulder to Callen.

"Come on, you idiot. We've got to go!"

"Well, I guess this is it," Callen said, his voice taking on a fake sad tone. "I will miss working with you two. You were a lot of fun. Ah, hell. Who am I kidding? No, I won't! I'll be too busy spending money and sleeping with models to think about either of you!"

Before Marie or Bryant could respond to the situation at all, Callen and Autumn exited the room, and three imposing men took their place. Marie eyed them, but they didn't seem interested in her or Bryant at all.

"All right, fellas," said the smallest of the three men. "We need to figure out how long the boss wants us to keep these two around before we put them on ice. You stay here and watch them. I'm going downstairs to get orders and our money. Sit tight."

"Hey, when's the kill guy getting here?" one thug asked before the man could leave the room. "I don't feel like sitting around all day babysitting. I'm ready to clean up the mess he's gonna make and get the hell out of here."

"You get paid to do whatever I tell you to do, remember?" the man snarled. "But you are missing out on a piece of the pie since you messed up and kept that track phone instead of ditching it at headquarters."

"We were too busy nabbing these two. I forgot!"

"Just shut up and keep a watch on them," he demanded. "I swear. I don't know why I put up with you effing morons. If you didn't work for peanuts, why I swear..."

The man continued grumbling all the way down the stairs. Marie listened to his footsteps fade into the distance before turning her attention back to her constraints and her desperate search for an escape.

"Man, I hope the kill guy gets here soon," one of the two men left in the room griped.

"Yeah, no kidding," the other said. "I'm getting hungry."

With nothing left to do but wait, one man plopped down in a chair and started playing on his cellphone while the other threw his on a table and started pacing around.

"Bryant?" Marie asked, a panicked tone creeping into her voice as she watched the men. "What are we going to do?"

"I don't know, Marie," he said. "I don't know."

Chapter 36

Thursday 2 PM – Anna and Joe

"DO YOU HAVE A LICENSE to carry that thing?" Anna asked as she eyed the side panel of Joe's jeep where he'd stashed a pistol.

"Why, yes," he said, not looking at her. "Yes, I do."

Before hitting the road, Joe had insisted on adding the pistol to their inventory. In fact, he hadn't even asked her opinion on the matter. Instead, he opted to leave her in his running jeep on a dirt path behind his house while he slipped into the workshop on the back of the property. When he returned, he put the gun in his side panel without looking at her.

"I swear, you're James Bond," she said, shaking her head and looking back to the laptop she held in her lap.

"Awe, come on," Joe said, glancing at himself in the rearview mirror. "You know I'm better looking than James Bond."

Anna laughed and considered agreeing with him but cleared her throat and changed the subject instead.

"So, where are we headed?" she asked.

"Just follow that signal there." Joe pointed at a flashing dot on the screen of the laptop Anna held while still paying attention to the road. "We just have to stay within three miles of it to know where we're headed. So, I need you to tell me when I need to exit and make turns and such."

"I can do that," Anna said and frowned at her phone as it started to ring. "Oh, no. It's Alex."

"You gonna answer it?" Joe asked.

"Uh, I probably shouldn't," she said and watched the phone ring several more times before it went silent.

Joe and Anna both sat in silence for a few moments waiting for it to ring again. Anna sighed when the phone alerted her that she had a voice message. Before she could listen to it, the phone dinged in response to the text Alex had just sent her.

"He sent a text. It says we need to stay at the apartment and he's coming to get us. They want to put us in protective custody."

"Yeah, that's not happening," Joe said.

"He will freak when we aren't there," Anna said.

"It'll all turn out all right. He might be mad at first, but he'll get over it."

"I hope so."

Anna gazed at the text on her phone again before listening to Alex's short message, all while trying to watch the dot on the screen as Joe drove down the highway. She leaned over and glanced at his speedometer and scowled a bit.

"Hey, you want to slow it down a bit?" she asked. "Normally, I wouldn't care how fast we were going, but the last thing we need is to get thrown in jail for reckless driving."

Joe's eyes followed her gaze to his speedometer and took his foot off the gas, allowing the jeep to coast to a respectable speed.

"You're right," he said. "Hey, we've been on this highway for thirty minutes now. They haven't taken any turns yet?"

Anna glanced down at the screen for a few moments before replying.

"It looks like we are coming up on an exit that looks promising. Here in two miles, the dot no longer looks like it's on this highway."

When they reached the exit, Joe maneuvered the jeep onto it and glanced in his rearview mirror to ensure they didn't have to worry about company. So far, the roads were silent behind them, and it looked like they were coming up on their destination without being noticed.

Coming to a stop sign at the end of the exit, Joe asked, "Which way?"

"They went to the right." Anna followed the dot with her finger. They continued driving and made several more turns before approaching a dirt road. "The signal stops about a mile up this road."

"I'm going to make a pass at it and see what we are dealing with before we do anything," Joe said.

He turned the jeep onto the road and tried to drive slow enough to avoid creating too much of a dust cloud that would alert their prey. "You keep an eye out for activity."

Anna nodded and peered out the windshield in front of her as they approached the end of the signal. They passed an old farmhouse complete with a rustic barn nestled in front of a sparse forest.

"At least it isn't out in the open," she said. "Maybe we can sneak up on them."

"Yeah," Joe said, doing his best to look at the property while maintaining a decent speed past it. "Let's just hope there is a place up here where we can turn around, park, and do some planning. I don't want to go into this blind."

The small woods grew thicker as they drove, and just a few hundred yards past the farmhouse, they noticed a short-secluded path large enough to accommodate the jeep.

"Perfect," Joe said.

He pulled his vehicle inside the cover of the trees and found a spot off the path to park.

"What now?" Anna asked, gazing toward the farm-house.

"Now," Joe said, taking his laptop back from her. "We need to figure out where everyone is."

Anna watched as he typed a few keys and broadened the parameters of his program. All the cell phone signals in the area came into view.

"I count at least three signals in the farmhouse." Joe pointed to the screen. "This one appears to be sitting still, so I bet it's on a counter somewhere."

"So, we're dealing with at least three people."

Joe pointed to another dot on the screen. "This phone is separated from the others, but it's moving around some. I bet these two over here are with Marie and Bryant."

"What's the plan?"

"I think we have to get a closer look and see if we can't take out these guys one at a time."

Joe opened the driver door and grabbed the pistol, tucking it into the back of his waistband and pulling his t-shirt over to hide it.

"I'm right behind you," Anna said and opened the door to get out.

She and Joe crept through the trees toward the farmhouse. The cover was just enough to get them close to the house where they could start seeing inside the windows and doors.

Approaching the area where the separate cellphone was, Joe put his finger to his lips and peered inside one of the nearby windows. When they heard a voice, he jerked back down and pressed himself up against the house straining to listen to what the voice was saying.

"Yeah, I know," a man's voice said. Hearing no other sounds, they could only assume the man was talking to someone on the phone.

"We can take care of it right now," the voice continued. "I don't know why we are waiting."

From the sound of the man's footsteps, they could tell he was pacing around the bottom floor of the farmhouse.

"Yeah, but Autumn can take care of that, can't she?"

The man fell silent again for a few more moments while listening to the voice on the other end of the line.

"All I'm saying is it's only one day," he continued. "The trial is tomorrow. That's a short enough window where no one will find their bodies. I guarantee it."

Anna looked at Joe in horror, and he put his finger back to his lips to ensure she stayed silent. She nodded, but her eyes filled with tears.

"Nah, man," the voice continued. "We'll off them right now, take their bodies where they won't be found for months, if ever, and make sure those other two don't have nothin' to say about it either."

"Yep, yep," the man said after another pause. "We'll make sure it isn't messy. We can be done and out of here in the next hour. You just make sure you send over the funds. I will check the account before I finish the job."

Joe motioned for Anna to follow him and led her back into the trees so they could talk.

"Joe, what are we going to do?" Anna asked in a panicked whisper once they were a safe distance from the house.

Joe gazed at the farmhouse with a stern and solemn look on his face before replying.

"I'm going in there to get them," he said. "You wait here."

"Are you crazy?" Anna retorted. "I'm not letting you go in there on your own. If you're going in there, I am too."

"No way, Anna!"

"My sister is in there! There is no way I'm sitting out here and just waiting for you to come back with them or not come back at all."

Joe sighed and gave her a strange look. "I was afraid you'd say that."

"I said we're in this together," she said. "You need someone to watch your back in there."

"I will never forgive myself if something happens to you," he said. "You've got to come out of there in one piece. Deal?"

"Deal."

"You need to call Alex first," he said. "He needs to know where we are so he can bring help. This will not be easy."

Anna hesitated but picked up her phone.

"He will be pissed," she whispered as her phone tried to connect with Alex's. She grimaced at the sound of his stressed-out voice when he answered.

"Alex? It's me."

"Anna!" Alex said. "Where the hell are you? We've been looking everywhere!"

Anna looked at Joe and scowled before replying.

"We found them, Alex," she said. "Joe and I found Marie and Bryant."

"Oh, God, Anna. Are they all right?"

"They took them to a farmhouse about forty-five minutes outside of town," Anna continued. "But as far as we can tell, they are still alive. We just...we just have to get them out."

"What do you mean? You don't go anywhere. Wait there and I'll bring a team to get them out!"

"Alex," she said. "You're too far away. We don't have time to wait for even a local team, let alone you. We need to get them out now. This conversation is wasting time. I will send you the address, but Joe and I..."

"Let me talk to Joe, right now," Alex said.

Anna gave Joe a look but remained silent as she held her phone out to him. He took it and held it to his ear, and Anna turned her attention back to the farmhouse and her sister's predicament.

Hesitating, Joe put the phone to his ear and said, "Hello."

Anna watched Joe's face as he had a conversation with her boyfriend. After listening to him, Joe replied with, "I promise I will keep her safe."

Alex had more to say on the subject and Joe sighed as he listened more.

Joe shook his head and said, "You're too far out. We only have 20 to 30 minutes to get them out, or they will kill them."

Joe hung his head as Alex finished up the conversation with him, Anna desperately trying to figure out what Alex was telling him. She knew they didn't have time to be arguing over whether she was going in there with Joe or not. If they wasted too much time, Bryant and Marie wouldn't be coming out of there alive. But there was no way she would agree to send Joe in there by himself.

Joe handed the phone back to Anna and brought her back to reality. She held it back to her ear again and turned her attention back to Alex.

"Anna," Alex said, his voice cracking with emotion. "I can't be there for you right now. I have to rely on Joe to keep you safe. But I need you to promise me you will be careful in there."

Relieved he had given up trying to convince her to not go in, Anna sighed and nodded her head.

"I promise to be careful, Alex," she said. "I love you."

"Tell me that when I see you again."

"I will."

Anna ended the call and looked at Joe, who was already preparing to enter the darkened building in front of them. Making sure the safety was off on his gun, he trained the weapon on the back doorway of the building before creeping forward and opening the door.

"Let's go," he whispered to Anna. "Stay close to me."

The two crept inside the building, both praying they wouldn't be too late when they reached Marie and Bryant.

Chapter 37

THEY COULD STILL HEAR the man talking when they slipped inside the farmhouse. Joe motioned for Anna to be quiet and led her across the old wood floor. The man was so involved in his conversation he never heard Joe's approach. Not wanting to trigger any alarms, Joe and Anna stayed in the shadows until the man ended his call and started to trek back upstairs again before striking.

It took little effort for Joe to subdue the man. After clubbing him on the head with his gun, Joe jerked the man into a chokehold until he collapsed in his arms. Glancing around, Anna saw an old curtain hanging from a rod in the room, removed it, and handed it to Joe so he could secure the man.

"Good idea," Joe whispered, getting to work on tying up the man. "After we get him tied up, we'll go find Marie and Bryant. I'm sure they are upstairs, especially since that's where he was headed just now."

Joe was still leaned over wrapping the curtain into knots around the man's arms and legs when a pair of strong arms wrapped around Anna's waist, causing her to stiffen. She tried to wiggle out of the grasp, but the more she struggled, the harder the arms gripped her. Her attacker jerked both her arms to her side, squeezing her against his body, one arm securing her arms to her side and the other holding her upper body against his.

"Say his name, sweetheart," a gravelly voice whispered in her ear.

Anna shook her head in defiance but stiffened when the man flipped open a knife and held it in front of her eyes. She still hesitated, causing him to take the edge of the blade and catch the collar of her t-shirt, cutting a clean slit down the front of it. She shivered as she felt the tip of the blade against her skin just under her collarbone.

"Joe," she said, closing her eyes and flinching as the man dug the tip of his knife into her skin, tracing a line under her collarbone, drawing blood.

Joe turned around, his eyes growing wide the moment he saw the man's arms around Anna.

"Why don't you put that down?" the man said, nodding to Joe's gun while holding Anna's arms to her side, the knife still at her neck. Anna kept her eyes closed gritting her teeth against the fear she felt, her heart racing that much more when she heard Joe drop the gun to the floor.

"Hey," Joe said. "Why don't we switch places. You let her go and...let's just switch places."

"That's awfully noble of you," the man said with a grin. "Isn't that noble, Anna?"

The man looked down at Anna and sneered when she didn't reply.

"Sorry, she's not in the mood to talk," he continued. "But, no. To answer your question, we are staying just like this for now."

Anna's mind raced, and she tried to calm it. But, try as she might, her nerves and body fought against her desires. She sucked in a deep breath as she felt the man holding her adjust his grip.

"I like to do research on my marks before I start," he said, neither Joe nor Anna knowing which one he was talking to. "But I have to say, being put in charge of siblings was interesting. It was like a bonus! I planned to use this knife on your sister, but I'll start with you first. You want to tell Joe here why this knife might make you nervous, Anna?"

Somehow Anna found her voice at last.

"He knows," she said, her voice shaky and brimming with anger.

"Well, good," the man said. "I would hate to be redundant on the information I share."

Anna took another shaky breath as the man took the knife away from her neck and began tracing his thumb down her ribcage.

"One, two, three, four…" he murmured in her ear. "That's about right, don't you think?"

Anna couldn't respond, her terror having taken hold of her. The man smiled at Joe.

"Do you know what someone sounds like when they have a knife slide through these two ribs?" he asked. "Anna knows, don't you, sweetheart? I also got my hands on your mother's autopsy report. Seven stab wounds are a lot to handle. You think you got it in you to help me recreate them?"

"You, son of a bitch," Joe muttered through gritted teeth. "Anna don't listen to him. Stay with me. I'm right here. It will be all right. I promised. Remember?"

The man laughed in Anna's ear, causing her skin to bristle with goosebumps.

"Yes, please listen to him lie to you," he said and traced his finger across her stomach all the way to the bottom edge of her t-shirt. Pulling it up, he slipped his finger under the fabric and traced a line just to the right of her belly button.

"There was another one right there," he whispered.

A small whimper escaped Anna's lips. A part of her mind balked at her weakness, but she also couldn't keep a tear from slipping down her cheek as she felt the blood from the cut run down her chest, her ruined t-shirt soaking it up.

"Anna," Joe pleaded. "Please ignore him. I need you to focus on my voice. Don't listen to him. I've got you."

"So, sweet," the man said, turning all his attention to Joe and loosening his grip on her. "But you've gone through this once already, haven't you? Well, I guess you haven't. Not really. You weren't there for her, were you?"

Joe continued to talk to Anna, ignoring the man's words, even though she knew they had to be sending daggers through his heart just like they had hers.

"Poor, Merida. That was her name, wasn't it?"

"You keep her name out of your mouth," Joe spewed, before turning his attention back to Anna.

The man smiled, knowing he'd hit a nerve. Anna swallowed the lump in her throat and somehow convinced her mind to focus on Joe's voice instead of the man's.

"Tell me? Would you have been able to save sweet MERIDA had you gone in there with her? Would we even be here right now if you had?"

Anna could feel the anger building up inside of her as the man spoke, but she tried to focus on Joe's voice to keep her mind from racing off in another direction again. His ability to stay focused on her and ignore the vile things the man said to him was admirable.

"Do you think Merida cried for you when they took her? I guess you'll get to know what Anna here does when I slice her open," he growled.

She finally met Joe's eyes and saw him shove the pain he felt back inside the deep hole he kept it in. But he wasn't quick enough for her to not notice it. Anna felt her heart break a little for him and glared up at the man holding her.

The man glanced back down at Anna.

"I'm thinking I should start with you. I thought this one would have been a little friskier."

Anna stiffened and stayed still while the man's attention was back on her again.

"I really, REALLY like frisky women," he whispered seductively in Anna's ear.

When she didn't respond, a disappointed look crossed his face, and he sighed before turning his attention back to Joe. Relaxing his grip on Anna, the man seemed indifferent to her, choosing instead to focus his attention on Joe.

Keeping her eyes on Joe's, Anna hooked her foot around the back of the man's leg, praying Joe would notice and jerked his foot out from under him, knocking him off balance. Surprised, he threw his arms out to balance himself, and Anna drove her elbow through his nose.

Grunting in pain, the man stumbled, which gave Joe enough time to lunge forward. Grabbing the hand that held the knife, he twisted the man's wrist and drove the knife straight through the man's knee, causing him to scream in pain and fell to the floor. His subject subdued, Joe grabbed Anna's wrist and pulled her away from the man and into the safety of his arms.

"Arrrg, you two are going to get it," the man said. He jerked the knife out of his leg and tried to stand but slipped back to the floor in pain. "I knew you were a frisky one. I just knew it. But just you wait. I'll get it out of you."

"If you liked her," a familiar voice boomed from the darkness behind the man. "You'll really like me."

Anna breathed a sigh of relief and buried her face in Joe's shirt when she heard Alex's voice. Joe kept his arm around her and watched as Alex jerked the man's hand behind his back. A team of police officers came pouring in behind him, followed by Agents Hoage and Kamera.

"This is police brutality!" the man screamed as Alex wrenched his arms behind him while driving his knee into the man's back. "You will break my arm!"

"Considering you just put your hands on my girlfriend," Alex said while securing the man's hands behind his back, "I would consider this gentle if I were you."

After ensuring the man was secured and being watched by someone, Alex stepped over and pulled Anna out of Joe's arms and into his own, letting out a huge breath.

"I need to get you out of here," he said, pulling away and taking in her distraught eyes. His eyes darkened as he gazed at the blood on her shirt and the thin cut on her chest.

"No," Anna choked out. "I need to know Marie is okay first."

"Stay behind me," Alex sighed and signaled his men to head upstairs.

Joe and Anna stayed back, keeping an eye peeled for their siblings. The men cleared the entire farmhouse, only finding two more kidnappers besides the two detained downstairs. Marie and Bryant were sitting back to back, zip-tied to matching chairs, but appeared in good health.

Anna rushed to her sister once the men set her free and wrapped her arms around her neck. Marie closed her eyes, returning the hug before pushing Anna away and turning to check on Bryant, sighing when she realized he was also unhurt.

"We need to talk with them," Carver said. "If you two are up to it anyway."

Anna nodded and pulled away from the group of men. She watched Alex lead his men back downstairs, barking orders and gathering evidence while the FBI agents took command of Marie and Bryant.

"All right," Carver said. "Marie, you come with me. Bryant, you can go with Kamera. We'll make it quick so you can get checked out by the EMTs. They should be here any minute."

As Carver took Marie and Bryant away, Anna slipped into a darkened room in the farmhouse and sank to the floor. She propped her back against the wall, dropped her head between her knees, and threw her arms over her head. She was trying to control her breathing when Joe found her and didn't look up when he approached.

Joe dropped to the floor next to her, gathered her in his arms, and wrapped her up in them. Anna curled up in his comfort, no longer able to keep any of her tears inside and let his shirt soak them up while she gripped it with both hands.

"It's all right," he murmured in her ear. "It's over."

Chapter 38

"WHAT THE HELL WERE you thinking, Marie?" Carver demanded once he had her alone. "That was the stupidest thing you could have done. Why didn't you call for help, first?"

Marie hung her head. She knew she didn't have a defense in any of this, but she stood by her decision.

"I didn't realize I was in any danger," she said.

"So, tell me what happened."

"I don't remember much," Marie said. "I remember parking my car in an alley and walking through those warehouse doors, but that's about it."

"They must have drugged you as soon as you walked in," Carver mused.

Marie continued, "I woke up here just a little bit ago, and Bryant was here, too. And then Autumn and Callen showed up..."

"What?" Carver asked, confused. "Callen? The guy that died in his apartment?"

"Yeah," Marie said. "Didn't someone tell you about him? He and Autumn are working together or something. They were both here, and they left when the crew you captured got

323

here. Autumn said she would finish out our case and make sure Haskell got off."

"All right," Carver said. "I need to make some calls and talk to your sister and Joe to see what they have to say about things. You head downstairs and get checked out by the paramedics."

Marie nodded and walked down the stairs to find Bryant already sitting in an ambulance that had shown up while they were upstairs. The agents met up outside and began talking to each other excitedly.

Seeing Marie's tired face, an EMT rushed to her and forced her to sit down next to Bryant, ignoring her pleas to let her find her sister. While still protesting, Marie found herself hooked up to several machines.

"Yeah," Bryant said. "They didn't listen to me either. I don't know where Joe and Anna are."

"They are with the other EMTs," the man checking Marie out said. "You two need to stop worrying about them. They are in good hands."

"That's easy for you to say," Marie grumbled.

"It'll be all right," Bryant said, leaning against the side of the ambulance and closing his eyes. "They'll be fine. I promise."

Marie shook her head and continued looking around the exterior of the farmhouse, trying to figure out where she was and what had caused her to lose an entire day.

AFTER MAKING SURE ALL the parties inside the farm-house were secure, Alex went on a hunt for Anna. He found her sitting on the back of an ambulance, a vacant look in her eyes. Joe watched over her while an EMT addressed the knife cut on her chest and glanced up when Alex approached.

"I'm sorry," Joe said. "I didn't do as good a job as I promised."

Alex shook his head and scrutinized Anna.

"She's alive at least," he said. "And in one piece."

"Still," Joe said, somewhat hanging his head before glancing at her wound.

Alex was still looking Anna over when Agents Hoage and Kamera approached.

"Tell me what happened," Carver demanded of Joe. "Marie and Bryant are fuzzy on the details, but they say Callen and Autumn were at the farmhouse."

"Which is impossible," said Renato, "considering Callen is dead."

"I know nothing about Callen other than he and Autumn are related," Joe said. "We found some stuff tracing Autumn's step-dad back to Haskell, though. And a huge money trail that connects everyone to everything."

"Anything you can prove?"

"Well, of course, it is," Joe said. "You think we would have gone to all the trouble to dig it up if it wasn't admissible in court?"

Carver laughed and glanced over at Anna, who still wasn't contributing to the conversation.

"You two are something else," Renato mused.

"How did you find them?" Carver asked. "I've got to know. All the resources at our fingertips and we couldn't find them. But somehow, you did."

"Ah, I'm just stubborn," Joe said.

Carver and Renato both narrowed their eyes at the same time and crossed their arms, causing Joe to shift uncomfortably.

"All right," he stammered. "I have this program I built that helped me find them. No, you can't see it. No, I don't use it a lot. No, it's not legal."

"Of course, you do," Carver said. "I'm just going to pretend like we didn't ask, considering you two just took down one of the biggest crime families around."

"We've got to get to Autumn and Callen before they split," Renato said. "You know they won't hang around if they get word of what went down here."

"Already way ahead of you," Carver said. "As soon as I heard where they were, I sent agents to their apartment to pick them up. If we're lucky, they'll be in our custody when we get back."

"And, hopefully, someone will talk."

"Oh, you bet they all will talk," Carver laughed. "Those clowns we just picked up were singing like songbirds as they went into those squad cars. Everyone else is bound to follow suit."

"We'll touch base with all you guys tomorrow to get final statements and to tie up any loose ends," Renato said to Joe and Alex. "Stay out of trouble."

As the agents were leaving, the EMT finished up with Anna and sighed.

"All right, honey. That cut is all fixed up," he said, looking at her with a concerned look on his face before turning to Joe. "Do we need to take her in so she can get some rest?"

Alex stepped in and said, "We've got it from here, thanks."

The EMT shrugged and looked back at Anna but didn't press the issue. When the EMT walked away, Alex stood in front of her trying to bring her back to him. "Anna, how about I take you and Marie home so you can get some rest?"

Her eyes focused on him for a second before turning to face Joe, confusion clear on her face. "But I road with Joe, right?"

Joe looked at Alex, not sure what to do, before turning back to Anna. "You rode with me. But Alex can take you back home."

"You'll have to ride home by yourself?"

"No, I will take Bryant with me."

"How will we know you get home?"

Alex drew her attention back to himself.

"How about we follow them home?" he suggested. "You and Marie can ride home with me, we'll stop and make sure Joe and Bryant get home, and I can take you home so you can get some sleep."

"OK," Anna said, still sounding confused but looking too tired to argue with him.

She leaned against the ambulance and closed her eyes. Alex sighed and looked her up and down again before turning to Joe.

"I'm putting her in my car," he said. "Will you be all right by yourself for a minute?"

"Of course."

Alex took Anna's hand and urged her into the front seat of his car before retrieving Marie and putting her in the back. When they were safely inside, he went back to Joe who seemed to be looking around for his brother.

"Bryant's over by your jeep," Alex said.

"I'm sorry..." Joe started but stopped when Alex threw up his hands to stop him.

"It's all right," he said. "Everything's fine. Anna just needs some rest and she'll be back to normal tomorrow."

"I'm sorry I couldn't have made things easier."

Alex glared at the squad cars holding the men who had done the damage to Anna. "Not your fault."

"You don't have to follow me and Bryant home. We can make it home on our own. You need to get Anna and Marie home."

"Nope," Alex said. "She won't be able to sleep if I don't make sure you guys make it home."

"If that's the way she wants it, that's the way she gets it, I guess," Joe said.

Before they could say more, Bryant approached, and Joe jerked him into a hug before stepping back to look his brother up and down.

"Man, it's good to see you," Joe said.

"Can we go home now?" Bryant replied with a pained look on his face. "I've got to go to work tomorrow."

"You aren't going into work tomorrow! Are you crazy?"

"I have to! We have to finish our trial!" Bryant argued. "And I need to see Allie. She is ticked I left like I did earlier without telling her where I was going. I have to see her and let her know I'm okay. She's worried."

Joe raised his eyebrows at his brother, rolled his eyes, and said, "Fine, Casanova. Let's get out of here so we can get you back to Allie."

Chapter 39

"I'M SO GLAD YOU BOTH are ok," Claire muttered for the tenth time since she, Frankie and Eddie had arrived at the apartment.

"You know," Frankie said to Marie as she picked up another piece of pizza. "I told you to follow a pattern, but I never said to follow it yourself, dummy. You could be dead right now! And who would visit me when I move to Atlanta?"

"Yeah, don't get me started," Eddie grumbled. "I can't believe you did something like this and lied about it! We didn't even know we needed to look for you."

"I'm sorry I wasn't honest about what I was doing," Marie said. "I didn't want to get anyone in any more danger than they already were."

"How'd that work out for you?" Alex asked before glancing down at Anna, who hadn't left his arms since they'd made it home. She remained detached from the conversation, and he looked at her concerned as her eyelids drifted closed.

"Anna, honey," Claire said, also looking at her friend with concern. "Are you all right? What can I do?"

"What?" Anna said, jerking awake and shaking her head before trying to put a smile on her face. "Oh, I'm sorry, Claire. I promise I'm fine. I'm just glad everything is over, and we can get back to normal."

"You and me both," Marie said. "Except I have to go in tomorrow and close out this case."

"At least you know you won't get any more surprises," Frankie said with a shrug.

"One can only hope," Marie said with a sigh. "It will be chaos in the morning. I can't imagine Autumn and Callen were the only ones involved in this. Agents Hoage and Kamera will probably be super busy gathering up everyone. No telling who will not show up tomorrow."

"Will you still have a job?" Frankie asked.

"I don't know!" Marie said, wringing her hands. "We got a lot of the people in our office arrested. And two people died! No one will want to work with Bryant or me. I feel tainted at this point."

Not knowing what to do or say, Frankie took her friend's hand to comfort her. Marie tried to remain positive, but the stress of the case and her future were wearing her thin. Everything seemed so helpless.

"That's enough of this, my love," Alex said as he noticed Anna's eyes drifting closed again. "Time to get you in bed."

"Yes," Eddie agreed, taking Marie's hand. "I think it's time we all called it a night. "Hopefully, the morning will bring around some sunshine to make things look good again."

Claire and Frankie both hugged their friends before heading out into the darkening night. Anna and Marie were both asleep in bed before their friends even made it back to their own apartments.

Friday 8:00 AM – Anna

ANNA WATCHED ALEX BUZZ around her apartment, getting ready for work. It was time for life to continue, as much as she didn't want it to, and Anna knew she wouldn't be able to convince Alex to delay getting things back to normal again.

She pulled the covers around her a little tighter trying to beat the cold chill that seemed to seep through no matter what she tried. Her movements caught Alex's attention, and he paused for a minute to lean down over her.

"Good morning," he said, a soft smile playing out on his lips.

"Good morning," Anna whispered back, gazing up into his eyes.

"I'm sorry if I woke you," he said, running a finger across her forehead to move a strand of hair out of her eyes. "I had to get ready for work."

"You could stay," Anna said. "I'm sure I'm way more fun than those guys you work with."

"You definitely are," Alex said with a laugh, "but I already missed most of the day yesterday. Any more will look bad."

"You're right," Anna conceded. "But I don't have to like it, do I?"

"No," Alex said before planting a kiss on her lips. "No, you do not."

"I sure hope everything works out for Marie," Anna mused as Alex resumed his routine. "I don't know what she will do if she can't be a lawyer anymore. She's worked so hard for it."

"I wouldn't worry about it," Alex called from the bathroom, holding a toothbrush in his hand. "These things always have a way of working themselves out."

"I hope you're right," Anna said, picking at her blanket.

"You know I am," Alex said with a smile, coming back to her side of the bed. "Now. I have to go to work. Will you be all right by yourself today?"

Anna put a smile on her face and tried to reassure him.

"I'll be fine," she said. "Nothing a little rest, and recharge won't fix."

"Good," he said before, letting his lips linger on hers for a few moments. "I love you."

"I love you, too," Anna said before snuggling back into the blankets. "See you tomorrow?"

"You can count on it," he said before leaving her bedroom and the apartment altogether.

The moment she heard the door click closed behind him, Anna began throwing the blankets off her and rounding up her usual barrage of items she took with her when she escaped. Throwing on her swimsuit underneath a pair of shorts and a tank top, she tossed her journal in her bag along with some sunscreen.

Seeing her phone lying on her nightstand, she grabbed it and hesitated, remembering what happened the last time she took it along with her. Shaking her head, she tossed it in the bag and scooped up the helmet that still sat on the floor from last time.

Before thinking much more about anything, she locked up her apartment and swung herself onto her bike, leaving the quietness of her apartment behind. As soon as she turned onto the highway, she felt her anxiety sweep away, and she felt free.

Typically, Anna tried to avoid paying attention to anything around her when she escaped, but this time she glimpsed something in the parking lot of a gas station on her route that made her pause. Frowning, she turned to look at the object as she passed but ignored it, only to change her mind a mile down the road and turn back.

When she reached the parking lot a second time, she cruised in and jerked off her helmet after she'd stopped.

"What are you doing here?" she asked, walking over to the subject that had caught her attention on her way by.

Joe smiled at her and leaned against his own bike. Glaring at him, Anna folded her arms across her chest and tapped her foot.

"I had a hunch," he said.

"Were you watching me again?" she asked, annoyance creeping into her voice. "You've got to stop that."

"No. I promise I wasn't watching you."

"What are you doing here?" she said through gritted teeth.

"I woke up and felt like going for a ride. I was in the neighborhood..."

He stopped when Anna continued to glare at him and sighed.

"I was worried about you. Yesterday was rough, and the last time I was with you and something was rough, this is what you did. I just popped over here just in case you came by."

Anna softened her gaze at him but still didn't reply.

"I'm sorry if I overstepped," Joe continued. "I didn't know what to do with myself this morning. We've spent all week chasing bad guys, and I got a little bored."

Anna shook her head but couldn't help but laugh a bit.

"You weren't watching me? Don't lie to me."

"I swear!" Joe said, throwing up his hands. "I was out for a ride and just stopped here for a bit in case you came by. And, here you are."

"And here I am," Anna said. "How long were you going to wait here?"

"I figured I would give it a half-hour," Joe said. "I do have things to do with my life other than waiting around for you, you know."

Anna laughed and shook her head at him again before picking up her helmet. "Well, come along then."

"Oh!" Joe said, smiling at her. "You want me to come with you?"

"Unless you have something better to do with your time," Anna said looking back at him.

"Nope," Joe said, pausing before he put his own helmet back on his head. "Wait, you just want me to beat you again, don't you?"

"Beat me? What do you mean?"

"At surfing," Joe said before popping his helmet back on and lifting the visor so she could see his eyes. "You want me to beat you again at surfing."

"You didn't beat me."

Joe laughed and started his bike, revving the engine over the sound of her voice.

"You didn't beat me!" Anna yelled over the sound of his bike, but Joe ignored her, lowered his visor, and headed out onto the highway.

"You didn't beat me," Anna grumbled to herself before following him.

Chapter 40

8:00 AM – Marie and Bryant

"HONESTLY, I CAN'T BELIEVE the two of you are here today," Judge Toland said. "With half your firm thrust into the middle of a legal dilemma and everything you went through yesterday I wouldn't have been surprised if you'd stayed home."

"We wanted to get Mr. Shaw the deal we had agreed on," Bryant said. "There was no sense in keeping him in jail another few days."

"Besides," Marie added. "With everything going on with the firm, we couldn't take the chance it would affect this case."

"Well," the judge said. "I'm quite impressed with your fortitude."

"Not to mention their diligence and dedication to me," Dominique Shaw muttered. The judge turned to look at him as he sat at the table in his suit.

"Ah, yes, Mr. Shaw," he said. "We need to get to the outcome of your case. I'm sure you are wondering what is left for you."

"Yes sir, Judge Toland," Shaw said. "I testified in Haskell's trial this morning, provided all the evidence I have, and everything is recorded for future use, so what's next for me?"

"Next," Judge Toland said. "We'll close your case based on the deal your fine attorneys and the D.A. arranged, and you will go into Witness Protection. After I strike my gavel, you're a free man, within the constraints of your agreement, of course."

"I can't wait," Shaw said with a smile.

"All right, well, if everyone will please rise," Judge Toland said, prompting the prosecution's side of the courtroom and Bryant, Marie, and Mr. Shaw to stand to their feet. "Are there any changes to the offer or motions being requested by either side in this matter?"

"No, sir," Bryant said.

"No," the prosecutor agreed.

"Well, in that case," the judge said, striking the gavel. "I declare this case closed, and the charges against Dominique Shaw dropped."

The moment the gavel struck, Dominique swept first Marie and then Bryant into a tight hug before pulling away.

"I can't thank you enough," he said. "You do not understand how much you've helped me."

"You're welcome," Marie said with a smile.

"I'm just glad everything came together," Bryant said.

"Me, too," Dominique said. "I'm so sorry my crime spree got the two of you tied up in something that almost got you killed, though. You are skilled attorneys."

"Thanks," Marie said, trying to put a smile on her face.

"Don't worry," Dominique said. "I'm sure the two of you will land on your feet."

Marie and Bryant glanced at each other and tried to put a positive look on their faces. Before they could talk with their client anymore, a pair of United States Marshalls swept into the courtroom and led Dominique away. Marie and Bryant looked at each other and sighed. Marie sat back down at the table to catch her breath.

"I'm glad that's all over and done with," Bryant said.

"Yeah," Marie said, putting her head in her hands. "Along with our careers."

"Try to look at the bright side," Bryant said. "At least we're both alive."

"I suppose you're right," Marie said, still covering her face. "But, let's face it. We're done. No law firm will hire us."

"I know," Bryant said, sitting down next to her. "Between working at a shady law firm and getting the whole place arrested, it's difficult to see the light at the end of the tunnel."

The two sat in the empty courtroom for several minutes before Bryant shook his head. "Stop it. We've got to stop feeling sorry for ourselves."

"You're right," Marie agreed but didn't sound convinced. "We need to get out of here."

"And, clean out our desks," Bryant said with a groan.

"I already packed everything this morning just in case."

Bryant shook his head at her and stood to exit the courtroom. "One would hope it won't be that bad."

"Well, I guess we're fixing to find out."

Back at the office, Marie and Bryant walked into a storm. Papers were strewn across the offices, and the few employees left looked lost. Allie looked up at them when they walked in and tried to put a smile on her face.

"Well, it was a good job while it lasted, at least," she joked. "Haven't even gotten a paycheck yet, and I'm already back out looking for work again."

"What happened?" Bryant asked, looking around the chaos-filled office.

"Well, Agents Hoage and Kamera somehow kept everything quiet," Allie said. "So, no one at the office knew a thing until the FBI came sweeping in this morning and started making arrests. Autumn and Callen and the rest of those guys they arrested started talking the moment they got in an interview room. Turned everything upside down in just a few hours."

"So, that's it," Marie said. "I knew this would be bad. Maybe we can move to California and change our names or something. Retake the bar. Start over."

Allie shook her head and looked at her desk, her eyes filling with tears. She went back to loading up the few belongings she'd brought in with her since her first day earlier that week. Bryant and Marie watched her for a few seconds before walking to their own offices and following suit. It wasn't long before the attorneys had cleared their offices and began turning off lights, not sure what else to do with their time.

"Well," Bryant said, standing next to Marie and Allie at the elevator as they waited for it to take them to the ground level one last time. "It was nice working with you."

Before the three could enter the elevator, a woman rushed off as the doors flew open and stopped them.

"Oh, thank goodness I found you," she stammered while dabbing away tears from her eyes. "I need your help."

Friday Noon – Anna and Joe

ANNA COLLAPSED IN A beach chair, pulled her sunglasses out of her bag, and popped them on her nose before turning her face toward the sun and allowing its heat to dry her wet skin. Joe plopped down next to her.

"I'm hungry," he said after a minute.

Anna looked at him out of the corner of her eye and grinned. "Are you always hungry?"

"Pretty much."

Shaking her head, Anna smiled and said, "How about we get something to eat and head back. I need to get back before Alex or Marie notices I'm not there. They will kill me if I disappear twice in one week."

"Well, you didn't technically disappear this time," Joe laughed. "Someone knows where you are this time."

Anna glared at him and tossed a handful of sand his way. "Yeah, not by choice!"

Joe was still laughing when both their phones started making noise.

"Uh oh," Anna said. "What do you think is going on now?"

"Don't know. But Bryant just texted that I need to call him."

Anna was already dialing her sister's number. "Marie did too."

She couldn't hide her relief when Marie answered her call. "Marie? Thank God. What's wrong?"

"Something interesting happened today," Marie said. "I need to talk to you. Can you meet me in town?"

"Uh," Anna hesitated. "I'm not in town right now. It will take me a minute to get to you."

"Anna," Marie groaned. "Where the hell are you?"

"When do you want to meet and where?" Anna asked, avoiding her sister's question.

"Can you meet me at 2 at the apartment?"

"I can do that."

"Great. If you can, get Alex to stop by. He might want to know what's going on."

"Now, I'm intrigued," Anna said. "Can I get a hint?"

"No. There's too much detail. Just wait until 2."

"Fine," Anna said, before ending her call and texting Alex.

Joe had taken the easy route and texted Bryant rather than call him.

"Meet at your apartment at 2?" he asked when she had hung up with Marie.

"Yep," Anna said, glancing down at Alex's text, confirming he could also stop by. "I wonder what's going on?"

"I don't know," Joe said. "But we are still stopping to get something to eat on the way back."

Anna shook her head at him but laughed before gathering up her belongings and heading back toward her bike.

Friday 2 PM

ANNA THREW HER FEET up on the coffee table and propped her hands up behind her neck while she waited for her sister and Bryant to get to the point of the meeting they'd called.

She glanced at Alex, who looked official in his police uniform and hoped he didn't ask about her day. When she'd gotten home from her rendezvous with Joe, she'd taken a quick shower and thrown on a pair of sweatpants and a t-shirt, hoping it made her look inconspicuous.

Alex seemed in a hurry to get back to work, so he didn't notice her distracted state. Bryant glanced at his watch, annoyed and sighed when a knock sounded at the door, ten minutes after the hour.

"Where have you been?" he asked when Marie opened the door to let Joe in.

"I was busy," he grinned before meeting Anna's eyes.

She glanced back at Alex, and Joe moved to the kitchen table turning a chair around and sitting in it backward.

"If you are ready to begin," Bryant said and glared at his brother. "We have something we need to talk to you two about."

"Fire away," Joe said, obviously fascinated with whatever his brother had to say.

"Well," Marie started. "The law firm is done. Finished. Closed."

"Oh, that's awful!" Anna interjected with a gasp.

"It's all right," Bryant said.

Marie shook off Anna's pity. "When we were leaving the office. A woman rushed off the elevator, saying she needed our help."

"She had already heard about the work we did with the Haskell case," Bryant continued.

"What does this have to do with anything?" Alex asked.

"I'm getting to it," Marie said. "She needs our help with a case."

"I'm not following how we're involved in this," Anna said, looking at Joe.

"She wants to hire 'our team,'" Bryant said.

"And she wants to pay a lot to do it," Marie continued.

"When you say a lot," Joe said. "What are we talking about?"

"She wants to put down a guaranteed retainer of $50,000," Bryant said.

"Plus, any other expenses we may have," Marie said.

Joe whistled. "That's a big retainer."

Anna looked at Alex. "And she wants our help? I don't know..."

Alex and Marie locked eyes, and he sighed, understanding why she invited him to the meeting. After thinking about it for a minute, he glanced at Joe before turning to face Anna. "I think you should do it."

Anna stood up and pulled Alex to the privacy of her bedroom, ignoring the uncomfortable gazes of the others.

"Are you sure you are all right with this?" she asked when they were inside. "You weren't too comfortable with Joe before. You will be ok with me working with him now?"

"That was before he saved your life. Anna, if I can't trust you, what's the point? Besides, if you are going to do this for a living, I want you doing it with someone who will be there to protect you."

Anna hung her head. "I need to tell you something. I wasn't here today. Joe and I went surfing."

Alex's eyes flared, causing Anna to glance away from him. Sighing, he pulled her chin to make her look at him.

"You're allowed to have friends," he said. "You're allowed to do things with other people besides me. I would like you to not hide things from me, though. No secrets, you hear?"

"I'm sorry," she said. "I just... I'm sorry."

Alex rubbed her cheek and gazed into her eyes. "I trust you, Anna. If you want to surf with Joe, do it. Just remember who you come home to."

Anna smiled. "Of course."

"Now. Let's go back out there and tell them you will do this thing."

Before they left her bedroom, Anna wrapped her arms around his neck and kissed him. Alex closed his eyes and squeezed her tight.

"So?" Marie asked when they had returned to the living room.

"I'm in," Anna said.

Joe grinned. "Well, Mary. I guess we will see more of each other then, won't we?"

Anna laughed, remembering their time at the HR firm earlier that week. "It seems this was just the start of our shenanigans, John."

"That reminds me," Bryant said. "We need to set some ground rules before we do this thing."

Marie folded her arms across her chest. "Yeah! No breaking and entering and no stealing things."

Anna glared back at her sister. "How about no going off on your own and getting kidnapped?"

Joe's eyes narrowed at Bryant. "Yeah, that seems like a good rule."

"How about no speeding?" Alex said, causing both Anna and Joe to jump. "And, no running from the cops...Anna."

"All right, all right," Anna said, ending the conversation. "We get it. Behave."

"Follow the law," Joe laughed, saluting Alex with his fingers. "Check."

Alex glared back at him, causing Joe to grin and look over at Anna.

"So, when do we start?" Marie asked. "We're all free tomorrow, right? We could go ahead and..."

"Marie," Anna said. "If you think I'm spending another day this week working on a case with you, you're crazy. We're going to the spa. We've earned it."

"Fine, fine," Marie grumbled, watching Anna head to her bedroom to pack a bag before picking up her phone to call Frankie and Claire. "But, this time, I'm driving."

Continue reading for a sneak peek at Book 2 – Forgotten Promises!

Sneak Peek
Forgotten Promises
A Hartman and Malone Mystery #2

Chapter 1

"WE ARE SO GOING TO get in trouble for this."

Joe peered around the edge of the building he and Anna stood with their backs against and gazed at the small house tucked against a serene cliff side.

"Well, when we do," Anna whispered back at him. "I will tell them this was all your idea."

Joe turned to glare at her, and she suppressed a laugh with her hand. Shaking his head at her while smiling, Joe began to take a step around the building when a gruff voice caused them both to flinch.

"What do you two think you're doing? This is government property, and you are trespassing."

Anna and Joe froze in place at the sound of the gruff voice. Before Joe had time to react, Anna slipped her hand into his, interlaced their fingers, and wrapped her free arm around him before addressing the man.

She allowed her voice to take on a surprised, yet sweet tone. "Oh, sir! My boyfriend and I are house hunting. We must have gotten turned around!"

The man sighed. "What address are you looking for?"

"Uh, 2601 Wordsworth Terrace?"

"Wordsworth Terrace is two miles to the south. This is Wordsworth North," came the reply.

"Well, that would explain our confusion, then!" Anna said and put a huge smile on her face. "I'm so sorry we disturbed you, sir."

Joe tugged on Anna's hand and began leading her away from the building. "We'll get out of your hair, then."

Anna held her breath and let Joe lead her a few steps away from the building and the man but sighed when he called out to them.

"How did you get past the gate?"

"I'm sorry?" Anna asked, turning back to face him.

"The gate," he said and put his hands on his hips. "How did you get past it?"

Anna didn't miss noticing the gun strapped to his belt.

"Uh, I think it was open, wasn't it?" Joe turned to look at Anna.

"Definitely," Anna agreed. "Definitely opened."

Joe pulled Anna a few more steps away before the man stopped them again.

"Where's your car?"

"Shit."

"If we chose to live here, then we wanted to check out the full property," she said, talking over Joe's grumble. "What better way to do that than a leisurely walk up the driveway?"

"You have an answer for everything?" The man cocked his head at her. "How about we go inside, and you answer a few more?"

"Well, I don't know what you want us to answer," Anna said. "Like I said, we were lost."

"I'm not buying that. Let's go."

Joe gave Anna a sharp look, stepped in front of her, and began following the man. When they got closer to the building, Anna peered around him at the man.

"You have a lovely home," she said. "I hope the place we are looking to rent has the same charm as yours."

He glared back at her and stomped the final few feet to the front door. He swung it open and motioned for them to enter, glaring at them as they passed by. Joe caught Anna's eye again and gave her a look that she hoped meant he had a plan.

Once they had passed through the door, Anna paused and looked around for a moment. Behind her, the man sighed and gave her a little nudge in the back, spurring her to continue walking. Anna's eyes slipped from one side of the house to the other as they walked through the rooms. The man encouraged them through the entire home and into a small kitchen that acted as a command station.

The man pointed at a pair of chairs at the kitchen table, and both she and Joe sat. Anna couldn't hide her curiosity at the surrounding devices. Phones and computers sat on counters, servers rested along the wall on the floor, and camera monitors plastered the walls. Anna allowed her eyes to sweep over the devices before turning to the man with a surprised look on her face.

"My goodness! You have some interesting decorating tastes!"

Ignoring her, the man turned to Joe. "What the hell are you two doing here? I've been watching you for 20 minutes.

You've been sneaking around this property like you're hunting something."

"Like she said," Joe said, leaning forward in his chair, his hands in his lap. "We were checking out the property. Our realtor is walking us through in about 30 minutes, but we got here early so we could check things out. Didn't want to bother whoever might be home while we were looking things over, so we were trying to stay quiet."

"I'm afraid it was my fault," Anna said, causing the man's eyes to shift to her. "I love spending time outdoors and I wanted to see what type of space we were dealing with."

"Can we cut the bullshit, please? We all know there isn't such a place as Wordsworth Terrace, and this ain't no Wordsworth North. What the HELL do you want?"

Anna and Joe looked at each other before both turning their eyes back to the man, neither willing to say anything more.

"Fine," the man said. "My team should be back in about five minutes. I'm going to search you two and secure you until they can get some answers out of you."

"You, stay there," he said, pointing at Joe. "And, you, get over here and let me make sure you don't have any weapons."

Anna felt Joe stiffen a bit at the order, but Anna gave him a look and complied with the man. She held her breath again and flinched when the man's hands found their way to her hips. But before he could conduct his search, Joe jerked him backward and to the floor.

"Go, Anna," Joe grunted as he subdued the man and made sure he was unconscious.

Anna didn't wait for him to follow her and instead took off running through the house and back to the front door. She burst into the sunlight just as three large SUVs were pulling up outside of the house. Several confused men poured from the vehicle and spotted her, which caused her to backpedal to a stop.

Before she could change directions, Joe sped through the door behind her and grabbed her hand, pulling her with him toward the cliffs. The men soon broke their startled trance and took chase. Anna could hear their combat boots rustling the grass behind her as they ran.

"Did you at least get the device in place?" she panted as Joe pulled her along.

"You would think you'd stop doubting me at some point," he said, not looking back at her.

He kept them on a straight path to the cliff, and Anna did her best to keep up with him. When he stopped at the edge of the cliff and looked down, Anna's eyes widened, and she froze in place.

"I'm sorry," Joe said. "This won't be pleasant."

Anna had just enough time to look down at the steadily flowing water below her in fear before Joe jerked her into his arms and pulled her over the cliff with him. Before she had time to scream, they hit the water, and it pulled them under.

Continue reading the exciting adventure by downloading the next installment of the Hartman & Malone Mys-

tery Series, Forgotten Promises (Coming Soon)!

Visit us online at www.paigehperry.com[1] for character profiles, short stories, and more team freebies and to learn how you can get a free e-book!

Follow us on Facebook at fb.me/PaigeHPerry[2] to stay up to date with the team and to learn about release dates for book 2!

| Page

CPSIA information can be obtained
at www.ICGtesting.com
Printed in the USA
BVHW081915240120
570269BV00001B/8